Dedication

In loving memory of my dear Aunt Alice

When Shadows Stir

The Kavenaghs 1870 - 1879
Book Two

Eden Monroe

Print ISBNs
Amazon print 9780228634324
Ingram Spark 9780228634331
Barnes & Noble 9780228634348
BWL Print 9780228634355

BWL Publishing Inc.

Books we love to write ...
Authors around the world.

http://bwlpublishing.ca

Table of Contents

Chapter 1 7

Chapter 2 26

Chapter 3 45

Chapter 4 65

Chapter 5 85

Chapter 6 104

Chapter 7 124

Chapter 8 143

Chapter 9 162

Chapter 10 182

Chapter 11 202

Chapter 12 222

Chapter 13 242

Chapter 14 262

Chapter 15.. 282

Chapter 16 302

Epilogue... 324

Chapter 1

1876 - Brogan Kavenagh

The day had begun with such promise. When he'd opened his eyes to see the sun about to rise in splendor above the tree line, he was reminded yet again of his good fortune. It was never far from his mind. He had a healthy, happy eight-year-old son, Luke, still fast asleep in his room, and his beautiful wife lay warm and willing in his arms. In fact it was her kiss that had awakened him, and he couldn't help but think that every man should start the day by making love to his wife. Their passion after fifteen years of marriage had not even begun to cool. He loved his Maggie with a fierceness that startled even himself.

But before the sun had fully set on this day, his entire world would be knocked sideways ... his final stop a hangman's noose.

* * *

Brogan set the double-bit felling axe against the trunk of a nearby birch tree. It was a warm day for the end of September, made even more so after swinging an axe for hours. Brogan had ditched his shirt and vest hours ago. His muscled shoulders and back glistened with a fine sheen of perspiration as he stretched large, then settled onto the ground, resting against the same huge white birch. Wiping his brow he took a long pull from the jug to slake his thirst. When he'd fetched the water this morning from the artesian well that fed the house, it tasted refreshingly sweet and cool. Now, the water was lukewarm, and the best he could say about it was that it was wet. But, he was glad he'd brought the full jug. He'd needed it.

He relaxed his long legs out in front of him, then drew his knees up to an inverted V. Tilting his head back, he peered up through branches that only partially shielded him from the punishing intensity of the sun. This thing must be almost fifty feet tall. A giant for sure, with wood enough to top up next year's firewood supply. He'd saved this tree for last. He smiled, his blue-grey eyes crinkling at the corners. Maybe he'd wait until tomorrow now that he thought about it. But nah, he reasoned silently, losing the argument with himself, might as well get it done today. He'd bring it down, then limb it and start chopping it up tomorrow before hauling it back to the homestead.

Getting to his feet he grabbed the haft of the axe up in strong hands and swung with years of practice. The razor-sharp blade hit the mark, the heavy head biting deep into the wood.

"Hey there! Brogan!"

Brogan arrested a second swing as he turned in the direction of the man's voice. It wasn't very often one saw Peterson Gault on foot, having climbed down from his wagon. He was now picking his way through the trees, both those that had been felled and the many still standing.

Brogan set the axe down again. "Thought I heard a rig passing by," he told his neighbour. "What brings you up in here?"

The effort of walking even this short distance quickly caught up with the old man, and he sank onto a nearby stump. Pulling off his battered hat, he mopped his brow again before settling his hat back onto his head.

"Oh nothin', just on my way back to my place and thought I'd stop by for a spell. Say hello." He eyed the jug sitting beside the birch tree. "It's uncommonly warm today, and I'm terrible thirsty."

Brogan smiled. "There's nothing but water in there, but you're welcome to a slug. It's a warm one all right." Retrieving the chipped earthenware jug he passed it to Gault who made no attempt to hide his disappointment.

"Thought you might have something a bit stronger than that with you, Brogan. You know, somethin' a little more interesting to cut the heat."

Brogan shrugged. "Sorry, just water, but have all you like. I'll be heading home in an hour or so anyway. You just stop for this?" he asked with a smile, holding up the jug.

Gault was well known for his love of spirits and for making it his business to know what was going on out this way ... either bringing news or carrying it away. Since Brogan could think of nothing to say worth carrying away, Gault must have something he wanted to tell him.

Gault took the jug reluctantly although he helped himself to a generous pull, wiping his mouth as he passed it back to Brogan. "That was one of the reasons," he said, nodding in the direction of the jug. "The other was to ask you what's wrong with your brother, Tabor."

"I didn't know there was anything wrong with my brother. What makes you think there is? You saying he's sick?"

Retrieving a decrepit corncob pipe from his shirt pocket, Gault methodically stuffed it with tobacco and set it afire with the scratch of a match against the sole of his boot. Following a series of firm and steady inhales, the tobacco caught, and he was in business.

"He had a good woman in that Julia Buckley," Gault said at last, "but she up and left him. Ran her off is what I heard."

Brogan puffed a long sigh. He knew very well that Tabor and Julia had, in essence, broken up, but both he and Maggie liked

Julia and hoped it was only temporary. "It's probably just a spat. Tabor can be a handful."

"I hope he didn't hurt her."

Brogan was already shaking his head. "Tabor's a hard man all right, but he'd never hurt a woman. I know he wouldn't. He knows I wouldn't stand for it for one thing, but no, he's just hard to get along with sometimes."

Gault nodded as he drew deeply on his pipe. "He's good to his boy, though. Pate's doin' just fine with those horses he's raisin'. He's growin' like a bad weed too, tall as you and his Pa now. He must be nigh on eighteen years."

"Pate's twenty-two ... and Julia will likely be back," he said returning to Gault's original concern. "They made it this far, six years and all. She'll be back."

Gault shook his head with the smugness of a man who prided himself on knowing more than his neighbours. "Not what I heard, but you never know."

"That's for them to work out. I got enough to do minding my own business," Brogan told him holding the jug up to offer the man another drink.

Gault shook his head, already on his feet to leave.

Brogan grinned. If there had been a little corn in the jug, Gault would no doubt have settled in for a much longer visit. He watched as the old farmer made his way back to his wagon, climbed up with surprising agility, and ambled on down the road.

He stood there watching until the wagon was out of sight, his mind on Tabor and Julia. Maybe Gault was wrong in whatever he'd been hinting at, but he knew the man had a well-trained ear for gossip.

It had been a while since he'd returned to the family farm, a couple of months anyway. He'd picked up on some tension during his last visit, but he'd just put it down to a bad day. Every couple had arguments. Even him and Maggie got into it every once in a while, although it never lasted long. It was usually when he'd done something stupid like drinking with his friends and then of course fighting. He never backed down from a fight, but he was thirty-four now and probably time to grow up as Maggie would put it.

Truth was he'd grown up young. When you had Bart Kavenagh for a father, you grew up fast and you grew up mean. Maggie had taken a lot of the meanness out of him, and the drinking and fistfights were meant to take care of the rest. Nevertheless, he'd left all that behind a few years ago. He wanted to be a better man, not only for his son but also for his wife.

He felt sorry for Tabor in a way. His father had been the toughest on him because he was the oldest, and it seemed he'd never gotten over it. He didn't imagine his brother had done anything to physically hurt Julia.

He better not have. Really though, Tabor could hurt you worse with words than he ever could with his fists. Brogan looked around at the work ahead of him. Still, maybe he'd get on down to the farm in another day or so and see what was happening. Have a talk with his older brother.

He'd just picked up his axe again to have a go at the giant birch when he noticed a plume of dust billowing from a fast-approaching wagon. The driver was pushing the horses much too hard on such a warm day. He didn't have to wonder who it was, guessing correctly, Latham Storey. They'd locked horns before, and he assumed from the man's haste that it wouldn't be any different today. He wondered who his two passengers might be.

He watched the driver, heavy with advancing old age, climb gingerly down off the buckboard, fire in his eyes as he started in Brogan's direction. He was carrying a shotgun.

"You get off my land, Kavenagh!" the man shouted, fairly trembling with rage as he marched toward Brogan, the shotgun leveled straight at him.

This was a dance he and Latham had done before. Brogan had purchased a ten-acre parcel of land from the John Millerton estate a little over a mile from his homestead down the road. He'd had it properly surveyed and deeded, but Storey had fought him every inch of the way, still maintaining that the land belonged to him.

Brogan set the axe down again. The birch tree would live another day. He eyed his Winchester, standing against a smaller birch a few feet away. He dared not make a move to pick it up, not with a shotgun pointed at him.

The shorter man finally came to a stop, winded from the energy he'd expended covering the distance between them so quickly. Overdressed in a woolen jacket, he was perspiring heavily.

Brogan faced him. "This is not your land, Storey," he said. "We've been through all this before. I bought this piece of property for my firewood."

"I don't know what you paid for, or where it is, but it's not *this* piece of land. I own all of this property running right back to the brook. It's Storey land, has been for many years. My father bought this parcel back in eighteen thirty-eight. Now I'm telling you to get yourself off it, or I'll put the lead to you and I mean it."

Brogan shook his head. "Nobody's putting the lead to anybody, Storey. I've already showed you the deed. The land belongs to me fair and square, so I guess if anyone is trespassing, it's you. Now go on home. As I've already told you, I bought this land from the John Millerton estate. His son Danford sold it to me. You already know all that."

Storey's chest heaved with unspent fury. "It was not his to sell 'cause it was bought by my father from old Millerton himself to go with his original land grant!"

"Everything was checked out before I bought it," Brogan explained patiently, "and the land was registered in Danford Millerton's name. That's what they go by, not who gave who what. And now that the sale's gone through, it's registered in *my* name."

Sparks fairly flew from the man's eyes, his face a dangerous purplish red. "It's mine I tell you!"

Brogan sighed. "Look, we've already had this conversation. I asked you to show me a deed in case there was a mistake made, but you've got no such document or so you say."

"Us Storeys don't bother with such doin's! My father made a deal with John Millerton. They shook hands on it. He took my father's money!"

Brogan rolled his eyes. "That doesn't matter if the sale wasn't registered. Millerton could have sold that land a dozen times, and if the sale wasn't registered, he still owned it. Apparently, that's what happened. Your father should have gotten a deed. I'm sorry, but I paid for it. I made sure the sale was properly registered with the government records. I have the piece of paper saying it's mine, and that's the end of it. You don't have a leg to stand on."

"That's not the end of it! I don't care about a piece of paper. I say this land is mine and I mean to run you off!" he shouted. "I told my nephew all about it and he tells me I still own the land and it's just one of those damned Kavenaghs trying to steal it out from under me. You're all a bunch of thieves. No good, the whole lot of you. I thought after I laid down the law to you the other day you'd see reason. Then my nephew and his wife came by earlier. That's them in the wagon. They saw you up here cutting trees on *my* land!"

"Your nephew."

"Yes, my nephew, and I'm indebted to him. If it wasn't for him, I wouldn't have known you were up here stealing my wood." The man looked around quickly. "And I see you've already got quite a few of my best trees down. I ought to kill you right here on the spot for that. I don't want no trees cut on this parcel. I was letting them get good and big."

Brogan looked pointedly at the birch tree he'd started to chop down. "That one's almost three feet at the butt. It won't get any bigger."

"It'll get as big as I want it to because you won't be cutting here no more. Go buy another piece of land. This is not yours, and I can fetch the sheriff to prove it."

Brogan spread his hands reasonably. "That would be a wise thing to do, Storey," he said, although he would rather deal with a snake than that crooked sheriff. "I can show him my deed, and it'll straighten out this whole matter. I could show it to your nephew, too."

The mention of a deed further inflamed the fractious man, who looked as though he was about to boil over. "I'll shoot you dead, Kavenagh, if you don't pick up that axe and your liquor jug and get out of here. I'm holding the gun on you until you do. And don't come back. I'm warning you. Now you git!"

Brogan could feel his own blood begin to simmer. "I'm not *gitting* anywhere. I came here to cut firewood, and by heavens, that's exactly what I'm going to do. I'm done for the day now, but you can be sure I'll be back tomorrow to do the same until I have all I need. Now you can like it or not like it, it's up to you. You can go and get the sheriff if you want to. I'll save you the trip though because he's only going to tell you the same thing I am. It belongs to me now. That's why they gave me the piece of paper that said so. Now you get off my land. I'm done fooling around with you."

Storey took another step closer, his finger on the trigger. Was the shotgun even loaded? No! He could see it in Storey's eyes that it wasn't, and he relaxed a little. The old fool was bluffing him.

"I'd like to see you try to put me off my own land! That'll be the day a Kavenagh tells me what to do. My nephew and his wife will back me up if I call them up here," Storey announced triumphantly glancing back at his passengers before turning to face Brogan again. "He figured I'd have trouble with you 'cause he knows the Kavenaghs. He's a good rugged lad himself and he's also armed."

Brogan glanced at the wagon. He didn't recognize the nephew, or the woman, but he sized them up quickly. The man he guessed to be a little younger than his own age, and a bully, the wife as timid as a mouse. The nephew had a gun, a Winchester like his own, and he knew there was about to be bad trouble. Someone was going to get hurt here today because, for sure, there'd be gunplay. He could feel it.

It happened so quickly that there was no time to react. Brogan watched in disbelief as the nephew raised his rifle, and a loud crack split the warm September afternoon. Fatally shot, Latham Storey crumpled into a lifeless heap.

Brogan knew he would never forget the look of surprise on Latham's face when the bullet smashed into his back, his mouth agape, and his eyes widened in horror.

The nephew now trained his weapon on Brogan. "You're next Kavenagh, if you make one move toward that rifle," he said, having already spotted Brogan's weapon standing against the tree. "If you don't think I'll do it, just look at the man lying in front of you. That's right, he's my uncle, and if I'd shoot my own kin, I sure as hell will shoot you. Make no mistake about it."

Brogan remained tensed and alert as the nephew got slowly off the wagon and walked toward him, rifle at the ready. The wife, her hands folded in her lap, sat crying quietly on the wagon seat.

The nephew glanced over his shoulder. "Shut up, Josephine! Stop that almighty blubbering."

The woman put her hand over her mouth, although her shoulders still shook.

The nephew kept his gun trained on Brogan as he picked his way forward until he was standing on the other side of his uncle's body.

"You don't know who I am, do you, Kavenagh?"

Brogan never took his eyes off him. "No, I can't say as I ever saw you before in my life. Am I supposed to know you?"

"Let's just say I come from a big family. There *was* nine of us boys, and the one thing our pa always knocked into our heads was to take up for each other. Anything wrong done to us had to be made right, no matter how long it took. And don't be stupid about it, he told us. When you get someone, get 'em good, but don't get any blood on your own hands."

Brogan was incredulous. "I'd say you've got blood on your hands here today. You just shot your own uncle in the back. You killed him in cold blood!"

"I didn't kill anybody, Kavenagh. You did. You're the one who shot him in cold blood."

"You're crazy."

"Not as crazy as you might think I am. My name's Ambrose Burk, Amby for short. Ring any bells now?"

Brogan knew in an instant who the man was. "You're Tuncy Burk's brother."

"Yup! And you killed my brother and got off with it. You walked away without so much as a slap on the wrist. I've waited a long time to even the score with you."

"Your brother jumped me. Everyone saw it. He started that fight, and he got the worst of it is all. I didn't mean for him to hit his head. He tripped over his own man and fell. Anyway, I was defending myself. There were plenty of witnesses who saw the whole thing. My friends and I were minding our own business and Tuncy came with that bunch he ran with and went after us."

"You killed my brother!"

"It was an accident! I didn't kill anyone!"

"You were the last one to have your hands on him, so it was your fault. I don't care what any sheriff said. They're all bought and paid for anyway, in my opinion. To our family, you were the one responsible for Tuncy's death. He'd be here with us right now if it wasn't for you."

Brogan watched the man in front of him with narrowed eyes. The Burks were clannish and ruthless by reputation. Sure, as a Kavenagh, he'd gotten into more than his fair share of fights, starting in the schoolyard, but he didn't go out looking for someone to hurt. Tuncy and his gang were mean-spirited, and he could see now that it ran in the family. He'd always heard it wasn't wise to have a Burk for an enemy, but he'd had no idea they'd go this far. The man had shot his own uncle with no apparent remorse. It made his blood run cold. He fought nausea. He'd never seen anyone gunned down.

"Look, Burk, I felt terrible that your brother died. I mean, I didn't like him, at all, but I didn't want to see him dead. It's something that still bothers me."

Amby's grip on the rifle didn't loosen. "Isn't that nice. You feel terrible."

"Well, I do! You doing this here today, though, is not going to bring him back. You've done murder. I don't know what you're working at, but you won't get away with it."

Amby shrugged in an exaggerated gesture. "What are you talking about? I already have."

"Whatever your game is, *you* killed your uncle. He thought you were coming to help him."

"Someone would have shot him sooner or later anyway. He fought with everyone, and no one in the family liked him. That's how us Burks operate. Things that need doin' get done, and we stay clean. Didn't you ever wonder why your brother, Garrett, left town so fast a few years ago?"

Brogan did recall that Garrett had found a good job at the carriage factory in Sackville. Then, all of a sudden, he was gone. He'd come back a few years after that, all married up and happy, but he'd never said why he'd moved to practically the other end of the province. Not that he worried too much about it. Garrett was a big boy and could take care of himself.

"Yeah, so, he left Sackville. So what?"

Amby laughed, but it was not a pleasant sound. "He left Sackville because my brother, Donnie, saw to it that he got fired and no one else would hire him. See that's what I mean. We get the job done, but we keep our hands clean. You killed *our* brother, so one of us hurt *your* brother, well, close to one anyway, although not as bad as he deserved. Donnie got him where it hurt most, in the money purse.

"Now you, Brogan, deserve a lot worse because you are a flat-out murderer. First you killed Tuncy. Now you killed one fine upstanding citizen, Latham Storey, my mother's dear brother. You shot an unarmed man. When the sheriff comes, I'll show him where you hid your gun. He'll see there was a shot fired because I assume you keep it fully loaded. Only now there'll be one cartridge gone. And guess what?" He pointed to his own gun. "I'm carrying a Winchester too. So, the bullet in Uncle Latham's back will also match your gun. Face it, Kavenagh, you're finally going to get what's coming to you."

"There's no shot missing from my rifle, but there's one missing from yours."

Amby smiled. "A warning shot. I had good reason to think you might shoot me too … or my wife."

Brogan could feel sweat trickle between his shoulder blades and on down the middle of his back. "You're crazy. It's my word over yours."

"Really!"

"Yes, really!"

"Make that two against one." He turned and called over his shoulder to his wife. "Josephine! Come up here!"

Josephine obediently climbed down from the wagon, seemingly having regained some of her composure. She came to stand beside Amby, averting her eyes from the dead man lying on the ground between them.

Amby didn't look at Josephine as he spoke to her. "Tell Mr. Kavenagh here what you observed as we pulled up at the side of the road."

Her voice was tremulous, but she was clearly well rehearsed. "I saw this man here," she said, pointing a finger in Brogan's direction, "shoot your Uncle Latham. Uncle was walking away when he aimed at his back and shot him. I saw the whole thing as plain as day. He intended to do murder, and he did."

Brogan felt anger dash through him at top speed. "You're a liar! You never saw any such thing. I never shot anyone. It was your husband who shot him. I saw *that whole thing as plain as day*. Both of you are trying to frame me, but it won't work."

Amby was shockingly nonchalant. "You don't think so? With your reputation? You already talked your way out of one murder. I guarantee you won't talk your way out of another one. Don't forget, my witness here saw everything. You stole my poor uncle's land, and when he confronted you about it, you shot him dead. And in the back, I might add. Oh, and by the way, my uncle told me he was afraid of you, on more than one occasion. He said you might try to shoot him so you could keep the land. Isn't that right, Josephine?"

She nodded obediently, although still white as a sheet. "I heard him say that this very afternoon," she told Brogan. "He said he was going to try to talk to you one more time before he sent for the sheriff. But then you went ahead and shot him anyway just as he feared you would."

Brogan's jaw muscles clenched. "You're not going to get away with this, either one of you."

"Get away with what?" Amby asked Brogan before turning to his wife. "Go get that rope from the back of the wagon and bring it up here."

Josephine hurried away to do his bidding, returning moments later with a length of hemp rope.

"Now tie him up," Amby ordered her. "And do a proper job of it, or he might shoot you too if you know what I mean."

Josephine somehow kept her tears at bay as she looped the rope around Brogan's wrists and tied them surprisingly tight until his hands were indeed bound fast in front of him. When Brogan was secure, Amby picked up the other man's rifle, discharged it once into the air, then flung it a few yards away into a thicket.

"There," he told Brogan, clearly pleased with himself, "one shot missing from your gun." He waved his rifle in the direction of the wagon. "Now get going, both of you," he added, scowling at his wife.

Brogan's jaw was clenched so tightly it hurt. "I'm not going anywhere with you."

Amby levelled the gun at Brogan. "I'm arresting you and taking you to the sheriff. Josephine and I will tell him what we saw, and they'll jail you for sure. You killed Tuncy, now I'm going to see you killed, Kavenagh. You're going to hang."

Chapter 2

Brogan knew real fear in that moment because that's exactly what would happen if Sheriff Ratchford ever got his hands on him again. Percival Ratchford didn't like the Kavenagh boys. He'd made no secret of that, and Brogan had played right into his hands when he'd been roughing it up around the countryside. Sure, things were different now, but Ratchford didn't care that Brogan had settled down and left his rowdy ways behind.

He well remembered that night in Ratchford's custody, the night Tuncy Burk had died. Ratchford had wanted to pin that death on him in the worst way, but there'd just been too many witnesses who told him otherwise. So, he'd had to let him go. Not before he'd manhandled him while still in shackles. That's where the broken arm and ribs had come in, although everyone thought it was Tuncy who'd done it. The last thing the sheriff said to him that night was: "I'll get you, Kavenagh, make no mistake about that, and then it'll be all over." He had no chance here, and Amby Burk knew it. That much was obvious.

Amby brought the rifle closer to Brogan's head. "I said, get in the wagon. You and I are going to see the sheriff. You done murder, and I'm going to make sure you pay."

In a lightning move Brogan whipped forward, headbutting Amby Burk with a mighty crash to the forehead. Josephine screamed as Amby crumpled to the ground, out cold, the gun slipping from his fingers as he fell. Josephine backed up, saucer-eyed.

Brogan held his hands out to her, his head throbbing. Blood had begun to seep from a cut above his eye socket. "Untie me!"

"No...." she whimpered. "I fear you'll harm me too."

"Do it!" he shouted at her. "Now, and be fast about it!"

Still, she held back. "Please don't hurt me ... don't have your way with me."

Brogan threw back his head in disgust, the sharp movement causing knife-like pain to ricochet in his temples. Have his way with her? Good lord!

"I'm not going to hurt you or have my way with you. I promise. Just undo the ropes," he added, trying to inject a gentleness into his words that he was far from feeling.

If he didn't try to calm her down, she'd likely dissolve into a useless heap on the ground and he'd be sunk for sure. He was used to women with a backbone, like his Maggie and his mother for that matter. He'd never thought it necessary to try to best a woman, browbeat her into submission, but the one he had on his hands now obviously had been. He had to consider that if he was to have any chance at all.

"Listen to me," he told her patiently, expecting more traffic along the road at any second. "Untie my hands as quickly as you can. Get hold of yourself and do it, and then I'll be gone."

Trembling violently, she struggled with the knot, precious minutes flying by. Finally, she loosened it and unwound the rope, her eyes wide with terror. He knew she was still pondering her own fate.

He briefly flexed his wrists before snatching the rope from her hands. "You sit down there by that tree," he said, nodding toward the large birch, "where I can keep an eye on you."

Josephine, seemingly used to years of blind obedience, did as she was told although she continued to sniffle noisily.

Brogan wiped a bare arm across his face, bringing it back with a mixture of sweat and blood. His eyes stung. Working quickly, he tied Burk's hands securely behind his back. The man would be coming around any minute, and he had to get out of there. He spied his shirt lying where he'd tossed it earlier. Grabbing it, he ordered Josephine to put her hands behind her back and secured them as best he could with the shirt. He then seized Burk's rifle by the barrel and hurled it into the woods.

Amby had already begun to moan as Brogan hurried to the road and climbed aboard Storey's wagon. Releasing the handbrake, he turned the team back in the direction they had come. The horse on the right appeared to be the more skittish of the two, so jumping clear of the wagon he gave its rump a mighty slap. As he'd hoped, the animal jumped ahead in the traces, his mate having no choice but to follow. The wagon rattled away down the hill. He knew they'd probably go only a half-mile or so. From their appearance, they were an old team and already tired from being driven here so hard. They wouldn't go far before needing a rest, likely right back to old Latham's place. That distance would give him the head start he needed. That would be ideal because a wagon sitting on the roadside or abandoned in a field was sure to raise suspicion before he was able to get out of there.

He knew Amby and his wife would be okay, although that headbutt would leave his opponent with a king-sized headache. Maybe worse than his own. They would manage to get themselves untied and find the uncle's wagon by following the tracks. All of that would give him time to escape.

He swiped at the cut on his eyebrow with no effect. He'd head for home, but not by the main road. There were plenty of footpaths around here from the early days, and one led right past his place. Breathing hard, he started through the woods. The sound of Josephine's weeping grew fainter in the distance. He expected the woman cried a lot with Amby Burk for a husband, and he pitied her. But right now, she was a very dangerous woman. Her lies could help get him hanged. He knew there was no chance of her going against her husband in this. If she'd said it in the first place, she would continue to do so. And it wasn't like she would be pressed about her testimony. Her words would be considered as good as carved in stone when they left her mouth.

His headache continued in a dull, aching throb, and he only hoped that Burk was suffering more. In his wildest dreams, he would never have imagined a man could do what Amby Burk had just done: murder his own uncle right in front of Brogan and appear indifferent about it as if he were pleased. It was unbelievable. How much hate could there be inside a person to do such a thing? Not only kill someone but do it to frame an innocent man. He'd heard of people who swore by vengeance. Now, he was experiencing it.

He thought back to the night Tuncy Burk had died. He remembered it all very well. Maggie had begged him not to go out that night. She'd had a feeling there would be trouble and was rarely wrong with such premonitions; she wasn't that night either.

At last, his homestead came into view. It could hardly be called a farm, they only raised what they needed. There was a large vegetable garden, and he could see Maggie in it now, likely picking the last of this summer's green beans. Luke would be on his way home from school.

His stomach churning, he called out to Maggie as he cleared the trees at a jog.

"I'm in the garden, sweetheart," she answered, raising her voice to be heard.

Time was a precious commodity if he intended to put any distance behind him before nightfall. He couldn't even afford the extra minutes to go as far as the garden.

"Maggie, come! Please hurry!"

He saw her jump up, recognizing the urgency in his voice. Dropping her bean basket, she ran for the house, meeting him at the back door.

"Dear God, Brogan! What has happened?" she demanded, her eyes wide, reaching up to touch the purple swelling under one eye, and then the large bruise forming on his forehead. "Were you in a fight? Your face is bleeding."

He placed his hands firmly on her shoulders. "I was in a fight, yes, but not of my own choosing. I don't have time to tell you everything, not now. I will try to come back later."

"You tell me now, Brogan Kavenagh! What has happened to you? You don't look well. I think we should fetch the doctor."

He tried to smile. "Now, my beloved, you have seen me look much worse than this. I'll be all right." Dropping his hands, he made to move past her into the house but she tried to hold him back.

There were tears in her eyes. "I certainly have seen worse, but it's been a while. Don't do this to me, Brogan! Tell me what happened. Stop pulling away from me!"

He took hold of her shoulders again. "Maggie, I need you to be strong. Something terrible has happened, and I have to leave. A man has been murdered, and they're blaming me. The sheriff will come and arrest me, and I will hang. I have no chance in this."

Her chest had begun to heave. "Why would they blame you? What did you do?"

"I did nothing!" he shouted in frustration.

"Was it an accident like before then?"

He squeezed her shoulders tightly. "Maggie, listen to me! I have to leave right now, or I'm a dead man. Throw some food together that I can take with me. Get my pistol and holster from the trunk upstairs while I go and saddle the horse. Oh, and I'll need a heavy shirt and my buckskin jacket."

"Brogan!"

"Do it! Please, Maggie, it has to be this way. I'll come back when I can."

"You mean *if* you can."

He nodded miserably as he pulled her roughly against him. "I'm so sorry about this.

Believe me, none of this is my doing. I have no choice but to leave, or they will kill me."

She raised her face to his, stricken. "Oh, my darling, Brogan. Why does it have to be this way? I can hardly take it all in. But time is of the essence, isn't it?"

"Yes, it is," he said, his chin resting on the top of her head. "I have to be on my way within minutes."

"But where will you go?"

"I'll decide that as I ride. I'll take the old footpath east that follows the river. It'll be rough going, but Dutch and I'll manage. That gelding is sound and as sure-footed as they come. He'll get me to wherever I'm going."

Minutes later, he was ready to leave, Dutch anxious as usual to be underway now that he was saddled. The five-year-old chestnut loved it when Brogan took him out for a fast run, and he'd get plenty of that today. Maggie could handle the big horse, too. She was as good a rider as he was, the only girl in a family of boys from up Dorchester way. She'd grown up as rough and tumble as her brothers. It'd take a lot to throw her, and not just with horses. That was the only thing that gave him any peace of mind to leave her and Luke as he was doing now.

They hugged urgently for only a few moments before he climbed into the saddle and was gone. For how long, he did not know, maybe forever, but he would not hang. Not for something he didn't do.

"I'm sorry to be going like this, Maggie. It's a terrible thing for you, I know."

She lifted her chin, a glint of defiance in those sparkling green eyes of hers. "I understand now it would also be terrible for you to stay. At least this way, I know you'll likely still be alive. I will not stand by and watch my husband hanged for something he didn't do. Don't worry about me, Brogan. I can take care of myself." She eyed the Henry repeating rifle leaning against the side of the house. "I know how to use that, and I will if I have to. And don't worry about Luke. He'll be safe here with me. As long as there's breath in my body, our son will come to no harm. Now you go, my love, and may God ride with you until we can be together again."

He didn't try to hide the tears that rolled down his cheeks. "I will miss you both."

Her tears ran unchecked as well. "And us you, Brogan Kavenagh. Remember our hearts are with you no matter where you go or how long you must stay away. Be safe, my husband."

* * *

Travelling was rough for the first couple of miles. Indeed, there was a footpath, but it was badly overgrown in a tangle of undergrowth and young trees. The going would have been even worse if Dutch hadn't been so surefooted. The river could be more accurately described as a stream. Still, it was a welcome source of water for the horse on such a warm day, although now that nighttime was close in hand, it was cooling off quickly. He'd already put on his jacket. He knew the buckskin would help stave off the deep chill when the late September night was full upon them. And he was hungry. He'd been starved after a full day's work, anxious to take his empty belly home for Maggie to lovingly fill. The provisions she'd been able to throw together without any notice were spare by comparison. His stomach rumbled. It was going to be a long night.

"Come on, Dutch, my boy," Brogan encouraged the horse, whose energy began to flag after several miles of tough travelling. "Just another mile or two, and we'll stop for the night," he told the animal, leaning forward to pat the big horse's neck.

At last, when darkness had begun to fall, Brogan pulled the horse up in a small clearing and slid wearily out of the saddle. He remembered this spot. He and Tabor had been up here hunting a few years ago and had found an old trapper's cabin. It'd been falling down back then, so most likely no more than a pile of rotten logs by now. And then he spotted it, over to his left. The building was nothing more than ruins, but not yet the pile of logs he'd imagined. Two sagging walls held together, the roof clinging to life in that corner. It would provide shelter for the night. The weather had turned over the past hour or so, dense clouds gathering ominously, thunder in the distance.

The clearing was no more than a wide gap among the trees, saplings having sprung up to reclaim what had been taken by the woodcutter. Still, there was grass growing in the spaces exposed to sunlight. Dutch immediately busied himself, munching hungrily to supplement what he'd gotten along the riverbank.

Brogan headed for what amounted to a lean-to, in its present condition. Striking one precious match, he took a quick look inside to see if it was already occupied, say by a bear. No sign of a bear, but it was obvious small animals took refuge there, evidence of raccoons everywhere. He wouldn't be able to do much about the droppings tonight, but he would at least get he and Dutch under cover. He had no sooner done so when a downpour drummed on the old thatched roof with the precision of a military tattoo.

A fire would be a most welcome friend, but he dared not light one in case his pursuers were close behind. But he would eat because Maggie had packed cornbread, cheese, apples, venison jerky, and water. It wasn't the meal he'd envisioned when he'd thought about home and hearth this afternoon, but he would be all right ... at least for the next couple of days. And then what? Certain death awaited him at home. Certain death lay in wait for him here too, if he couldn't find a way to live off the land. How long could he manage with winter not more than a month away? His tired mind thrust the question at him, and his answer came back just as quickly. He would manage somehow.

"Let's get settled down for the night," Brogan told the horse as he pulled off the saddle and blanket. "I'm sure you're just as tired as I am, so let's get at it."

Dutch nickered. He knew the horse understood something was not right, but if he had anything reassuring to say to the animal, he would have said it to himself first. Damned if he could think of anything.

* * *

Brogan wasn't sure what had wakened him, but the first thing he realized was that the rain had stopped. Slowly, he shook off enough sleep to listen clearly. There it was again! Something *or someone* walked around outside the old cabin. His muscles tensed as he reached for the Colt pistol, feeling only marginally better with the weight of it in his hand. The gun belt had plenty more ammunition in it come to that, but it occurred to him that if he did have to shoot anyone, he could very well kill whomever it was. Then he *would* be guilty of murder. His stomach soured. He held his breath as the footsteps came closer to what used to be a window, but had long ago been boarded up.

He expected any second to hear: "Brogan Kavenagh, come out with your hands in the air!"

However, Percival Ratchford wouldn't give anyone even that much of a chance. He was a dirty one, although he played the part of an upstanding government official to keep his political connections happy. He would shoot first and claim it was self-defense. That was especially true in his case, since he'd sworn to get him. Brogan's breath was painful in his chest, hardly daring to breathe, his head still aching. And then Dutch nickered softly. The footsteps outside quickened.

"Eeurghhh!"

The call of the cow moose startled Brogan, Dutch blowing hard in alarm. He spoke to the horse in an effort to quiet him. The moose called again. Of course, this was the fall rut and there were plenty of moose in the area, an encounter like this was not at all uncommon. It wasn't as though Dutch had never heard such a thing before either, or himself. Brogan and Maggie had often lain in bed at night and heard moose calling, both male and female, in the woods nearby.

"Settle down, boy," he spoke softly to the horse. "It's just an old moose. She'll be moving off soon."

And it wasn't long before the cow moose did leave, her call now much further away.

Relief flooded through him that it was only an animal outside, but the hard truth of his situation continued to settle over him like a cold, wet blanket. He was a man on the run, a wanted man. The fact that he'd run would be taken as proof of guilt by those who expected nothing less from a Kavenagh, but what other choice did he have? It made absolutely no sense at all to stay and face his accusers. The dice had already been cast, and he was on the losing side. And, despite the fact that his tired brain continued to circle the problem, there were no answers of how to help himself that made any sense. His only hope was that Josephine Burk would eventually weaken and tell the truth, but the chance of that happening was so remote it was ridiculous to consider it. She looked like a woman completely under the control of her husband. She would do exactly as she was told or face something even more awful than the law.

And now he'd added assault, and heaven only knew what other crimes they would tack onto him, doing what he'd done to get away. Even carrying this pistol was breaking the law here. He would get six months jail time just for owning the thing, unless he had it for just cause, such as defending his life or his property. He was pretty sure they wouldn't consider escaping a murder charge as just cause.

It was a beauty though, a single-action six-shot revolver that had belonged to his father back in Hamilton County, New York. He remembered seeing him carry it, and his mother had brought it with them when they'd fled to Canada. Since he wasn't even supposed to have it, he kept it locked in the trunk upstairs. Luke already knew how to handle the Winchester and the Henry, but he didn't want his son to know about the handgun.

* * *

It might have been an hour or more, but he did manage to go back to sleep. It was Dutch's pawing the dirt floor that woke him at daylight. The gelding was a pasture horse. He disliked being in the barn for any length of time, and that's what this was to him, a small barn. He was anxious to get outside for fresh grass.

Rousing his stiff body from the corner where he lay on some boughs he'd scraped together last night, Brogan led the animal outside and tied him next to an ample growth of grass.

* * *

Later that night, Maggie was putting Luke to bed when there came a loud pounding on the back door, rattling it on its hinges. Fear dashed through her. That would be the men looking for her husband. She had been waiting for this moment, dreading it.

"Ma!" yelled Luke, turning to his mother. "What's happening? Why is Pa not here to help us?"

Maggie worked to keep her voice even. "I told you, Luke, your pa had to go away, but we're going to be just fine. Now I've got to go down and see to whoever's at the door. You go to sleep, dear. You've got to go to school in the morning."

Luke was already out of bed, pulling his britches on over his nightshirt. Almost nine, he was as tall as an eleven-year-old, and well built like his father.

"I'm going downstairs with you, Ma."

Maggie looked back at him. There was no time to argue. It would be a wasted effort to do so anyway. Down the stairs the two of them hurried to see who was causing the commotion. Taking a deep breath, she turned up the lamp and unlatched the door just as another volley of fist pounding thrust it open, forcing her to step back or be knocked down.

Sheriff Ratchford stood ready to attack the door again. "Where is that no good husband of yours, woman?"

She squared her shoulders. "If you're talking about Brogan, I have no idea. He left late this afternoon, and I haven't heard from

41

him since. I would imagine he's a long way from here by now."

Pushing past her, Ratchford marched into the room as though he owned the house. He was followed by three men, mean looking and plainly driven by bloodlust. All carried weapons. Brogan was right. These men were no better than rabid dogs bent on capturing their prey.

Maggie stood her ground, and Ratchford sneered in her face. "I don't believe you. You've got him hid in here somewhere." He turned to two of the men. "Boys, search the barn and the outbuildings, Whitlong and I will look in here."

The two tasked with searching the outside buildings left with torches aloft.

Ratchford turned to the third deputy, a squat man with a bushy red beard and lifeless eyes. "Tear this place apart."

"Search if you must," Maggie told him, struggling to keep her voice even and remain calm. Intimidation was the currency of these men, and she refused to give them the satisfaction of reacting to it.

If they thought she was going to cower and succumb to the vapours, they had another think coming. Besides, she had Luke to consider. She and Brogan understood that to help make Luke strong, he must be taught such things through example.

Maggie reached out a hand to her son. "Come over here, Luke, and stand by me. These men have a job to do. Let them do it and see that your father isn't here, then they can be on their way."

Ratchford and Whitlong searched the premises, the house now nearly in shambles. As though Brogan would be hiding in the sewing basket, they spitefully turned upside down, scattering the contents across the floor. It was the same with the flour bin. They would have done worse at that point if the other two men had not trotted back into the house.

"There's an empty stall in the barn, and there's tack missing. So, he must have left on horseback," the taller of the two informed the sheriff.

That stopped Ratchford in his tracks, wheeling on Maggie. "So, he left on horseback, did he?"

Maggie stood her ground, her chin raised defiantly. "I told you he was gone, and I doubt you'll catch him. He's got at least a four-hour lead. You've wasted your time searching here."

Maggie had never seen a man's face go purple.

Ratchford looked as though he was about to explode. "We'll find him, don't you worry. He's done murder, shot a man down in cold blood."

Maggie worked to keep her temper under control. "My husband would never do such a thing. You're mistaken. Besides, isn't a man entitled to a trial? Innocent until proven guilty?"

Ratchford's smile was feral. "He's guilty, all right. He escaped the hangman's noose once. I assure you he will not do so again. I'd tear him to pieces with my own hands before I allowed that to happen."

"My pa could lick you with one hand tied behind his back," Luke told Ratchford recklessly.

Maggie hated that her son had to be subjected to this. "Luke! That'll be enough, son. This will all be sorted out." She turned to face Ratchford. "You'll see."

She could well understand why Brogan had run. His life was indeed on the line. If he faced this howling mob, he'd never make it to the shiretown alive to stand trial.

"I'll see nothing!" Ratchford roared at Maggie. "You're just as bad as he is. Any woman who would lie down with the likes of Brogan Kavenagh isn't much. Matter of fact, maybe you would like to lie with one of us before we go. Maybe all of us."

Her hand, with a will of its own, reared back and slapped him soundly across the face.

Ratchford grabbed her by the hair, twisting it painfully. "You'll pay for that, you little...."

Luke had somehow managed to inch his way to where the rifle stood in the corner and got hold of it. Lifting the Henry, he aimed it straight at Ratchford. "Let my mother go...."

Chapter 3

"Luke! No!" Maggie shouted, wincing, her hair still firmly in Ratchford's vice-like grip.

Luke never wavered, his thumb slowly pulling the hammer back to the full cock position. "Let her go, or I'll shoot. I mean it."

Maggie was horrified at the look in her son's eyes. They were his father's eyes, and they burned with the same intensity. Just like his father, even at such a young age, he did not make idle threats. But this was her son, her eight-year-old baby. She could not allow this to carry through to a disastrous conclusion. If Luke shot Ratchford, one of the other men would shoot Luke. They might just as well shoot her, too, if she had to watch her son die.

Ratchford was smart enough to know a genuine threat when he saw one. This child was capable of ending his life. He let go of Maggie's hair, which now hung free from its coil atop her head, falling in an auburn waterfall to her waist. Her scalp was on fire.

"We're wasting time here with them while Kavenagh is getting away," Ratchford announced to the three men watching him closely, waiting for orders.

Even these ruffians who threw their weight around under the guise of law enforcement did not want the blood of a child on their hands.

The stout man with the red beard said, "We can't track him in the dark, Sheriff. He's likely miles away by now anyway."

Ratchford's smile was malevolent, one that pulled his lips back over discoloured, uneven teeth. "He's not miles away, men. He's probably much closer than we think. If he's not here, I know exactly where to look next. Come on! We've no more time to waste."

Within moments, the sheriff and his motley deputies were gone, although the air remained thick with the stench of their sweating bodies. That they'd come up empty-handed had only added to their bad temper. Hoof beats pounded out of the yard and down the road, torches high in a fiery macabre spectacle.

Maggie began to shiver, steeling herself to hold her nerves in check. She'd known this was coming but had not imagined it would be so soul-rending. Ratchford had come for her husband before, although he'd not been as ravenous as he was tonight. He'd been only a year or so into his job as sheriff that first time, a strutting cock consumed with his own importance. Now, with more time under his belt to relish his position of unquestioned authority, he was to be truly feared. And the cronies he deputized shared his malicious zeal.

"It's over, Luke," she told the child, who seemed rooted to the spot, the gun frozen in his grip, although now lowered. "Put the rifle down, son."

Luke carefully uncocked the Henry rifle, just as he'd been taught, and set it back against the wall in the corner. He looked at his mother with questioning eyes, and then suddenly, he was a little boy again, unsure and very badly frightened.

Crossing the room quickly, she took him into her arms. At first, he became rigid and resistant. Then she felt his muscles gradually relax until he sagged against her as his tears flowed. She let him cry it out. She felt like doing the same thing but would not allow that. Her muscles remained stiff, poised, ready for whatever came next.

"There, there," she said, comforting the boy. "It's all over now. They're gone."

"He's going to come back and arrest me, isn't he, Ma?" Luke sobbed. "I pointed a gun at the sheriff and threatened to shoot him, but I couldn't let him hurt you. Pa wouldn't."

She stroked his hair, as black and thick as his father's. "You were defending me, Luke. Sheriff Ratchford is a bad man, and he does bad things. It's true, though, you must think carefully before you point a weapon at anyone. You can't threaten to shoot people, but this was a very unusual circumstance, and it's over. Now, we'll lock the door for the night and go back to our beds. Remember that you have school in the morning, and I have plenty of work to do around here ... now, besides my regular chores. Everything can't stop just because your father is away for a while."

Luke still clung to his mother. "They said he done murder."

Maggie took a deep, steadying breath. "They're wrong. I don't know all of the details yet. Your father didn't have time to tell me the entire story before he left, but know one thing, Luke Kavenagh, your father would not do what they're accusing him of. Your Pa is a good, decent man. He regrets he had to go so quickly. He didn't have a chance to say goodbye to you, so try to imagine that he's right here with us now. Go on back to bed, son, and know your pa is with you in your heart."

Settled down now, he went back to bed. She doubted he would get much sleep, although she was hopeful. Shaken herself but determined to overcome it, she stoked the fire before heading to bed. It was then that the tears came, and she held her pillow close to her face lest Luke should hear her. She longed for Brogan's reassuring arms around her and hers around him. Where was her husband at this very hour? Was he safe?

A barred owl hooted in the nearby forest. Its haunting nighttime cry was answered a short distance away by another of its kind. Normally, she loved the sound of those birds, especially on such a beautiful clear evening. It had rained earlier, but the full moon was out now and impossibly huge. Countless stars bedazzled the inky heavens, but nature had no joy tonight.

She pulled Brogan's pillow against her chest again, burying her face in the white cotton where his scent lingered. Little had she known when she'd made love with him at daybreak how different their world would be when darkness fell. She missed him desperately. Steeling herself, she knew she must refrain from giving in to her emotions any further. There would be some very difficult days and possibly weeks ahead, but she would never accept the possible loss of her beloved husband when all of the dust from this nightmare eventually settled.

* * *

Tabor Kavenagh had just finished laying another log on the fire before returning to bed when he heard an almighty banging on the kitchen door. What in the! He was out of bed in an instant as the racket at the back door continued. Pulling on his pants, he shoved his feet into his boots and nearly ran into Pate as he hurried out of the bedroom and down the stairs into the kitchen.

Pate lit the lamp and turned it up as his father went to see who was at the door. He'd just finished undoing the latch when Sheriff Ratchford and his men stormed into the room. Tabor and Pate had to step back or be knocked to the floor.

Tabor was incensed. He knew Ratchford. Everyone around here did and rightfully feared him. It was worse if you found yourself on the wrong side of the law.

The sheriff yelled, "Where is he? Where is that devil of a brother of yours? You've got about five seconds to drag him on out here so we can take him into custody."

Tabor's fists balled at his side. "Are you talking about Brogan?"

Ratchford took a step closer. "I'm talking about Brogan. He's done murder. Your brother shot a man down in cold blood, and we're taking him in to be hanged."

Pate stepped forward. "Don't you mean you're taking him in for trial, or does a Kavenagh even get one of those around here?"

Ratchford swung his attention to Pate. "You watch your mouth, boy, or you'll end up in jail too. We've got lots of room for Kavenaghs. Hell, that's why they went to all the trouble of building the place. Now, where is he?"

Tabor was seething. "I haven't seen my brother for weeks. He's not here."

Ratchford eyed Pate again. "What about you, boy? You seen your brother tonight? Think careful before you lie to me."

Pate returned Ratchford's glare without blinking. "He's not my brother, he's my uncle, and no, I haven't seen him either. Same as my father said, not for a few weeks."

Ratchford looked back at his goons. They were like mad dogs waiting to be let off their tethers. "Search the place, boys. Pete and Edward, you take the outbuildings, same as before. You, Whitlong," he said to the stout deputy, "help me go through this place."

Tabor started forward. "Now, you just hold on there. No one's going to go through my home. You've got no reason to."

Ratchford was lightning quick with his rifle butt, and Tabor collapsed to the floor, knocked cold. The sheriff then turned his attention to Pate. "You want to be next? I can oblige you, ya stinkin' whelp. I'd just as soon lay all you Kavenaghs out, so one more won't matter to me."

Outnumbered, Pate reluctantly stepped aside, and if looks could kill, Ratchford and his deputy would be the ones laid out cold.

Ratchford and his man made a methodical sweep through the small house, coming up empty-handed. That didn't improve their already irascible mood. When the two deputies returned from searching the outbuildings and reported that Brogan Kavenagh was nowhere to be found,

Ratchford doubled his efforts indoors. Again, they went from room to room, turning over furniture and emptying any spot large enough to hide a man of Brogan's size.

When they returned to the kitchen, Tabor was coming around. The room spun, his stomach soured with nausea, and his head pounded. His first thought was for his son as he struggled to stand up and was relieved to see Pate unharmed. The room still felt tilted as he noticed Ratchford standing nearby.

"Tell me where he is, or so help me, we'll torch this place," the sheriff told Tabor in ominous tones. "He might not be in this house, but you know where he's gone."

Tabor tried to shake his head for no, but it hurt too much. "I told you I don't know where he is. Neither one of us does. You said he did murder. That's the first I heard about that. Where was it supposed to have happened?"

Ratchford took a step closer. "You calling me a liar?"

Tabor would give anything to get his hands on the sheriff, but he held his temper. If anything happened to him, they'd get Pate. "I'm saying I don't know anything about a murder. But I know my brother, and he wouldn't just shoot a man in cold blood."

Ratchford stepped forward, his face mere inches from Tabor's. "And I'm saying he did. We have witnesses, one of them being a woman. She and her husband saw the whole thing. This is your last chance before we set fire to this shack. Where is your brother? You don't tell me, and while this place is burning, I'll be running both of you in for harbouring a known criminal and getting in the way of justice. The choice is yours."

Tabor was getting his equilibrium back now, but there were still plenty of cobwebs. "You want to burn this house down, Ratchford? Then get to it, but it's not going to get you any closer to my brother. I have no idea where he went. He could have found a ship sailing out of Sackville and be on it for all I know. Ever think of looking down there?"

Tabor could tell by the light that suddenly sprang to life in Ratchford's small eyes that he had not considered such a possibility. The sheriff did not like being denied. He was a violent man who abused his authority, and his blood lust was obviously getting in the way of rational thought.

Ratchford watched Tabor. "You better hope we find what we're looking for there, Kavenagh, because if we don't, we're coming back here and finishing up."

Pate could stay silent no longer, his jaw muscles working furiously. "Leave my father alone! He's not guilty of anything, and besides, you can't just burn down somebody's house because you don't get what you want."

Tabor turned his head slowly in his son's direction. "Shut up, Pate!" he shouted.

Pate's chest was heaving. "Well, he can't!"

Tabor leaned against the doorjamb to steady himself. "Pate, be quiet, I say!"

But Pate had drawn Ratchford's attention. "I can't? You just watch me. Accidents can take place at any time. You push me, I push you, a torch gets dropped, and before you know it the house is afire. You best listen to your pa here and mind your tongue, or that could happen."

Ratchford turned his attention to his deputies. "Come on, men. He's not here, but we'll get him. Maybe we *will* find him in Sackville."

* * *

The search in Sackville didn't produce any better results. It was late when the group of four riders arrived at the waterfront, and it was plain to see there hadn't been any activity there for the past several hours. When they did manage to find someone in authority to ask, the answer was the same. Nothing had sailed from there for a week.

It was well past midnight when the four lawmen found an inn for the night and a stable for their tired horses. Their strategy to track Brogan on the well-travelled road was a fool's errand, its deplorable condition making it almost impossible. Likewise, the search of Brogan's homestead and the Kavenagh farm had proved fruitless. Sheriff Ratchford finally determined they would seek out any sign of travel on the old footpath that followed the river to the east. The going would be slow with four of them on the narrow trail, but they'd be able to determine very quickly if Kavenagh had chosen that route as a means of escape. Early the next morning, they set out with renewed enthusiasm.

* * *

Josephine Burk couldn't find sleep no matter how hard she tried that night. Her husband was a hard-hearted man with a quick temper who'd been raised to believe that women were to be kept firmly in hand. Did she love him? She realized with shame that she might have at one time, but she'd experienced the full brunt of his foul disposition too often over the past eleven years to still feel that way. But honour him, she would because that's what she'd been taught was right. She'd grown up bearing witness to it in her parents' marriage.

"If you are fortunate enough to have a man choose you for his wife, then you must never forsake him," her mother had drilled into her. "It's your job as his wife not to displease him and your lot in life to suffer when you do. Remember, Josephine, obey is set out in the wedding vows for a reason."

Josephine held fast to those vows and would continue to do so no matter what. That included telling falsehoods. The latest, that she'd borne witness to Brogan Kavenagh murdering Amby's uncle. It had been the worst. However, her husband had offered a reasonable explanation. The Kavenaghs were no good. What would it matter if one of them hanged? As much as she tried to use that to rationalize her actions, it did not make sense. When you looked a man in the eye, no matter how bad he was, and he told a bald-faced lie, it didn't set well in the stomach.

Also, Amby had made it good and clear that if she ever opened her mouth about what had really happened, he'd hurt her bad, then say she'd lost her mind before he threw her and their six children out. Even if she survived, how on earth could she ever provide for herself and six young ones? Her parents would never take her in, so it would be the Almshouse for them. No, she would do as she was told and learn to live with it.

The events of the previous afternoon were indelibly etched in her mind. She'd been nearly paralyzed with fear when Brogan had knocked her husband unconscious. She thought he'd turn his wrath on her, but he hadn't. He'd just wanted to get away, not wreak vengeance on them. She hadn't figured on him being so handsome, not at all like the bad man who'd been described to her. To hear Amby tell it, Brogan Kavenagh was no better than the devil himself, bloodthirsty and violent. She'd seen for herself how capable Brogan was at taking care of himself. She had hardly dared move a muscle until he was out of sight. She'd thought about the children at home. Ten-year-old Nellie had seen to her younger siblings until her parents returned from their gruesome mission.

Amby had taken a while to come around, bloody and bruised, and by then, she'd freed herself from the shirt Brogan had tied her hands with. She had then unbound Amby. He'd cursed at her the entire time as though it was her fault they'd ended up as they had. And all the while, a dead man laid an arm's length away, staring with unseeing eyes. It'd been like something out of a nightmare.

And, of course, she'd had to stay with Uncle Latham while Amby went and fetched the wagon and then, horror of horrors, helped him load the body. They'd driven the seemingly interminable distance to the sheriff's office to report the murder. Sheriff Ratchford was practically salivating as he took their statements, Josephine, the good wife, doing exactly as she was told. She just wanted it over with.

"And he shot the man in the back? Is that what you saw?" the sheriff had demanded, his eyes blazing.

"Yes, that's what I saw," said Josephine.

"And you are prepared to swear on the Holy Bible in a court of law to the truth of your statement?"

"Yes," she'd told him, scared witless of the man. If she feared the consequences of going against Amby, it bore little resemblance to the terror the sheriff had instilled in her.

Within a half-hour the sheriff and three men from the town, duly deputized, had been mounted and, on their way, fired up at the prospect of bringing down an accused murderer.

Josephine turned carefully onto her side. She thought about Amby's Uncle Latham. He'd always been quarrelsome and struggled to get along with people. It hadn't taken much for Amby to fan the flames and get Uncle Latham stirred into a rage over the land. As a matter of fact, it had been ridiculously easy, the poor old man heading over to Brogan Kavenagh's woodlot to set things right once and for all. Little did he know he only had minutes to live. It would be his own nephew who would lay him low.

Uncle Latham had been good to her and the children. Why just last Christmas he'd carved a sawhorse for the youngest, Ambrose Junior, or as the family called him, Junior.

"Now you make sure you feed and water him, Junior," Latham had told the curly-headed child. "And put him in for the night so's the bears don't get 'im."

To be sure, Uncle Latham had a kind side, and she would miss that about him.

She turned again.

"If you don't stop flopping around in this bed, you can get out and sleep on the floor," Amby told her sternly, still in a surly mood. "I've got work to get to in the morning, and I'll not have you robbing me of a night's sleep."

"I'm sorry," she apologized. "I'll lie still."

* * *

Brogan was cold and muscle sore as he sat on a nearby stump and ate cornbread and cheese. He'd save the jerky for later. He thought about the day ahead, deciding which direction he should go. Having left the footpath behind temporarily, he spied a game trail to his left. That would make for easier travelling, and he decided to walk with the horse rather than ride him, which would make for less obvious tracks. The carpet of fallen leaves was a blessing, in that regard, for as long as they were travelling through a hardwood forest. When he felt he'd covered enough ground and the going was considerably less difficult, he would ride again to put as much distance as possible between himself and his pursuers.

When he felt Dutch had enough of a feed and drunk his fill in the nearby brook, he went to fetch him.

"Come on, old boy," he told the horse. "Time to go to work. Going to see some new sights today," he said lightly, giving the horse's rump a good-natured smack.

But he was feeling anything but light-hearted. He had escaped with his life so far, but by now Ratchford would be hot on his trail. He even imagined he would pop up any second in front of him, maybe shoot him dead. On immediate second thought, he might not want to deny the hangman his pleasure. It would be any man's guess.

He tried not to think about Ratchford going to his home because he knew Ratchford would. He tried to drive the awful thought from his mind that Maggie and Luke would be at the mercy of the detestable sheriff. It roiled his stomach, the cornbread and cheese threatening to reverse direction. And it was him, Brogan Kavenagh, who had sworn to be a better man, to be there with his wife and son — to protect them as was his duty as a husband and a father, who had brought it on them.

And Ratchford had probably gone to Tabor's too, although he and Pate could take care of themselves. So could Maggie, come to that, but to put her in this terrible circumstance made him feel like less of a man. Worse yet, not a man at all. He shoved those thoughts from his brain. He had to think of better things, or else he would lose his mind. He had no idea how to get out of this mess, but somehow he would. The alternative meant that Maggie would be a widow, and Luke would lose his father.

Striving for more pleasant thoughts, he forced himself to think about when he and Maggie had first met. He'd felt like he'd gotten hit with a wagonload of fieldstones when he'd first laid eyes on the tall, slender young woman with hair the colour of an autumn sunset. Those were the best words he could find to describe the light auburn.

"Don't ever cut your hair, please," he'd told her. "That would be a terrible shame."

She'd laughed and tossed that beautiful mane, her dark green eyes sizing him up saucily. She was like no other woman he'd ever seen and knew he had to have her for his own. But courting her wasn't easy, not when you were a Kavenagh. Her father tried to keep them apart, but Maggie was a lot like Brogan. When she wanted something, she went after it, and so she had.

"We met in the middle," he often liked to tease her, and she would laugh in that special way of hers.

He never had to wonder if she loved him. He knew she did, and he loved her back with everything he had. He thought about Luke and how thrilled he'd been when Maggie had given him a son. He was a good boy, and both, he and Maggie wanted the very best for him.

"When I grow up, I want to be just like you," Luke had told him proudly not two days ago.

Tears brimmed in his eyes as the game trail came to an end, and they were now negotiating heavy forest again. Tying Dutch's reins to a spruce bough, he let the horse rest after hours of walking. Sinking wearily onto the ground, he rested his elbows on his knees as he leaned back against a hardwood tree.

"I've got to get settled," he told himself aloud. "I've got to come up with a plan. I've got to believe that something will go my way."

And something did, when minutes later he picked up another game trail as he and Dutch left dense woods for slightly easier travelling. Now leg-weary, Brogan climbed into the saddle to rest himself a little. It was late afternoon when he started to think about finding a place to stay for the night. It wasn't as warm today as it had been yesterday, and he was glad all over again that he'd remembered, in his haste, to bring his jacket. It'd been sunny today, although it now felt like rain. He would have to set up a lean-to because no one would do well this time of year in the rain. It could turn cold fast.

Resting his head against the tree trunk, he glanced around. Suddenly straightening up, he shielded his eyes with his hand as he stared into the distance. It looked like a clearing up ahead. Could it be a meadow way back in here? Clambouring to his feet, he unwound the rein and climbed into the saddle. Sure enough, within minutes, they found themselves in a small clearing, and off to one side was a log cabin. It was rough-cut and low to the ground. Not large by any description, but it looked in good shape. There was even a hovel attached to the back of it.

"Hello in the house!" Brogan shouted through cupped hands. No answer. He waited a few minutes and then repeated the greeting. Nothing.

Riding closer, he dismounted and knocked on the door. Still no answer. The door was open, so he let himself in, calling out his presence as he did so. It was obvious no one was about. What a turn of good fortune! But, it was apparent that someone called this place home. Going around to the back of the building, he inspected the hovel. There was space enough for two animals, and there was even hay in one of the mangers. It was then that he noticed a much wider trail off to the right, nearly hidden from view with the regrowth of a young forest.

Whoever lived on this property was away at the moment, and he was sure they wouldn't mind if he sought shelter here for the night. The sky had darkened, and rain had already begun to fall in huge splatters as he unsaddled Dutch. He tied him up in the hovel, then hurried into the cabin. He even took the chance to light a fire and was soon fast asleep in front of it.

It was just coming on dark an hour or so later when he was awakened. It took him only a few seconds to realize there was a gun barrel pressed firmly against the side of his head.

Chapter 4

"I can see you're awake," said a raspy voice. "Who are you and why are you in my camp?"

Brogan was now fully alert. "Take that gun barrel off me, and I'll tell you."

"It stays where it is until I know who you are, Mister."

"I thought wilderness camps were left unlocked in case someone needed shelter. I needed shelter, somewhere to get in for the night out of the rain. I'm sorry. I'll leave as soon as you take that gun off me."

The man was undaunted. "That takes care of why you're here. Now, what's your name?"

Brogan knew the moment he spoke his name he would be in big trouble. "My name is Thomas," he lied. "Thomas Roderick," he quickly improvised making good use of his middle name.

The gun stayed in place. "What are you doing abroad at this hour of the night on horseback way out here? I saw your horse in the hovel."

"Just out and about," Brogan said lamely, his tired brain unable to come up with anything better. "Look, I said I'd leave."

"And go where?"

'Anywhere but here,' he was tempted to reply, his neck beginning to cramp with his head virtually pinned to the floor. "It doesn't matter where I go does it as long as I'm away from here. Again, I apologize for being in your camp, but I didn't exactly knock down the door. I've done no damage. I didn't steal anything."

The man hesitated, but Brogan could sense his indecision. At that moment, it could go either way and so he was greatly relieved when the pressure of the barrel eased and he was at least able to sit up. He didn't want to make any sudden moves though. He knew what a double barrel felt like and he didn't want to fool with a shotgun that was maybe adjusted to have a hair trigger.

"All right, get up and get over to that chair by the table so's we can talk some more."

Brogan did as he was told. Straightening to his full height and spying the chair the cabin owner referred to, he placed himself in it. Finally, he was facing the man who was holding the shotgun, only now from a more comfortable distance. If there was a comfortable distance in a room this size.

"I told you who I was and that I didn't intend any harm to your home. So how about you take that shotgun off me?"

"In case you haven't heard, young fella, there's a dangerous murderer abroad at this hour. A man was shot down in cold blood and the killer escaped. They said the man who did the shooting was tall, muscular build, black hair and had light blue eyes. I'd say you look a lot like him, wouldn't you? I might be getting on a bit, but my eyesight's still good."

The man was half Brogan's size, but wiry-looking under his layers of weather-beaten clothing. It was only his long grey beard that spoke of any real age, a slouch hat pulled low on his ears. His eyes were his most compelling feature, and they burned a bright shade of blue. He guessed the man to be well into his seventies.

Brogan laid his head back against the wall. Closing his eyes, he heaved a deep sigh.

"It's you ain't it? I'm a good judge of a man's character."

Brogan sighed again. The man had him stone cold. "Yes, it's me."

"And your name ain't Thomas Roderick, is it? It's Rogan something or other."

"Brogan Kavenagh."

"Yeah, that's it. Brogan. Well, you make one move against me, young fella, and I'll level you. Matter of fact, I might just shoot you now and have done with it."

"You'd be shooting an innocent man if you did."

"Innocent ... ha! That's what they all say."

Brogan ran his hands over his face wearily. "Look, put the gun away. I'm not going to hurt you. I never killed anyone and I don't intend to start now. I have a wife and a young son. I might be a little rough around the edges but I'm no murderer. You'd think with you being such a good judge of character and all you could see that for yourself."

The man pushed his cap back off his forehead, puzzled. "How's that?"

"It's in the eyes, it's always in the eyes. Take a look in mine and you can tell I'm not a murderer."

To his credit the man did take a closer look, although his bravery didn't extend beyond the length of the shotgun barrel. "You're a nice-lookin' feller, I'll say that, but you might just be a dandy, lying to me."

Brogan had to chuckle despite the gravity of the situation. "Look again. Are these the clothes of a dandy? I'm dressed for working, and that's what I was doing when this whole thing took place yesterday afternoon. It doesn't pay to have any enemies because when you do, they'll say anything, do anything, to get back at you. That's what's happened here. A man got shot, but it wasn't me who did the shooting. But it's me who's getting blamed. I say again,

I didn't kill anyone. I might if my back was against the wall and that's what I had to do to survive, but I wouldn't go out looking for it."

Maybe it was his imagination, but it seemed as though the gun barrel had been lowered a bit.

The man adjusted his hat again. "You got enemies Mr. ... what did you say your last name was?"

Well, that tied the cat! He didn't think there was anyone around these parts who wasn't familiar with the Kavenagh name. Maybe he'd have a chance after all.

"Kavenagh. You never heard of us?"

"Nope, that name don't mean nothin' to me. I'm from further over in the county. I come out here years ago. I looked the countryside over and decided it was a good place to stay, me and old Queenie. That's my horse. Now you said enemies, you got some do you?"

Brogan folded his arms and settled back as comfortably as he could in the wooden chair. "Yeah, I got some. One of them is the sheriff for this county, Percival Ratchford. Ever heard tell of him?"

"Now him I heard of. He's a mean one they tell me. Would hang his own mother if she crossed him, but he's got the right politics. Or I should say his family does. How's it they come to say you done murder?"

Brogan told him the story. All of it, including the not so pretty parts.

The gun barrel was now pointing at the floor. "That's a sad tale, young fella. I'd have run too if it was me."

Brogan nodded. "If that Ratchford got his hands on me there'd be a farce of a trial with those two liars telling their story. I'd be hung the next day. That's the way it'll be if they find me."

The older man stepped forward and extended his hand. "My name's Ezekiel Loughty. I had a little trouble with the law a few years ago myself. I was accused of thievery by my next-door neighbour, the lying scoundrel. The truth finally won out, but I'd had enough of neighbours by the time I was done with the whole thing. I never married so I was as free as a bird to come and go as I pleased. So, I came as far away as I could get and still be in the area. I built me a log cabin, and this is where I stay. Queenie and I go into town every month or so to get what I need, everything else I shoot. Been out here now for nigh on to twenty years, and I like my own company just fine. But you! You said you were married. Had a boy. It's only been a day or so, but you must be missin' them somethin' powerful if you're on the run."

Brogan fought the tears that sprang to his eyes. He was trying not to think about Maggie ... Luke, who he imagined was doing his best to be the man of the house while his pa was away. He wished he'd had a chance to speak to his son before he'd left, but it hadn't been possible. It was probably better that he hadn't because the child would likely not have understood. *Him begging me to stay would have been my undoing.* No, it had to be the way it was, at least for the time being.

If this whole thing hadn't happened, he and Maggie would be in their nice warm bed together right now, in each other's arms as they were every night. He missed her soft body next to his. Her passion and kisses that drove him wild with desire. Instead, he was here, in the middle of nowhere sitting in some old hermit's camp. But it could be worse. Ezekiel could still be threatening to shoot him. As it appeared now, he might have found a friend.

Brogan unfolded his arms and tested his and Ezekiel's newfound friendship by standing up to stretch. He was relieved when the old man didn't react by raising the weapon.

He reclaimed the wooden chair. "I am missing my wife and my son. They're my whole life and I've had to leave them behind to fend for themselves. That kills me, worrying that someone could come along...."

"You mean like that sheriff."

Brogan sighed tiredly, a wealth of uneasiness in the sound. "Especially the sheriff. But my Maggie's strong. I actually pity the man who thinks he can best her, but still...."

Ezekiel sauntered to the corner by the table and set the shotgun on the floor, butt first. "When was the last time you ate, young fella?"

"I've been eating right along. Maggie sent some cornbread and cheese, and some jerky with me. I gave the apples to my horse."

Ezekiel shook his head. "Don't sound like much for a man your size. I've got some venison in the larder and I'll hack off a couple of steaks and get some biscuits going in the oven."

Brogan's mouth was already watering. "That sounds mighty fine to me, Ezekiel. Mighty fine indeed."

Later, with his belly full for the first time in two days, Brogan could feel sleep pulling at him. Try as he might to keep his eyes open, he drifted off while still sitting at the table.

He didn't hear Ezekiel rustling in the cupboard by the door. He woke with a start when the old man shook his shoulder and pointed to two large bear rugs on the floor by the hearth.

"One is for over you and one is for under you. Go get the sleep you need, young fella. Tomorrow's going to come whether we're ready for it or not, might as well be rested when it gets here. A man can think a lot clearer on a mind that's had enough sleep. So, take your full belly and get to your dreams."

Brogan wondered if he'd get to those dreams any time soon, now wide awake after that initial wave of drowsiness had passed. He lay with his eyes closed anyway, not interested in talking. Instead, he enjoyed the smell of Ezekiel's tobacco smoke that filled the room with a pungent haze, then slowly dissipated after the old man's one and only cigarette. His host threw another log on the fire, then shuffled off to bed. Climbing into the bunk built sturdily into the corner, in a remarkably short time he snored loud enough to wake the dead.

Brogan thought he would lie awake the entire night, but when Ezekiel lit a fire in the hearth early the next morning and woke him, he realized he hadn't.

"Good mornin', young fella," Ezekiel told him pleasantly. "Thought you'd never stop snoring."

Brogan had to smile at that, along with his new name: young fella. He could call him whatever he liked. Not only had the old man had the courage and good sense to believe him, but Ezekiel had fed him and given him and his horse warm shelter for the night.

* * *

Sheriff Ratchford and his three deputized men had left Sackville early the following morning. Since they'd be travelling into the wilderness, they had to fit what supplies they could into their saddlebags. And then they were off, the sheriff elated

73

when he indeed found hoof prints along the old footpath that followed the river.

But if Brogan had struggled on Dutch to negotiate the somewhat overgrown path, it had proved an even more onerous task for four horses. Especially when Ratchford continued to hurry the process. At one point, the sheriff had tumbled into the water and was on the receiving end of a sound drenching. It had been no problem to clambour out once the horse got his footing, but with the air somewhat cooler, he'd soon become thoroughly miserable. That much was evident by his rapidly deteriorating frame of mind. However, the temperature still provided sufficient warmth for the mosquitoes and blackflies that plagued the men as they picked their way along.

By late afternoon, with the sun disappearing altogether behind a thick wall of gunmetal grey clouds, the four stopped to make camp for the night. They busied themselves erecting a modest lean-to. However, the rain beat them to the finish line, falling in earnest and making Sheriff Ratchford even wetter. Stripping to the skin, he arranged his still soggy clothes around the sputtering fire in hopes they'd be dry by morning. Of course, that made him fair game for the blood-sucking insects that tormented him throughout the night adding to his distress. Bug-bitten and chilled, Ratchford was not fit company by morning when he had no alternative but to pull on the cold, damp clothes.

"I think he might have crossed the river and kept heading east," Ratchford told his men over campfire coffee a half hour later. "So that's the way we'll go. He can't have just disappeared. We're bound to pick up his tracks again soon and be upon him. With any luck, we'll have Kavenagh before the magistrate by the end of the week. So that gives us two whole days to find him. There are four of us and one of him. We'll simply outsmart him."

Soon they were mounted and, on their way, but they hadn't gone far when Pete's horse began to limp. The deputy climbed down and inspected the horse's shoes. The back left shoe was missing. Giving his mount a reassuring pat on the rump, Pete Brown straightened up. "Probably lost it on one of those rocks," he said, pointing to the stone-littered forest floor. "They're sharp. He's likely bruised the sole of his foot."

Ratchford was uninterested in the horse's foot. "It's only one shoe. Keep going. He should be able to keep up if it's just a stone bruise."

Pete climbed back into the saddle and started ahead with the other men. They hadn't gone far when it became apparent the horse was lame, the animal now limping noticeably.

Pete dismounted. "Can't ride him like this, sir. I don't want to cripple him."

Ratchford let loose with a long string of oaths. "What good is a horse that can't be ridden? All right, you're all done here. Take your horse and get back home the best way you know how. We three will carry on without you."

Pete looked as though he had something he wanted to say, but wisely held his tongue. Turning back the way they'd come, he led the ailing animal behind him. It wasn't long before the others were out of sight.

* * *

None of the men spoke as they rode on, all keeping their focus toward the ground in hopes of picking up some sign that Brogan had been here. When all hope seemed lost that they were even close to following in the right direction, they happened upon the ruins of the cabin where Brogan and Dutch had spent the night.

Ratchford leapt off his horse and all but ran to the tumbledown shack. "Look at the tracks! He tied the horse up here while he scouted the place out before overnighting."

They all trooped inside, the telltale manure droppings proof that indeed Brogan and his horse had taken shelter in the fallen-down building.

Ratchford's disposition was only marginally improved. "They were here all right, so I'd say he's got a good day's ride on us. There's no real roads back here, so he obviously found a game trail. They're all over the place. Come on, men, he's not that far ahead of us. We've got a few hours of daylight left, and we're good trackers. We'll get him. He'll be tied over his horse and headed back with us by nightfall."

Edward laughed, as much of a thug as the man who'd deputized him. "I doubt he would survive the ride back, belly down on the saddle. He would be dead by the time we got there."

Ratchford grinned as though picturing the spectacle. "Yeah, he just might be. I'll have to think of something better because I mean for him to hang."

Edward headed with the others back to their horses. "What if the magistrate don't see it your way, Sheriff? Don't think he should hang?"

Ratchford wheeled on him. "You buckin' me?"

Edward blanched. "No, Sheriff. I ain't buckin' you. Just wonderin' if that's the way it might go is all."

Ratchford gave Edward a long withering look. "We got the evidence we need. He'll hang all right. I'll personally see to it."

Once the three set off, it didn't take them long to find the game trail Brogan had used. They surged ahead with renewed eagerness. At least the rain had stopped, although storm clouds still hung low in the sky. Up ahead a cow moose trotted along the path, spooked by the horses running her way. With surprising agility, she crashed into the underbrush and was gone.

* * *

Brogan stretched and pulled himself out from under the bear rug. It'd been a while since he'd had a more comfortable sleep. He didn't much care for bears, recalling a close call he'd had once while working in the woods, but they'd certainly provided him with a good bed last night.

"You know how to make biscuits, young fella?" Ezekiel asked him cheerfully.

Brogan smiled. "Sure do. I'm a good biscuit maker as a matter of fact. Maggie says so anyway. So does my son, Luke."

Thinking of them brought the expected stab of pain. Lord how he missed them.

"Well then get to stirring. I'll cut us another couple of steaks and set the coffee to boiling. The flour's in that tin over there in the larder, and the salt beside it. Lard on the shelf above. I don't know about you, but I could eat the hind end off a billy goat. I'm that hungry."

Brogan smiled again as he assembled what he needed to make the biscuits. "I'm right there with you, Ezekiel. That was sure some good supper last night though. You're a good cook."

"First of all, call me Zeke," the older man cackled. "That's all I ever got when I was growin' up. As for my cooking, I worked in quite a few lumber camps. I had to do it right or they'd have bounced me out on my ear. I figured I had to learn how to cook anyhow since no woman would pay me any attention."

"You're being too hard on yourself," Brogan chuckled.

Ezekiel laughed, enjoying his own joke.

Within minutes the biscuits were in the hearth oven, live coals banked around the heavy pot with its tight-fitting lid.

Once the coffee was made, Ezekiel rolled another cigarette and leaned back with his metal cup full of the aromatic beverage. "Now this is the life," he said with a smile, setting fire to the end of his cigarette. Smoke curled lazily around his head. "There's nothing like it. 'Course if I'd taken a wife, I figure I could have been happy with that too. You sure seem to be."

Brogan took a long leisurely pull on his coffee. "That's the life for me."

Ezekiel sobered. "What are you going to do, son? How you figure to get out of this bind you're in and get back to that wife of yours, and little boy?"

Brogan's mood took a nosedive. "I have no idea. I've been praying to my Maker for an answer, but everything just seems so impossible. When you got a man who's taken an oath to see you dead, there doesn't seem any possible way of getting away from it, but I'll think of something. Until I do, I have to keep moving. And speaking of moving, I think I'll go let Dutch out, tether him in back of the cabin where there's grass."

Ezekiel nodded. "Good idea, but leave old Queenie where she is. She likes the barn. Just throw some more hay in her manger, if you don't mind."

The biscuits and steak were ready by the time he got back inside, and they sat down to polish off their breakfast.

Ezekiel grinned. "You're right, young fella. You sure can make biscuits. I don't know who taught you to do it, but you had a good teacher. I hate to say it, but I think they're even better than mine. I won't admit that to anyone though, 'cept you."

"Glad you like them." Brogan grinned. "You won't mind if I take a few with me when I go do you?"

"Not at all. You figurein' on leavin' soon?"

Brogan shrugged, trying his best to keep the feeling of utter hopelessness at bay. They were bound to catch up with him sooner or later.

"After we finish eating, I should be on my way."

"It looks like it might rain again. You got anything to put on against the weather?"

"I got a rain cape in my saddlebag if gets wet out. I'll be all right."

When they'd finished eating, they pushed the plates aside. Ezekiel reached for his tobacco pouch, and Brogan poured himself another cup of coffee. He was comfortable here, but he could hardly afford to waste time on comfort, not with Ratchford no doubt bearing down on him. He could feel it in his gut. He had to get going. He'd get this cup of coffee into him and then he and Dutch would take to their heels again.

"Where you going to go?" asked Ezekiel, interrupting his thoughts.

Brogan sighed, shrugging his shoulders. "I have no idea. Just keep moving I guess."

Ezekiel studied him for a moment. "I have a nephew. He and his wife got a nice little cabin about fifteen miles due north of here ... northeast really. If you can get that far, they'll put you up for the night ... longer if you need them to. His name's Jedediah and hers is Tilda. My nephew can be a might crusty at first, probably introduce himself at gunpoint same as I did, but tell him you're a friend of mine. That'll smooth things over fast enough.

"Now pay a close mind to the directions I'm goin' to give ya. Travel north of here, I'd say a good ten miles until you come to a lake. It's big, but this time of year it's low. Can't be more than six or seven feet of water in it. Now if your horse is a good swimmer...."

"He is. Dutch loves to swim."

"Great! So go the entire length of the lake, and when you come out the other side, you'll see two smaller lakes. Take the one to the east. Same thing. We've had some rain the past couple of days, so they'll be up a bit but nothing your horse can't handle if he's a good swimmer. Then head east again another few miles. Keep a sharp eye out for the cabin. It's hard to find. I don't know how long you can stay there, but Jedediah's got a couple of good hounds. They'll hear you comin', but so will they hear anyone else comin' who's looking for you. You make it to that cabin, and I'd say you've got a place to stay for as long as you need it."

"Ratchford and his men will find it."

"Not easily they won't. Even if they do track you, it'll be mighty hard for them to sneak up on you. My guess is that they'll be expectin' you to go west to find a farm for food and shelter. They *won't* be expectin' you to go past them lakes. It's high rocky ground back where I'm talking about, not good for a man on horseback. No, they won't be lookin' for you to cross them lakes on horseback. And if you can't, they can't."

"I thank you, Zeke, for everything you've done for me," Brogan said, shaking the old man's hand. "Now I've got to get going. If anyone comes here looking for me, you tell them you never saw me. Don't get yourself mixed up in this."

Ezekiel was as quick as a squirrel despite his age, springing from his chair and grabbing up his shotgun. "I always got my hand near to this, so don't worry. Anyone comes by here I'll tell them I never heard of you. If they don't take that for an answer they'll be dancing on the end of some buckshot. That won't feel too good. Besides if someone does get me, you remember this. I'd far rather go out in a hail of bullets than lay about in old age not able to take care of myself. I'm old, son. Don't worry about me. Whatever happens, happens. I'm not sorry I helped you. Now go!"

Brogan laughed. Ezekiel was a character, and well able to fend for himself.

* * *

Brogan had no sooner gone out back when he heard horses break from the cover of the forest and descend on the camp. Shotgun blasts rang out from the cabin. He could tell Ratchford and his men had not expected to run into a volley of buckshot, both barrels. He couldn't desert his new friend in his hour of need, though, so crouching down, he pulled his pistol and crept around to the front of the camp. Two men lay on the ground, likely Ratchford's deputies. They weren't moving. Ratchford himself had gone inside the building, and he knew by the gunfire that ensued that it was too late to help Ezekiel.

Moving as soundlessly as possible, he hurried around back and grabbed Dutch. He led the horse a short distance away before leaping into the saddle and urging the gelding away at top flight.

Ratchford was not fooled. Already back outside, he fired his pistol at the outlaw, and Brogan gritted his teeth as a bullet pierced deep into his right thigh.

Chapter 5

Ratchford watched as Brogan raced away on his horse. He fired again, but missed. He knew he'd hit him the first time, though, and that made him feel mighty good. He'd seen the blood spray from the wound, but those Kavenaghs were tough. He had to take that into consideration.

Spinning on his heel, he looked around frantically for his horse, but of course, all three animals had run off amid the barrage of gunfire. He whistled sharply, jogging the length of the clearing in search of them, but they were gone. Curses! Then he noticed the hovel. There had to be a horse in there! Racing for the door he nearly tore it off its hinges and was elated to find a horse, such as it was. That mare had to be more than twenty-five years old, but she would have to do. Quickly untying the animal, he backed it out of the stall and into the yard. He didn't see a saddle nearby and not wanting to take the time to look for one, launched himself onto its back and kicked her hard on the sides. Brogan could be slowing down. He might still be able to catch him if he hurried.

Queenie had no intention of going anywhere, and certainly not with this lout on her back. She balked, then lowered her head between her front legs, arched her back and kicked up her hind legs. Off went Ratchford, flying ingloriously through the air and landing in a heap a few feet away.

"You old wind-broke bag of bones," he yelled at the animal, climbing up on her back, only to have to endure being thrown off again.

This time the landing was more painful, his leg buckling under him. He heard the bone snap and the next few minutes were spent crawling to the camp. However, the pain in his leg at that moment was far outdistanced by the frustration of Kavenagh escaping his clutches. But then, he reasoned to himself, how far could Brogan get with a bullet in him? He would bleed heavily from that wound and in all likelihood, die soon enough anyway. In the meantime, he himself had a broken leg to contend with. First, he had to get it set. Then somehow, he had to find his horse and ride out of here. He whistled again for his mount, but the animal, normally obedient, did not respond to his summons.

He could always ride that old palomino back to civilization, but he doubted she'd let him anywhere near her now. He didn't need to be thrown with a broken leg. That he hadn't been wounded in the shoot-out was a miracle in itself. Compared to being either dead or shot full of holes, a broken leg was the better part of the bargain, although unbelievably painful.

Fury raced through him that he'd been denied getting his hands on Kavenagh, yet again, because he couldn't very well continue the chase with a broken leg. He tamped down his anger and schooled himself into thinking about more rational things, like finding something to use for a leg splint. He could always use saplings in a pinch, but he hoped to find something closer to hand inside the camp. An old broom was the first thing he spied. Good. He could break the handle free and use that. Now for the second piece. Ah, the fireplace poker made of steel would certainly be strong enough and the ideal length.

Before setting to work, he pulled a blanket from the cot. After several futile attempts to tear it into strips for binding the splints, he finally managed it and set them beside him. With a roar of pain, he got the leg somewhat aligned, tying the improvised splints securely into place. Wiping the sweat from his brow with the back of his sleeve, he crawled to what he guessed was the larder where he found a half-full bottle of rum. Snatching the cork free with his teeth, he downed the contents in two tries. That should help with the pain.

Crawling back outside, he was about to whistle again for his horse when he noticed with profound relief that all three animals were now standing just outside the camp. He had a good mind to give his horse a sound beating for running away, but there was no time for that. At least it was here now, and he'd make good use of the opportunity.

Now to mount up. Seizing the saddle horn in a death grip, he climbed into the saddle in about as half-assed a manner as was possible. But he was finally aboard, and grabbing the reins of the other two horses, besides his own, he began to pick his way through the trees and onto the trail they'd followed to find this place. He would send people back for the bodies.

The return trip to the shiretown was torturous. Twice he lost the trail in the dark, but he had to keep going. If he were to dismount, there would be no getting back on. He was dizzy and weak from pain when he at last rode into Doc Seeby's yard in Dorchester and shouted for him to come and help.

Fortunately, a young man was passing by the office just then, a big strapping lad. With his help, they were able to get the sheriff off his horse and into the house. Once the injured man was arranged on the examining table, the young fellow left while Doctor Seeby finished straightening the leg and applied a cast.

"I've given you some laudanum, Percival, so you should sleep for a while," said the doctor. "That'll help you deal with the pain."

"I don't have time to sleep!" Ratchford announced irritably. "I need to go back out in a few hours with a fresh horse. I'm tracking a murderer, and I almost had him. I got a bullet into him, but he managed to get away."

The doctor was already shaking his head, his shoulder-length salt and pepper hair swaying with the effort. "The circulation was very poor in that leg when you got here, Percival. I'd say you reached me just in time. It could still give you trouble. If anything, you may be able to get about on crutches when I say it's all right to do so, but you won't be on a horse again for several weeks ... if then."

* * *

Brogan kept the palm of his hand pressed firmly against the bullet wound, but it did little to stem the flow of blood soaking his pant leg. And the pain! Now that the initial numbness had worn off, it was like someone had set fire to his thigh, and yet, he rode on. Dutch covered the distance to the lake in ground-eating strides as though he understood his master's life was on the line. It was.

It was funny how a man could think he had reached the limit of his endurance only to dig down deeper and find plenty more —

especially when death was nipping at your heels. The energy and grit required to survive. And he would survive.

However, he'd never again bring down another animal to put meat on the table without understanding the sacrifice that animal was making for his family's subsistence. He now understood what it felt like to be hunted. Running on aching legs to put distance between yourself and a relentless pursuer. And now he and Dutch stood on the shores of the first lake. Ezekiel had been right. The banks were steep, the surrounding countryside wild and rugged as though compensating for the relatively flat land of the hardwood forests they'd just come through. If the old man hadn't assured him the depth of the water wasn't going to be a problem, he might have turned back and sought another route.

He couldn't stop thinking about kindly Ezekiel, who had taken him in, helped him, and then died for his trouble. He'd brought that trouble to the old man's door. But for him stumbling upon his camp, Ezekiel would be drinking coffee right now, enjoying one of his five-puff cigarettes. Guilt made him feel sick to his stomach.

"All right, boy," Brogan told the big horse. "I know you like to swim because I've seen you do it many a time. You're not afraid of a little lake. Come on now."

But the animal shied away from the water's edge, seemingly unwilling to try. He couldn't really blame the horse because he was already tired, and it was a sizeable lake. It stretched far beyond what he'd imagined when Ezekiel described it to him earlier. But there was no other way. On the far end of those lakes, a few miles distant, was shelter. Hope. He was sure that people who lived by their wits this far out in the wilderness would know a thing or two about taking care of a gunshot wound. He wasn't gut-shot. He knew nobody could help him if he was. It would just be a matter of time. No, he felt sure this could be fixed. He'd never been shot before, but he understood it had to be dealt with as soon as possible.

"Come on, boy," he urged the horse again with a sterner voice. "Come on, Dutch, we've got to do this." He brought his heels against the big horse's sides, and the animal started tentatively forward.

"Come on, Dutch!" he shouted at the horse. "Go, boy! Now! Do it!"

Dutch hesitated a moment longer then plunged forward, water arcing from the animal's body. And just as Ezekiel had assured him, the water only reached the horse's chest. Encouraged, he kept going. The water now rose to his neck, and Dutch snorted as he swam. Brogan half expected to hear shouts from the shoreline behind them at any moment, along with pistol shots as another bullet pierced his body to finish him off. But the only sound was Dutch swimming easily through the pristine water.

He'd pushed the horse hard today, and he knew this swim would be exhausting for him. He would give him a well-deserved rest on the other side, but somehow they'd have to keep going. It was now late afternoon, and darkness would overtake them in another two or three hours. Maybe sooner given the dense forest around them.

He was grateful when they reached the shore, Dutch shaking his coat free of the cool water. The lake had washed away a good deal of the blood on Brogan's thigh, but it wasn't long before his pant leg was crimson again.

He couldn't afford much of a rest, but he did give the horse a few minutes before they started for the next lake a short distance away. This time Dutch did not hesitate, plunging into the water without any encouragement from Brogan. Ezekiel was right again. The lake at first appeared to be quite shallow, but recent heavy rains had probably raised the water levels. Still, it was much smaller than the first, and they were out of it within minutes, making a sharp turn as directed. And now, another few miles to the cabin. How would he ever stand it? He tried to think of something other than the knife-like pain in his leg.

Onward they went. Dutch had slowed considerably, his muscles likely too tired to carry them him much further. But Brogan knew he had to stay in the saddle. He couldn't travel any distance on his leg the way it was. It was still bleeding steadily. If he tried to walk, it would likely pump out. He slowed Dutch to a walk, grateful it was still daylight. How would they ever find a cabin in the dark that was by all accounts almost impossible to see in the full light of day? Had the Almighty given up on them entirely?

Suddenly Dutch stopped, muscles tensed, his neck arched as he blew a warning snort. Dear God, had Ratchford found them already? How was that possible? His fingers touched the grip of the pistol in the holster at his side. Could he use it? Could he kill another man to preserve his own innocence? And who would believe him? If he were already accused of killing one man, they would blame him for this one too, and likely the two dead deputies back at the camp, and even Ezekiel. It was unbelievable how one lie could result in such chaos, and he, an innocent man, had become thrust into the middle of it. He was also shocked at how easily it could be accomplished. He thought of the old saying: *A thief can only rob you, but a liar can hang you.* He'd never realized how true that was, until now.

Dutch was rock-hard with tension, ears sharply forward, ready to flee at any moment. It had to be Ratchford. There was no remedy but to run and take his chances in the forest. But he knew his energy supply was just about depleted. Dutch's too, and there was no shelter nearby.

And then a most remarkable thing happened. He heard a woman singing. Her nice voice, soft and lilting, lovely in its simplicity. Was his mind playing tricks on him? No, Dutch heard it too, his tension slowly dissipated. Horse and rider stood as though transfixed, listening. It came from the opposite direction in which they'd been looking for the cabin. The cabin! That had to be it. It must be that woman, the nephew's wife. What was her name? Oh yes, Tilda.

Brogan carefully turned the horse in the direction of the sound, walking slowly toward it. He didn't want to frighten her by riding right up to the spot where she clearly thought she was alone. And it wouldn't be wise to do such a thing anyway. Her husband would be armed, or she would be, or both. As Ezekiel had warned him, they wouldn't take kindly to strangers. Probably shoot first and ask questions later.

"Hello in the house!" he called out in the normal fashion. It was the polite way to announce yourself.

His greeting was met with silence. "I say hello in the house!" Brogan called out again. "I'm riding in."

A shotgun blast seemed to miss his head by only inches. Dutch jumped sideways in alarm and almost unseated him. "Oh, no you're not! My husband and I both have our guns on you. That was a warning shot, but I still have one barrel left. I promise you the next one's going to hit you."

Brogan tried again. "I mean you no harm. I'm a friend of Uncle Ezekiel. He sent me here. I'm badly shot and need help. Please."

Silence.

Moments later the woman spoke again. "How do you know Zeke?"

"I stayed with him last night. He told me where you lived, and said you'd treat me kindly."

"Is the law after you?"

Great! "Yes, the law's after me, but I didn't do what they're accusing me of. Ezekiel understood that, and it's why he helped me."

"It wasn't him who shot you?"

"No, Zeke didn't shoot me."

"Was it the law then?"

"Yes, it was the law. I'm bleeding bad. I need someone to take the bullet out for me. Got a horse here that needs a rest and something to eat. A barn for the night."

"Where you shot?"

"In the leg, my thigh. It's hurting something awful and bleeding heavily."

"Leg shot's not too bad. Not like some gunshot wounds."

"It's bad enough that I'm going to come off this horse in a minute. I'm feeling mighty poorly. I need your help, and I need it soon."

He heard a rustling in the trees, and then saw movement in a grove of young spruce that was bordered by common buckthorn. A young woman pushed her way out to where Brogan and Dutch stood. She seemed short because he was used to a taller woman in

Maggie. He guessed she could be considered of medium height. Her hair was flaxen and hung in waves well past her shoulders. If this was Tilda Loughty, she was a beauty and probably no more than twenty years old.

The shotgun was still trained on Brogan as she eyed him suspiciously. "Why should I help a man running from the law?" she asked. "How many people have you killed exactly?"

"Exactly none. You don't need to hold that gun on me. Just send your husband out here, and I'll talk to him. I can understand you'd be frightened."

She lifted her chin stubbornly. "I'm not half as frightened as *you're* going to be if I open up on you," she told him, holding his gaze without effort.

She had him there because the idea of being shot again was not at all an inviting prospect.

"I've already been opened up on, and once in a day is enough. So, can you help me or not? I've got to get this bullet out of my leg."

She did not lower the gun.

"Please," he said, "I'm not going to do anything to hurt you."

"You're armed. Take that gun belt off and throw it with the pistol over here to me."

"I'm not inclined to do that."

"Well, then I'm not inclined to help you, Uncle Zeke or not."

Brogan could feel himself growing weaker. If those were her terms, he had no choice but to abide by them. He was going to die from blood loss or worse anyway if he didn't get this bullet out. So maybe, like Ezekiel, it was a better option to get it over with quickly. He slowly undid the buckle and gathering the holster and pistol, tossed them onto the ground at her feet.

"*Now* will you help me?"

Thankfully she finally lowered her weapon, then picked up Brogan's gun and holster. "All right, get down off there and follow me inside. There's a path on the other side of these trees."

Brogan shook his head. "Fetch your husband for me, please. I think I'm going to need some help getting off this horse. A shoulder to lean on getting into the house. I'm not feeling so good right now."

She hesitated.

"Call your husband, please."

She watched him but didn't move.

"What's wrong?"

"My husband's not here right at this moment. He's out hunting. He'll be right back though, armed and all."

So, she was here alone. Not much wonder she was acting so nervous. He suspected the husband was further away than she was letting on.

"All right. I'll talk to him when he gets here," he told her, going along with the charade, "but you're going to have to give me a hand. Just steady me if you can."

She made no reply so he considered she was in agreement. She set the firearms aside and approached the horse.

He felt completely lightheaded as he swung his bad leg over the saddle and made to dismount. He didn't loosen his hold on the saddle horn as his feet touched the ground. He leaned against the side of the horse, attempting to stop his head from spinning. Funny how those trees were suddenly at an angle. His knees buckled, and he was about to go down completely when he felt a firm grip around his waist. He was amazed at her strength as he sagged against her. Together, they made their way through the perimeter of trees, down a narrow path, and into the cabin. And when he thought he couldn't possibly go another step, he was helped to the side of a bed. That's when the exertion took its toll, and after climbing onto the bed, he fell back, and passed out.

He wasn't sure how long he'd been out when he was suddenly and forcefully brought back to the present when the woman lifted his injured leg onto the bed as well. She then began to undo his belt buckle.

"What are you doing?" he asked, but his voice sounded as though it was coming from another room, the words belonging to someone else.

"I've got to get your pants off. I've tried to tear the fabric, but it's too strong. Besides, you'll need your pants later, so I don't want to destroy them. My husband has pants here, but they'd be much too small for you. Help me get them off."

There was no fight left in him at all. Fumbling with the buckle, he managed to get it undone, and clumsily undid the buttons on his fly, one by one. Easing his hands inside the waistband, and with her tugging in the other direction, his pants slid down. She was able to complete the job without his help.

"That's a bad wound," she told him. "I'm going to get that bullet out, but first I've got to heat the knife in the fire. Do you want something to bite down on? I've got some whiskey, but I'm going to use that on the wound. I'm afraid there's nothing here to dull the pain."

"Just do what you have to do," he managed through gritted teeth. "I'll take it or die trying."

He had never imagined anything could hurt as much as when that hot knife went in after the bullet. It seemed to take forever before she declared she'd found it and dug it out. Then he had to endure the agony of cauterizing the wound before he passed out again. He came to minutes later while she was wrapping the bandage into place. It was good the bullet was gone, but the pain didn't feel any less because of it. It felt as though the red-hot knife was still lodged in his thigh, and he grimaced against the misery of it.

Exhaustion, blood loss, and pain all worked as one to pull him under once more. When he surfaced again it was dark, save for an oil lamp that burned in the adjoining room. He lay in shadows.

Miraculously the pain seemed to have lessened, although only minimally. Good! He became aware he was covered with a heavy quilt, and he pushed it aside in favour of the warm room. It was then he realized his shirt and jacket had been removed, along with his pants. He reached down. Yep, his short drawers were still where they should be, although, at the moment, he wasn't worried whether he was naked or not. Men had suffered worse indignities than to be undressed by a beautiful woman.

A moan escaped his lips when he tried to move his leg. He wouldn't be doing that again soon.

The woman appeared in the doorway holding the lamp. "You're awake," she told him unnecessarily. "How do you feel?"

"Like a man with a gunshot wound."

"Ever been shot before?"

"Nope, this was my first time, and I don't recommend the experience. I've had plenty of bones broken, but this is a helluva lot more painful."

Suddenly the clouds parted in his tired brain. "My horse! Dutch!" he said struggling to an upright position.

"Shhh, now. Don't fret about your horse. He's all bedded down out back in the barn, tucked in there very comfortably. He wasn't all that thirsty, so I guess he drank his fill at the lakes. I assume that's the way you came because your pants and boots were still wet. Anyway, I gave your horse some grain that I use to make flour. He seemed happy to get it, along with lots of hay. Like I said, he was already settled down for the night when I last checked on him."

Brogan sank back. "Thank you. I appreciate you doing that for me."

"You're welcome. I'll wash all that blood off him tomorrow. Maybe turn him out in the pasture. Do you figure he'd run away if I were to do that? It's not fenced."

Brogan thought for a moment. "He's steady, but I'd tether him all the same. If something wild came along, he might run."

"Then tether him I will." She smiled.

"You mentioned a barn. You have other animals?"

"No, nothing now. We had a milk cow once. She walked all the way out here with us, but she was old, and it was too much for her. She only lasted a few months. Didn't even get to eat all that nice hay we made for her from the meadow east of here. So don't worry about having enough for your horse. There's hay aplenty in the mow."

Still holding the lamp, she sat down on the edge of the bed. "I expect you could use a drink of water yourself, maybe something to eat? I've got some stew left over from yesterday. I could do up a bowl if you thought you could take some nourishment.”

He thought about that. He had a powerful hunger but his stomach was still a bit on the flighty side. He decided to wait a while. “The stew sounds good, but maybe later. I’ll take that cup of water though. Is it nice and cold?”

She truly was beautiful when she smiled. She tended to do so more often now that the preliminaries had been gotten through, and she wasn’t shoving a shotgun in his face. “Carried it from the spring this morning, and I keep it outside, so yes, it’s nice and cool.” She hesitated. “I’m sorry I didn’t ask your name.”

“I’m Brogan Kavenagh, and I assume you’re Tilda.”

“That’s right, Tilda Loughty. I’ll go and get that cup of water now. I’m sure you must be parched, probably riding all day without anything to quench your thirst.”

Setting the lamp down, she went for the water and was back within minutes. Going to the head of the bed, she slipped a hand behind his shoulders to help lift him up to drink it.

“I’m all right, Tilda. I can do it on my own,” he assured her, raising up without her help and draining the cup.

She took it from him gently. “Would you like another?”

It felt good to lie back down. “No, one’s fine for the moment.”

She set the cup on a nearby chest of drawers and then returned to sit on the side of the bed. "Is your leg hurting a lot?"

He tried to smile, but it didn't work. "Yeah, a lot, but I want to thank you for taking the bullet out. There's still plenty of pain, but at least I'm on the mending side of things now. It's bound to hurt for a while. You did a fine job, and I'm grateful."

"How grateful?" she asked him.

Chapter 6

"I beg your pardon?"

"I think you heard me. I said how grateful are you, Mr. Kavenagh?"

She was direct, he'd give her that. "I'm as grateful as I can be. You saved my life, and I do owe you something for that, but...."

She blushed. He was sure of it by the sound of her voice although it was impossible to tell with the room in such deep shadow from the pale lamplight.

"I hope you don't think me forward, but I need help with winter coming on and all."

He stopped for a moment, perplexed. "Where is your husband? I assume he's not hunting in the dark. Is he staying overnight somewhere?"

"He's gone."

"He's gone? You mean you're all the way out here by yourself?"

She began to cry softly. "I would say that is my predicament. I know I didn't make you very welcome when you first arrived because a body can't be too careful when they don't know who's abroad. But you are like an answer to my prayers. You came here at just the right time."

"But I can't stay, surely you know that."

"Didn't you say you were running from the law?"

"Well, yes … but.…"

"They'll never find you here."

"I wouldn't say never. You don't know Percival Ratchford. He'd search for me to the ends of the earth. It's surprising what a vendetta will do to a man. It makes him mean, bloodthirsty. He's no better than a dog who's been too long on the end of a chain. Now tell me about your husband. Did something happen to him?"

She shrugged, dabbing at her eyes with the edge of her apron. "That's just it. I don't know. The only thing I can think is that he's run off and left me."

He couldn't imagine anyone running off and leaving this sweet young woman, but you never knew. "What makes you think he'd do something like that? How long has he been gone now?"

"Jedediah left in the spring, so six months come Wednesday. We used to have two dogs, Brooker and Caesar. Brooker died when he got in a fight with a bear and my husband took Caesar with him. I sure wish I at least had Caesar here with me. I'd feel a lot better."

"He's been gone six months? Where on earth did he go, Dorchester?"

"That could have been where he went, but he also knows people in Port Elgin. I just hope something hasn't happened to him. He was on foot."

"Why on foot? It's a long way back here."

"We don't have any real grazing room for stock so that means we don't have a horse. We travel by foot when we go for supplies. But we do just fine with what we can bring home from the forest. There's also plenty of fish out this way. There's a brook not far from here and we get a lot of fine trout in there. And, of course, the lakes are within a day's walking distance. We never go hungry. We like it out here all by ourselves, but I don't think many women would have agreed to live like this. I love it, 'cept it gets a might lonely now with no one to talk to. I can't imagine that Jedediah planned to leave me alone for so long."

He felt sorry for her situation, but he had no intention of staying here any longer than he had to. He couldn't. He'd only intended to maybe layover for a few days, get healed up, and then decide what to do next — where to go next. He would do whatever chores needed to be done, but then he had to keep moving.

"I'm sure something took place that has delayed him, Tilda. He'll likely be along any day now."

"Or maybe a sow bear got him."

"He didn't go unarmed, did he?"

"No, of course not, but sometimes a sow can get the drop on you before you can get a shot off. Not that we're bothered much by bears, although we've seen plenty of them. But I'd hate to think that's what's happened to him." She began to cry again. "What am I going to do? I always travelled in and out with Jedediah so I know I couldn't find my way out of here on my own. I didn't pay proper attention. Besides, I don't much relish the idea of giving up my home. I like the quiet nights, seeing all the stars. Nothing bothers me out here, but I miss my husband something awful. I'm lonely."

The more he listened to her talk, the more troubled he became. Unless he missed his guess entirely, she needed more than a man to help her get ready for the winter. Lay in enough wood and such. No, he guessed her situation to be much more dire.

"Tilda," he said gently, "are you with child?"

He wasn't surprised when she cried harder and that answered his question. He'd thought so when he first laid eyes on her, but sometimes it was hard to tell behind full skirts. It had looked a little fuller in the front, but it wasn't polite to assume that pregnancy was the reason. Still, when he'd leaned against her on the way in....

"When are you due to give birth?"

She looked away. "I'm getting near to my time. Two or three weeks at most I think."

She certainly didn't seem far enough along to be that near. Maggie was huge at that late stage, but then again Luke had been a big baby. But birth a baby? What did he know about that? Nothing, except he'd helped deliver any number of calves, colts, and anything else that was born on a farm. Yet, he was reminded unpleasantly of women who'd died in childbirth. It was not uncommon.

"I can't see your husband abandoning you at a time like this. I think he's just delayed," he offered hopefully.

She wiped her eyes again. "Do you know about children, Mr. Kavenagh?"

"I have a child," he said. "A little boy. He's eight years old now and a fine strong lad."

"I'll bet he looks just like you."

Brogan smiled despite the pain. "Everyone says so. My son and his mother mean the world to me."

"Is she beautiful, your wife I mean?"

"She is."

"Tell me how you came to be running from the law. Did you kill her, or your son?"

"Good lord, no!"

"So, you're not looking for a woman."

"No, I most definitely am not."

She heaved a sigh, and there was a wealth of desperation in it. "But will you at least stay with me until the baby is born?"

If he hung around here, Ratchford would have him for sure. He was surprised that he hadn't already caught up with him. Ratchford was no slouch when it came to knowing the countryside. He was like a bloodhound when he got on a scent, and that would be the next thing. They'd have the dogs on him. It would be like signing his own death warrant to stay here with the law on his tail, but he certainly couldn't leave her alone either. Again, he didn't know much about midwifery, but she, or the baby, likely wouldn't survive such an ordeal if she were here on her own. There was no question he'd have to stay, unless her husband happened to find his way home again. It wasn't unheard of that a man would abandon his wife when she became pregnant. Maybe he'd been scared off by the responsibilities of impending fatherhood. If he was that heartless, she was well rid of him. Should that be the case here, he would like to have a few minutes alone with *Jedediah*. Explain a thing or two to the young man.

In any event, he was putting his own neck in the noose by staying, and he would suffer the same fate if he were to take her back to Dorchester, and a doctor. The latter was not an option for her at the moment anyway, not at this late stage.

He thought about Maggie and Luke and wanted them so badly, he thought he would start to cry himself. Damn that Amby Burk and his milksop of a wife. They had set out to ruin his life, and they were doing a fine job of it at the moment. Add that mad dog, Sheriff Ratchford, and his future seemed utterly hopeless. At this point, he likely didn't have a future at all, except with the hangman.

* * *

Luke carried another armload of firewood into the house and dropped it with unnecessary force into the woodbox next to the cook stove.

"Luke, dear, can you drop the wood in with less force? I have a cake in the oven, and I don't want it to fall, which it will if you keep dropping the wood like that.

The boy didn't reply, just left for another armload and upon his return, dropped it just as loudly into the wood box.

"Luke! Didn't you hear me, dear? You don't have to drop the wood so hard."

He turned to go, and it was then she noticed the tears on his face.

"Luke, honey, come here. I want to talk to you."

The boy turned away from his mother, his shoulders hunched angrily. She went to him and put her arms around him. He snatched himself out of her embrace, his eyes blazing as he rounded on her.

"I want my father! Why did he run off like he did and leave us? The boys at school were calling him names today. So were the girls but I don't care about them. Everyone was calling him a back shooter. They said he shot a man in cold blood, which I don't even know what that means. All I know is that he must have done what they say he did if he ran away. Even the sheriff thinks he did it, remember?"

He began to sob. "I'm not ever going back to that school. I already know enough anyway. I'm going to stay home with you and help take care of this place."

Maggie was sympathetic, but firm. "Luke, you're going back to school. You're a strong boy. You have to learn not to pay attention to such things. People tell falsehoods, and when they get a rise out of you, they tell them all the more. It's like a bad game, and you play your part when you get angry at them. Ignore them." She knew as she was speaking those words of advice it was wholly too much to expect of such a young child. "Your pa and I taught you to be strong, Luke. It's at a time like this you must use those lessons."

"How can I do that when everyone is laughing at me because of Pa? When will he be back?"

Maggie sighed miserably. "I have no idea, dear." *Maybe never* a cruel voice in the corner of her mind mocked her, but she silenced it. "We just have to wait here and pray your father will find his way back to us soon."

Luke scrubbed at his eyes. "I don't know why he couldn't take us with him. Why do we have to stay here? We could help him if he needed it."

He allowed her to put her arms around him, pulling him against her. "The best way we can help your pa now is to wait here and take care of this place so he has something to come home to. And believe me, Luke, he will come back as soon as he is able.”

“But those bad men who came here the other night want to hurt him,” he worried, his face buried against her apron. “I could help him like I did the other night. Maybe if I *had* shot that man, it would all be over, and they’d leave him alone.”

She held her son at arm’s length so she could see his face. “Luke, you are not to speak like that ever again. There’ll be no more talk of shooting and killing, do you hear me? It is very serious to say such a thing, and even worse to think about doing it. It is never the answer. And you listen to me, your father did not shoot anyone like they say he did. There are some wicked people about, and they’re telling very dangerous falsehoods about him. Your Pa is trying to take care of that, find a way out of this, so he can come back home and be with us like he wants to.”

He raised a tear-stained face. “I miss him, Mamma.”

She pulled him close again. “I know you do, sweetheart. So do I.”

* * *

That night as she lay in bed, her ears were tuned for even the slightest noise out of the ordinary. She wondered where Brogan was. It'd been a week now since he'd left so quickly. Was he safe? Was he hurt and in need of medical attention? Had he found shelter? Her husband was a very resourceful man, and people took to him when he allowed them to. He'd had a huge chip on his shoulder when they'd met, ready to fight at the drop of a hat and defend the Kavenagh name. It had taken years before he'd become calmer. She'd helped him see the senselessness of fighting the world, and he had seemed so much happier when he'd finally given in and settled down. She'd always known he loved her. That had seen her through many difficult times during their marriage. Now, just when their lives were at last on a smoother path, something like this had to happen.

She couldn't even bear to think about losing him. She thought of women who'd been widowed, weeping beside the casket of their dearly departed husband, taken too soon. She prayed that would not be their fate. That she and Brogan would live into happy old age together, but one never knew. She began to pray again.

* * *

Ratchford thrashed in his bed, in agony. His fever had continued to worsen as evening approached and by nine o'clock, his wife, Rachel, could no longer stand it.

"I'm going to fetch the doctor," she told him.

He turned feverish eyes on her. "You'll do nothing of the kind. If a man can't take a little pain, he's not worth very much," he shouted back at her. "I will not incur the further expense!"

She did not often stand her ground, but she was frightened by this turn of events. What had seemed like a simple broken leg appeared to be turning into much more, and she had to do something to help her husband. "Percival, you need a doctor. I implore you to let me fetch Doctor Seeby. Something is wrong other than a broken bone."

"All right! Do as you please then," he bellowed, then added in a more congenial tone: "I'm sorry, Rachel. Maybe you're right. Just fetch something more for the pain if he has it and hurry back."

Without further delay, Rachel pulled on a heavy shawl against the cold night and made haste to the doctor's office.

Age was catching up with old Doc Seeby, but tall and as spare as he ever was, he still worked to keep pace with the medical needs of the town. He was much loved in the little community. He could always be relied upon in an emergency as he hurried back with

Rachel to the Ratchford residence, and was quickly ushered inside. Upon being shown to Percival's room, he made his way to the head of the bed and laid his hand on the sick man's forehead. He then pulled the bedclothes back so he could examine the affected leg.

"What's wrong with me, Doc? I've broken my leg before but it didn't hurt this bad. It must be that you put the cast on too tight. Maybe that's what the problem is. Cut it off!"

Doc pursed his lips as was his habit. "Your leg is swollen, that's one reason you're in so much pain. Your leg above the cast has nearly doubled in size."

Rachel hovered nearby, still clutching her wool shawl. "Isn't swelling part of having a broken bone? It seems his leg was swollen last time too."

Doc Seeby nodded. "It's normal to a certain extent. It's been almost a week, and the swelling should have gone down by now, not gotten worse."

Percival was beside himself, his face drenched in perspiration. "Just do something, Doc. Now that you're here, take the cast off, I beg you."

Doc studied him briefly. "Percival, I can indeed take the cast off." He turned to Rachel. "Rachel you go back to my office and get some splints. You'll find them in the corner by the big glass cabinet. And fetch some white bandages while you're there.

They are inside that same glass cabinet on the first shelf."

Rachel dashed off to get the needed medical supplies

The doctor returned his attention to Ratchford. "I'm going to take that cast off, Percival, but I'll have to re-splint the leg. If what I think is happening is true, it's not the cast that's the problem. It's the injury itself."

"What do you mean? A break is a break, isn't it? If someone breaks a bone, it gets set and heals. Why isn't mine healing the way it did before? I never went through anything like this."

"Well, first of all, you had a much worse break this time than you did before. You're a big man and falling on your leg the way you did caused excessive swelling. When a leg swells, it puts pressure on the blood vessels in that area and that means the flow of blood can be restricted. It's not common, but that's a very bad thing to have happen because the leg can become damaged further. It's not getting the blood it needs to stay healthy. The location of the break can also be a factor in the lower leg. You not only broke the bone, you twisted it badly when your weight came down full force upon it, judging by the way you described the fall. I'll have to see the leg, and I will as soon as the cast has been removed. What I'll need you to do is lie quiet, because it won't be without considerable pain. I've given you some laudanum and that will help."

When the cast had been removed and the leg re-splinted, it was obvious the doctor's suspicion was true.

"Percival, your leg is in very bad condition," Doctor Seeby told him quietly. "I'm afraid it won't be possible to save it."

Percival reared up. "What are you saying? You want to take off my leg? That's preposterous! I will not allow it!"

Rachel shrieked, then covered her mouth with the palm of her hand, embarrassed at her outburst. "Isn't there any other way?" she finally found the courage to ask.

"No, I'm very sorry, but I will need to take the leg. I should amputate as quickly as I can. I shouldn't wait another minute to get started."

"You will not take my leg!" Ratchford shouted. "I'll kill you with my own bare hands if you do."

The doctor was unfazed, likely having heard it all before. He took nothing about his practice of medicine lightly and cared deeply for the people he treated. He waited until his patient had vented his anger. He knew it was only the shock of receiving such a devastating diagnosis. Any other reaction would have been out of the ordinary.

Rachel left the room, overcome.

"Percival, if I don't amputate this leg of yours, you could die. It may already be too late but I have to try."

"Then I die," the sick man roared back, "but I will not give up my leg!" Spying the bottle of laudanum on the bedside table he swept it, and everything beside it, away with the swoop of an arm. It all crashed to the floor in dramatic fashion. "And don't think you're going to give me any more of that stuff to dull my senses," he yelled in reference to the laudanum. "The moment I'm asleep, you'll be cutting, and I forbid you to do that. I have the right to decide for myself. Besides, every man who has a fever doesn't die. Every man who happens to be so unfortunate as to break his leg does not die. You doctors don't know everything there is to know. Everything that happens in life cannot be found in a book."

"Percival...."

"My leg already feels much better with that cast off."

"You don't feel as much pain because you've already got laudanum in your system, but I can assure you the danger is very real. The leg itself is dying, the tissues within. You have gangrene, and if you don't allow me to take your leg, you could be dead within a few hours. Think about your wife and children. You are a young man, Percival. Don't cheat yourself out of the years you still have ahead of you."

"Can you promise me if I let you take my leg this very hour, that I will not die? Hmmm?"

The doctor sighed heavily. "No, of course I can't promise you that, but it would give you a better chance to live. I should have been sent for two days ago. Even now, with the time that's passed while you argue with me, your chances are diminishing. Don't be so hardheaded!"

Ratchford fell back against the pillows closing his eyes, seemingly exhausted from his battle with the doctor.

Doc Seeby stepped closer to the bed and laid a hand on Ratchford's arm. "You're scared, Percival. I can understand that, but...."

"Do you recall Hiram Fowler from over across the way?" the sheriff asked him. "You amputated his leg and he lived to be eighty-nine."

"That's what I'm trying to tell you. If I hadn't, he'd have died from gangrene. Luckily, we got it in time."

"And how are we to know he would have also lived to be eighty-nine if you hadn't touched that leg? We don't. I think you doctors are too quick to start cutting sometimes."

Doc scrubbed his face with his hand tiredly. "He wouldn't have lived if I hadn't done the amputation, and that's a fact, but I'm not going to stand here and argue with you. The final decision is yours, certainly, but I can't save you if you don't let me try."

Ratchford opened his eyes, too sick to continue the fight. "No, Doc. I'll pull through this. Just give me whatever medicine you have in that little black bag of yours and leave me to get some sleep. I've got to get back on my feet. I have a dangerous outlaw to capture, in case you haven't heard. It would be mighty hard to chase him down with only one leg."

* * *

Rachel Ratchford thought there would have been more people at her husband's funeral. After all, he had served the county well as sheriff. He'd taken pride in the job: running elections, summoning jurors, calling and chairing political meetings, and any other of a myriad of duties. She knew there were some people who disliked him, but she'd always admired his doggedness when it came to dealing with apprehending lawbreakers. He was relentless in his pursuit of criminals, but in the process, he kept the kind folks in his jurisdiction accountable. She was especially disappointed that the magistrate hadn't shown up to pay his respects at the funeral. That sent a terrible message. The two had never seen eye to eye, that was true, but certain things transcended petty differences.

One thing was for sure, Percival never forgave anyone who he believed had crossed him. Not taken him seriously enough.

"Their name is on my black list," he'd tell her the odd time he chose to discuss his work with her, "and they will eventually face my wrath."

She also knew that the wrath of Percival Ratchford was indeed a formidable thing. She'd always felt her husband loved her, as much as he could have loved anyone, but she was astutely careful not to incur that famous hot temper of his.

His children had not been so fortunate. Their oldest, Billy, was seventeen when he'd left home after that final set-to with his father. And since she'd always taken the side of her husband, Billy was estranged from her as well. The last she'd heard of her son he'd gone to sea, but that was two years ago. He could be just about anywhere by now. There were still three younger children left at home, and she would have to see to them now the best she could. Life carried on whether one was ready to face it or not.

* * *

The news of Sheriff Ratchford's death reverberated throughout the county like a never-ending rifle shot. He was a hated man, much feared by his own design and all and sundry wondered who would succeed him. His successor could be worse — or perhaps more fair as others had been in the past.

Maggie couldn't believe her ears when Tabor pulled up in the wagon that frosty October morning with the tidings. There wasn't a soul alive who didn't welcome the news, well with a few exceptions. But what did that mean for Brogan? He was still a wanted man, a charge of murder laid against him by way of first-hand witnesses. The death of the man who'd hunted him would not change that. She worried if he did get the news, he might feel free enough to come home under the cloak of darkness to see his family, but that decision would be foolhardy. The hysteria for his capture could mean he'd likely be shot on sight. She realized, on second thought, he would not chance it.

"He's in no less danger," she told Tabor. "But how will this turn of events affect him? Do you think he has a chance since the man who wanted him dead is now dead himself?"

Tabor stirred his coffee slowly, the spoon clinking rhythmically against the inside of the cup. "You're right, Maggie. Not much has changed. But I did hear they were having trouble getting men to help search after those two deputies got killed."

"They'll likely accuse him of that too."

Tabor shrugged. "Probably, but those men were done in with a shotgun. Did Brogan take the pistol with him?"

"Yes."

Tabor shook his head. "Well, he couldn't very well go unarmed, but they'll get him for carrying that too when they catch him."

"Everything's going against him."

"I'd say the weather is in his favour at the moment, but it's going to change. We had a good September before that killer frost came and finished everything off. There's going to be an early winter and a hard one. All the natural signs point to it, including geese and ducks leaving earlier than usual. You must have noticed how thick the onion skins were, and the corn husks. I'm thinking we're going to have a nor'easter in the next couple of weeks, with lots of snow. That would make woods travelling mighty hard. Wherever Brogan is holed up, I hope he's good and comfortable because he's probably going to be there for a while."

Chapter 7

Brogan knew he had a fever when he woke up the next morning, the site of his gunshot wound fiery hot. His body ached with his rising temperature, and chills raced up and down his spine.

It was early morning, the first light of dawn not yet fully illuminating the small bedroom. He could hear Tilda bustling about in the adjoining room. The clang of cooking utensils was likely what had awakened him. Moments later, she swept into the bedroom, dusting her hands on her apron.

"You feeling poorly this morning?" she asked in that soft-spoken voice of hers. "You were making noises in your sleep. Thought you must be fevered."

At times he had to strain to hear her, but it could be because she often seemed bashful around him, although she'd been anything but shy with that shotgun yesterday. Or when it came to undressing him. He guessed that Tilda was a girl who saw what needed to be done and got straight to it. The efficiency with which she'd relieved him of his trousers was proof of that. Most women he knew would have considered it too bold to strip a man of nearly all of his clothes. However, that's what the situation required, and so she'd wasted no time taking care of it. It was purely divine providence that had put him in such capable hands.

"Let's just say I have felt better," he said. "My leg is hurting something terrible. It feels as though it's on fire."

"I checked it earlier while you were sound asleep. The wound is very hot."

Oh, so that's what had wakened him. Tilda would have made a good nurse.

"I think we need to...." he began.

"I already know what needs to be done," she stated matter-of-factly. "I was waiting for you to awaken before I painted the area with iodine. We keep lots here in case either my husband or I sicken or get injured. After that, I'm going to apply a poultice. I have water on to heat now, and I've got the salts ready to put together. When I have everything ready, I'm going to bind it in place. That should help settle everything down."

He tried to smile, although it was a weak attempt. That's what he'd been about to suggest, a poultice. His mother had sworn by them. She'd kept iodine in the house too, at the suggestion of the doctor, after Pate had stepped on a horseshoe nail years ago.

Tilda set to work, and the iodine stung like he never imagined it would, but if it helped, then by all means put lots on. When the fire in his thigh began to cool, she announced that the poultice concoction was ready. That, too, hurt like anything when she laid it gently on the open wound. She wrapped it to contain the moisture as best she could. He could tell Tilda was a natural healer, but, oh, for something to dull this pain.

"There," she said once everything was in place. "I'll change it again later so you'll have a fresh one for overnight. That poultice will make quite a difference within forty-eight hours I expect. Now, I'm fixing some sausages and buckwheat pancakes. Do you think you can get some of that into you?"

Eating did not appeal to him in the least at the moment, but if he expected to regain his strength, he would need nourishment. However, there would be no point to it if it didn't stay down, but he would try a little. The throbbing in his leg was all-consuming.

"Maybe I'll have a sausage. I'm afraid I don't have much of an appetite, but I know I have to try and eat something."

She smiled, which now, in the full light of day, was a wonderful gift of nature. What a beauty she was!

"All right, I'll bring just a little at first," she agreed. "Of course, I'm eating for myself and the baby, so it doesn't take much to tempt me. A big breakfast sounds wonderful because I'm famished."

He pulled the heavy quilt back into place once she'd left. Unfortunately, though, it felt like the weight of a stone on his injured leg.

After several adjustments, he came to the frustrating conclusion that there would be no comfortable position. So, he lay there with his eyes closed, trying not to think about his predicament. Maggie and Luke were constantly on his mind. He wondered how they were faring in all of this.

He wasn't aware he'd fallen back to sleep until she touched his shoulder and he jerked awake.

"I didn't mean to startle you, Brogan, but I have your breakfast."

The agony of his leg was also reawakened. He glanced at the plate, and it was rather full considering his original plan to try one sausage. "I don't think I can eat all of that," he told her. "Sorry."

She smiled at him, understanding in her eyes. "I know, but I agree with you. It's important to try. You're a big man so you need plenty of sustenance. Really, there's only two sausages."

He glanced at the plate again. "Two very big sausages, and a buckwheat pancake the size of this room," he observed with a feeble attempt at a smile. "Did you make the sausages yourself?"

"I did. It's a big job, but I love the taste of them. So does Jedediah. He says I make the best sausages he's ever eaten."

Her smile disappeared when she mentioned her husband, and that was understandable. So in an attempt to cheer her up, if for no other reason, he took the plate and pulled himself into an upright position. After all her work, the least he could do was eat what she'd served him.

Brogan surprised himself by not only downing both sausages, but also the huge buckwheat pancake that had competed with the meat for the lion's share of the plate. Actually, he wolfed it down not realizing how hungry he was. It tasted delicious.

"I can bring more if you'd like," she told him when she checked on his progress a few minutes later. "There's a sausage in the pan, and I can fry another pancake very quickly."

He was already shaking his head as he passed her the empty plate. "That's fine for now, Tilda. I'd like some hot coffee if you have it, but don't bring it to me. I am perfectly able to get out of this bed and come out and get it."

She held up her hand. "Absolutely not. I don't want you to get that wound bleeding again. I'm afraid it might set you back. The idea is for you to get well, not worse."

"I'll be fine," he argued, throwing back the cover, remembering as he did so that he was only wearing short drawers. He lowered his feet to the floor. "Get me my pants, please. I'm coming to the table."

But his foolish act of bravado had already drained him of what little energy he had. Lying back down he waited for the room to stop spinning.

"There, you see?" she admonished him gently. "You need to stay in bed for a few days. You have to remember that you lost a lot of blood, and it takes a while for your body to regenerate it." She bent and picked up his feet and helped him swing them onto the bed, pulling the patchwork quilt back into place. "I'll pour that coffee for you, and then you can get some more sleep. It's plain to see you've been through an ordeal, and would be unwise of you to overdo it. If there were a doctor here, he'd tell you the same thing. My Grandpa tried to carry on as usual even when he had a bad sickness, and it weakened him even more. He died, and the doctor said it didn't need to happen. He said rest was what a body needed most of all to recover, so that's what I'm telling you."

And *he* had been put in his place by a woman half his size. He had no alternative but to listen because he knew she was right. Maggie wouldn't have taken any guff off him either, not that he gave her any. Well, not very often. That was just one more reason why he loved his wife so much. She was ... interesting. He couldn't stand weak women. His mother, for all her faults, hadn't been one, and neither was the woman he'd married. He wanted a woman to be his equal, not his doormat. It would be hard to love someone he didn't respect.

With a full belly, he fell into a sound sleep and dreamt about Maggie. She was looking for Luke. They both were, running through the forest and calling his name. He tried to catch up with his wife, but no matter how fast he ran he couldn't seem to do it. And where was Luke? They were going too far! The child couldn't possibly have covered this much distance. Hadn't he just seen him in the barnyard, feeding the chickens? How had he gotten away so fast? And Maggie! He had to catch her because he knew there was something dangerous ahead. He had to protect them both. "Maggie, wait!" he shouted. "Maggie! Maggie!"

He came to with a jolt, realizing he had been shouting in his sleep or else it seemed as though he had. It was hard to tell with dreams. As he came more fully awake, he was aware that Tilda was bending over him, straightening his covers. How had they gotten into such disarray?

"I think you were dreaming," she told him, laying the back of her hand against his forehead. "You've been asleep for hours, and I think your fever has broken. You're much cooler to the touch than you were earlier and that's a most encouraging sign."

"It must be those sausages," he said, trying for lightness as the dream still lay heavily upon him.

"Or the pancake," she returned the joke. "Don't forget about the pancake. Did you know that buckwheat is actually an herb used to treat swollen feet and it helps veins as well? Next time you have a chance, look at the red colour of the buckwheat stem and think of blood circulation. Now, I'll check your leg again," she said, already pulling back the quilt and laying a hand on the dressing. "I don't see any blood leaking, so I think I'll leave it there for a few more hours to allow it to work. If your fever has broken already, I would say it's doing its job. We were fortunate to be able to treat the wound before it got any worse. We'll leave the poultice undisturbed for the rest of the day."

Still trying to collect himself after such an unsettling dream that was still all too vivid, he tried another weak smile. "You sound like a doctor."

"I picked up a lot from my father. He's a doctor back in the town. Doctor Seeby. He used to let me help him sometimes in his office. He always said I would make a good nurse, but what I really wanted was to be a doctor. I've always been really excited to learn about medicine, but I don't know of any women doctors around these parts. My father said he would teach me what he knew, and I loved the learning while it lasted. It was fun being his nurse."

"I've heard of Doctor Seeby, and I would say your pa taught you a lot. How old were you when you came out here?"

"I was seventeen when I met Jedediah. We fell in love right off and didn't see the need for a lengthy courtship. My ma died when I was a young girl, and since my pa approved of Jedediah, we decided to marry early. I wasn't yet eighteen, but I'd been keeping house for years, so there wasn't much else I had to learn about that. I was ready. I hated leaving my father behind though. I was their only child, but well, you can't argue with a woman in love."

"And how old are you now, Tilda?" he asked, still guessing her to be about twenty years of age.

"I'll be twenty-one in a fortnight. I already told you how much I love it out here. I miss my father and I know he misses me, but Jedediah says my loyalty has to be to him now. He is the man of the house, not my father, and of course, I must obey him. The preacher said I should remember that if I wanted a long happy marriage, and Jedediah agreed."

Love and honour were also part of the vows Jedediah Loughty must have spoken to his bride on their wedding day. Those seemed to have been conveniently forgotten given the young man's long absence. But of course, it was possible he might have met with misadventure. Anything could have happened, but he had a gut feeling about this. It sounded more like the rooster had flown the coop. The idea of leaving a pregnant woman alone in the wilderness, purposely, really raised his hackles. And she was such a sweet young woman.

"Tell me about this Jedediah of yours, Tilda. A good man, is he?"

She flushed. "Yes, my Jedediah is a good man. That's why I love him. Oh, he has his ways and he gets to feeling on edge every now and again. I try not to bother him when he's in one of his hateful moods."

Brogan wasn't surprised somehow to hear that Jedediah could be difficult. However, Tilda gave him the impression she could stand her own ground, but he did wonder how bad it actually got.

"Does he beat you, Tilda? I mean, when he gets in one of his hateful moods as you put it?"

"He did, once," she said, and he was surprised to hear her admit it. "Or I should say he tried to. He pushed me down but that was only because he got into the whiskey. Jedediah isn't one to drink, so it hit him hard. My father said you can always find the devil waiting at the bottom of a whiskey bottle, and Jedediah certainly did that night. But I got a great big ole stick and whacked him with it. That wasn't long after we got this place up and running. He has never tried anything like that again. I hurt him with that stick, and I meant to, right where it would do him the most good, on his bottom."

Brogan laughed out loud. "I'm sorry," he apologized. "I shouldn't have done that. It's not funny. It was just that I could picture.... Never mind. I can't abide a man who'd hurt a woman. That's no kind of a man to me."

"That's what I told him." She agreed with a smile. "And I think he learned his lesson. There was just only ever that one time. Like I said, Jedediah is a good man."

Maggie was collecting eggs in the barn the next forenoon, what few there were. The chickens were now laying less because of shorter daylight hours along with colder temperatures. They'd still have to be fed though. She scattered grain for the small flock and made sure their water dish was kept fresh.

The slamming of the kitchen door interrupted her work, and she hurried from the barn with her egg basket to see who was about. There was no one in the yard, no horse and wagon, or even a saddle horse tethered to the hitching post beside the apple tree. Hmmm.... Who could it be? Luke was at school. It was a windy day but she was sure she hadn't left the door open to have it blown shut. Heat was too precious to leave doors and windows open at this time of year.

Wood supplies were tended very carefully, especially with Brogan gone and not able to top up what they already had on hand. But she should be all right through the winter if this thing dragged on that long. Tabor and Pate had gone to the woodlot and chopped up the trees Brogan had felled for next year's supply, then hauled the firewood home and ranked it in the shed in back of the house. It wouldn't be properly seasoned until next fall, but in a pinch, she would make it work. She was mighty grateful to Tabor and Pate. Even Luke had helped, piling what he could handle. Her son was doing his best to be the man of the house during his father's absence.

She made her way quickly toward the house, wondering with a sense of foreboding what she was to expect inside. A few more steps and she knew exactly what she would find when she got there. She could hear Luke crying noisily.

Hurrying inside, she set the egg basket on the table, then went to Luke's room at the end of the hall. The door was ajar, so she knocked lightly and went inside. Luke was lying face down on the bed, his shoulders shaking with sobs.

Brogan's absence was terribly hard on the child. She knew how difficult *she* was finding the days, not knowing what had happened to her husband. Whether he was dead or alive, and when he was found, what awaited him? It must be torturous for Luke.

She sat down beside him and laid a hand gently on his shoulder, then began to stroke his hair. "Luke, can you tell me what upset you so? Did something take place at school?"

He nodded, crying all the harder.

"Tell me what happened. Maybe we can talk it out."

She jumped when he suddenly twisted himself into an upright position, his eyes red and swollen. "No, Ma, we can't talk it out. I'm never going back to school again. The other children are nasty, and now they're saying Pa killed a bunch more people. They're telling lies about him, and I don't want to hear them say those things. It's not fair. They're all a bunch of ratbags!"

"Luke! Watch your tongue, young man. Who told you about that word?"

Luke had only begun to vent his fury. "Uncle Tabor said that's what people around here were, all a bunch of rogues and ratbags, and I don't want to be around them anymore."

"Well, Uncle Tabor shouldn't be teaching you those kinds of words. You'll learn them fast enough on your own."

"Uncle Tabor is right because that's what they are."

She reached to pull him toward her, to put her arm around him in comfort, but he wasn't to be placated. "No, Ma! I won't cuss anymore, but I'm not going back there. Not ever."

It was a few more moments before she could finally gather him to her. By that time, he'd dissolved into tears again. "I want Pa to come home," he wailed. "I miss him. He's been gone for a long time."

She stroked the back of his head. Such a wise boy for his age, but still a child crying for his pa. It tore at her heart. It had only been a little more than two weeks since he'd left, but how interminable that time must seem to one so young.

"Luke, dear, we have to be strong. It's what your pa would want. If he'd had a chance to speak to you before he left, that's what he would have asked of you. To be strong while he was gone."

The unfairness of what she was telling her son ate at her, but she could not give in. She had to help him stay strong. She hated that she was asking too much from him at such a tender age, but if that's what held everything together, then by the Almighty, that's what she must do.

Luke was still hiccupping on sobs. "I am trying to stay strong," he told her, his voice so unbearably young and naïve that she fought to keep her own tears at bay. It would not serve either of them if she went to pieces.

"Oh, and you are, Luke! You are, my boy! I feel so safe with you here to help me look after things. But we have to carry on until your pa comes back to us. I wish I could tell you when that will be, but I cannot. I am also trying my best to be strong. Can you help me too? We could do it together."

The sobs had all but subsided. "Yes," he said. "I can help you, Mamma. What do you want me to do?"

Leaning him back, she brushed the damp hair from his forehead. "What I need you to do for me will take a lot of strength, Luke. More than *you* think you have, but I know you've got it in you."

"Do you want me to lift something out in the barn?"

"No, honey, a different kind of strength." She tapped his chest gently with a forefinger. "The strength I'm talking about comes from inside. It's not muscles, it's what we refer to as strength of character because that's the real measure of a man. Your father has it, and I know you do too. It just needs a little more practice, although you do very well for your age. That's why your pa and I are so proud of you."

Luke studied his mother. "So, what do you want me to do?"

"What I'm going to ask you to do is not easy, but I know you can do it. It's what your father would want you to do too, and that's go back to school."

He started to pull away as his face clouded over again.

"Now wait a minute," she rushed to explain. "You don't have to go back there today. As a matter of fact, I would suggest you don't. But I do want you to return on Monday morning, same as you always do."

"But, Ma. The other children say...."

"Ahh, that's the part where you 'have to be strong' comes in. They may say it, but you know in your heart it's not true and that's all that matters. Just pretend you don't hear them. There's an old saying that goes something like this: No one can get your goat if they don't know where it's tied. What that means is if you ignore them, they won't get any pleasure from trying to upset you and they'll stop. I think I'll just walk up there

with you on Monday anyway and speak with
your teacher."

"No!"

"Why ever not?"

"Because then everybody will think I'm a
baby."

She sighed. "All right, Luke, but I just
want to say that it's very important to your
father and I that you get your schooling.
Now, do you think you can go back to school
alone on Monday and know that when you
do, you're doing it for your father? He would
be so proud you were strong enough to do
that."

Luke was solemn for a moment, then
stuck his chest out. "I'll do it for my pa. I'll
show them."

"Good boy! Now, I've been thinking
about baking a lally cake. Would you like
that?" she asked, knowing molasses cake was
his favourite.

His eyes lit up in little boy fashion. "All
right! Can we put fresh cream on it?"

"Yes, we can! I've got a pitcher of heavy
cream cooling in the root cellar. It's for
butter making, but I think I can spare a little
of it for your lally cake."

* * *

Tabor Kavenagh was right. A nor'easter,
the likes of which hadn't been seen in the

area in fifteen years, descended on the countryside. Before the blizzard blew out forty-eight hours later, it had dumped almost two feet of snow. And then the temperature plummeted to freezing temperatures that lasted for several days before returning to more seasonal values. But it was apparent the snow was here to stay unless much milder weather arrived.

* * *

John Vailor was chosen as the new sheriff for the county to succeed the late Percival Ratchford. It was who everyone suspected would be Ratchford's successor, although given Vailor's seemingly mild manner, it wasn't at all who the former sheriff would have wanted to take his place. Ratchford was overzealous in the execution of his duties, a man who made enemies easily and held grudges. Vailor, on the other hand, was coolly efficient, although no less ruthless when it came to dealing with lawbreakers.

"What about this Kavenagh character?" the magistrate asked the newly minted sheriff when they met in the privacy of the magistrate's office. "What do you intend to do about him?"

Vailor casually crossed his legs at the ankle and folded his arms loosely across his chest. "Nothing for the moment. What *can* we do?" he asked reasonably, spreading his hands for effect as he looked out the window at the banks of snow. "But bad weather or not, there's a distinct lack of interest in his pursuit since those two deputies were gunned down. Besides, I think he's already dead. Ratchford was able to tell us he managed to get a bullet into the fugitive. He saw the blood fly himself. Now it was in the leg, I believe he said, but with no shelter or medical treatment, what chance would he have to survive? None. He'd either die from blood loss or sepsis. No, I think at this point, it'll just be a matter of waiting 'til spring and then go and recover his remains — if there are any left by then. Even if the gunshot wound didn't kill him, the exposure would. Ratchford did manage to save us the cost of a hangman and rid us of a very dangerous man. We should be grateful to him for that."

The magistrate, a bald, rotund man, steepled his fingers, his elbows on the arms of his wooden desk chair. "I concur, there's probably no way you can get in those woods after this kind of a storm, at least not easily. I expect the going would be most treacherous back where you think he might have gone. If he's on the ground, he would likely be drifted over. It seems winter has overtaken us much earlier than expected this year. No man wants to go far from hearth and home for any reason."

Vailor smiled, but it did not reach his eyes. Heavily lidded and as dark as midnight, he was impossible to read. "Divine providence is what I would call it. There's no way he could find adequate shelter and sustenance out in those woods, especially now that the weather has turned. I would say Ratchford's shot felled him, and nature took care of the rest."

"Has his family been told?"

"No, not until we have something definite to report to them."

"I understand Kavenagh has a young son and a wife."

Vailor smiled. "From what I understand, a very beautiful wife."

Chapter 8

By the second day, the bonfire in Brogan's thigh had all but been extinguished, and he'd begun to feel much better. Even his fever had cleared up and he knew he had Tilda to thank for her excellent nursing skills. Not only with the surgery and wound dressings but also for bringing food to nourish him. She'd even mended the bullet hole in his trousers and laid them folded on the chair beside the bed.

On his third day at the cabin, she looked up as she was making breakfast and was surprised to see him standing in the kitchen, leaning heavily against the doorjamb.

"What are you doing out of bed, Brogan? You shouldn't be walking on that leg. It's not healed enough."

"It's healed enough," he answered her stubbornly. "I'm not going to lie in bed and have you wait on me any longer. It's time I started pulling my own weight."

"And it's pulling that weight that's going to get you in trouble. Please go back and lie down. I have breakfast almost ready."

"Tell me, Tilda, have you been tending my horse?"

She chuckled. "Of course. You don't think I'd just leave him out there untended do you! I've been feeding and watering him."

Brogan cursed under his breath. "And you over eight months gone."

"Just because I'm in a family way doesn't mean I'm not able to work, Brogan."

"And I assume you cleared the snow away to get to the barn."

"I'm not used to being pampered."

"That much is apparent," he groused, "but from now on I'll tend to my own horse and take care of any snow that needs to be cleared."

She straightened up from where she'd been crouched by the hearth seeing to the sausages. "Brogan, I'm telling you your leg isn't strong enough, and you haven't had a chance to get your strength back."

"Then find me something to lean on while I work," he said, giving in because his thigh was already beginning to throb and he hadn't gone but five feet. "And tell me something else," he said looking around. "Are there just the two rooms in this cabin?"

"Well, except for the larder off the kitchen there."

He held her gaze. "So, one bedroom, one kitchen, one pantry."

"That's right."

"And since I've been using your bed, where have you been sleeping at night?"

"Right here," she said, pointing to the floor. "I have a rug under me and a hand-worked-quilt over me. It's lovely and warm in front of the fire."

Brogan swore aloud this time. "You're going to have a child and you've been sleeping on the floor."

She was looking at him nonplussed. "I could hardly share the bed with you, now could I?"

"Of course not, but I can assure you it'll be me sleeping on the floor tonight. Not you."

"But your leg...."

"My leg is going to be fine. It won't hurt it any to lay on the floor."

"No! You must stay in bed. You have to get well, Brogan, and you can't do that lying on the floor. I have not been inconvenienced in any way with this arrangement. I sleep like a baby at night."

"Tilda, I'm not going to argue with you," although he did wonder how he would be able to get up and lie down without having to endure excruciating pain.

Oh, how he wished for a good dose of laudanum given how badly his leg was aching, but there was no time to worry about that now. First of all, he had to go and take care of Dutch. That gelding was fractious and very high-spirited. Not at all suitable for a pregnant woman to be handling, and her half his size. The thought of her doing that while he lay in bed made his blood boil. He silently cursed both Amby Burk and Percival

Ratchford for putting him in such an untenable situation.

And what a time for an early winter! October! He'd been counting on better travelling weather, although the recent snowstorm would also slow up the search party. And what about Maggie and Luke? For all intents and purposes, they would be on their own, although he knew Tabor and Pate would have finished getting his firewood in for him and they would see to whatever else was needed. That at least gave him some peace of mind, but it did little to improve his mood.

Tilda held up her hands in mock surrender. "Have it your way. You're making a big mistake, but if you intend to go see to your horse, I can't stop you." Hurrying to the corner opposite the hearth she returned with a carved walking stick. "Here, use this. Jedediah had that when he hurt his ankle a year or so ago. It's good and sturdy so you can lean on it."

He took it from her, and it helped take the weight off his leg. "Where's my coat and boots?"

"There by the door," she said, pointing to the same corner where she'd gotten the walking stick. "Just sit down and I'll get them for you."

"No!" He hadn't meant to shout, but he couldn't allow her to keep waiting on him like this. "I can take care of it myself. Look," he said, gentling his tone when he saw her stricken expression, "first of all you don't need to wait on me for something like that. I can see to my own coat and boots. I don't mean to sound ungrateful, but you shouldn't be doing heavy tasks, like shoveling and lifting. Reaching."

"I'm hardly fragile, Brogan. Like I told you, I'm used to hard work."

"I don't mean you should just sit on a chair and do nothing, but things can happen by taking on heavy tasks. You should know that already if you learned about medicine from your father. A pregnant woman, especially one so close to delivering, has to be careful. You could injure yourself ... lose the baby, and I'm no doctor. There would be only so much I could do to help you, Tilda."

She nodded. "I do try to be careful, but all right. I'll let you spoil me. But your leg, it was a deep wound and it's trying to heal. You have to allow time for that to happen. You're not going to be completely recovered in a couple of days."

Brogan had to smile, despite himself. "We make a good pair you and I, don't we? I guess we'll have to help each other, but if there's any more heavy lifting to be done, either I do it or it doesn't get done. Understood?"

She smiled that radiant smile of hers. "Yes, sir!"

"I'm serious."

"I know you are. So am I. Now breakfast is ready and I assume you'll be joining me at the table this morning. Have a seat and I'll get the crockery."

He was more than glad to sit down. "It sure smells good. I didn't realize how hungry I was until I smelled breakfast cooking."

She set the crockery on the narrow wooden table, followed by the utensils. "I hope you don't mind eating the same thing every day."

"When food is this good a man doesn't mind how often he eats it. I thank you, Tilda. If it weren't for you, I would be eating stale cornbread and beef jerky, well, for a couple of days and then I would be fresh out of food. I thank you for all you're doing for me. I tell you again, you saved my life, and make no mistake about it, I'm grateful."

Tilda lowered her head, and this time he *could* see the blush. It didn't seem she was used to receiving compliments.

They ate in silence. When the meal was finished, she was immediately on her feet clearing everything away. Brogan pushed himself away from the table.

"All right I'm off to the barn," he said, hoping she didn't notice his reaction to the stab of pain when he slowly got to his feet.

Walking was even more painful, even with the cane. It was helpful, but it had been fashioned for a much shorter man. Still, he knew he couldn't function without it as he pulled on his buckskin jacket and fastened it up against the howling wind.

He'd thought to bring the shovel with him because of the blowing snow. Sure enough, a high drift had blown against the barn door. He heard Dutch nickering inside, stamping restlessly knowing his master was close at hand. He spoke to the horse to quiet him.

Still frustratingly weak, it was hard going with the shovel. Knowing Tilda had been out here doing the same thing in her condition reignited his anger. She could tear herself inside and die, and likely, the baby would too. Tilda was a strong woman. That was easy to see, but he couldn't allow her to take any more foolish chances with her health or that of her child.

It was long minutes before he'd dug his way into the barn, and unless she had been shoveling manure, there would be a sizeable job waiting inside for him too. He couldn't abide people who let their animals stand knee-deep in their own waste. But just as he'd figured, Tilda had been keeping the horse stall shoveled. There were only last night's droppings to contend with. He couldn't shovel very well leaning on a walking stick, so he'd set it aside and endured the pain until the job was finished. Next came the hay. He gritted his teeth as he slowly climbed the steps to the mow and forked down a generous supply, which he stacked neatly in the corner of the small barn. There was plenty, so he used some for the horse's bedding, too, just as Tilda had been doing. Dutch had been well taken care of.

He wanted to turn the horse out as he would have if he'd been home, but there he'd had a large pasture. Dutch could do with a leg stretch, and as soon as the weather improved, he would tether him in back of the cabin. The grass grew long there so he could forage through the snow. Tomorrow might be a better day he told the horse, and Dutch seemed to understand, munching contentedly on the hay in his manger.

On the way back to the cabin, he re-cleared the path as best he could. Unfortunately, the cabin had been built in the path of the prevailing wind. His work would be quickly undone. He would come out later to tend to Dutch for the night. Hopefully, that northeast wind would have blown itself out by then.

Brogan was glad to get back inside the warm cabin, and Tilda was not in the main room when he came in. He figured she must be in the larder. He'd stopped to get more wood for the fire because if he didn't, Tilda was sure to do that herself too. He made a note to watch her like a hawk. She was young and inexperienced. She seemed to have no idea what could happen if she wasn't careful. Barney Milburn's wife had torn herself inside just hanging out a wash. The doctor had told Barney she'd been reaching too high, straining herself and they couldn't stop the hemorrhaging. He'd lost both his wife and the baby.

Maggie was also one of those women who it was hard to keep from overdoing, but she'd been more careful, more mindful of the baby. Thinking of Maggie made his heart squeeze with longing. How he would have loved to hold her in his arms right now, embrace his son. Soon, he told himself. Things will turn around soon. He just had to hold onto hope.

He was shaking the snow off his coat and hood when Tilda walked into the room. She shrieked when she saw him, her hands flying to her mouth.

"What's wrong!" he demanded, following her gaze to his thigh.

His pant leg was crimson, his wound bleeding profusely. Of all the damned luck.

Tilda grabbed a sugar bag tea towel from the table and hurried to where he was standing, pressing the cloth against his thigh. "I told you it'd open everything up again if you started walking on it too soon."

Still wobbly, he kept the tea towel pressed in place as he made his way to the chair by the table and sank heavily onto it. "It's bound to bleed a little, Tilda."

"A little maybe, but not this much. You've probably managed to tear it open again. I'll have to examine it. Cauterize it again."

Another round with a red-hot knife wasn't at all appealing. "I don't think so," he said, holding up a hand in a stay-away gesture. "Once was enough, thank you."

Tilda wasn't to be bested. It was apparently not in her nature to take a step back. "Once would have been enough if you hadn't started walking on it. Working in the barn. I'll have to take a look at it."

Brogan waved her away. "It's fine. It just bled a little because I put weight on it. Give it a few minutes I tell you. It'll stop. It's not the first time I've ever had a cut."

She shook her head, every bit as stubborn as he was. "A cut, yes, but not like this, Brogan. That bullet went deep into the muscle, and I had to dig for it with the knife which injured it further. If my father was here, you wouldn't be getting out of bed so soon."

"Tilda," he said looking up at her from the tops of his eyes, "stop acting like a mother hen and fussing around. I haven't had anyone hovering over me for a very long time and I don't want it now."

"But my father...."

"Is not here," he finished for her, "and my leg is going to be all right."

It was still bleeding heavily minutes later, the tea towel soaked, and he knew he had to give in and get off his feet. That meant the bed again. He had to acknowledge that given the condition of his leg, getting up from the floor, or down onto it for that matter would put undo pressure on the injury. And aside from those concerns, it would be extremely painful.

"Brogan...." Tilda started again, seemingly ready to dig into another argument in favour of the bed.

"You win," he told her tiredly. "I have to go and lie down, get this thing stopped." He glared at his leg as though it had betrayed him. "And stop worrying about me. Everything's going to be fine."

She tilted her chin which he'd come to recognize as an outward sign of spirit. "I have to take a look at the wound, so kindly remove your trousers if you would, once you're there and comfortable. I would offer to help you make the trip," she said retrieving the walking stick from the corner, "but you would only insist on getting there under your own steam. So kindly let me know when you've arranged yourself for my examination."

He stared at her for a moment, then couldn't help chuckling at her temerity. "Yes, Doctor Loughty," he said, taking the walking stick from her and hobbling into the bedroom.

"It's just as I feared," she told him minutes later when she had examined the wound. "My stitches have held, but it's bleeding deeper down. I would say it's in the muscle. And you know what that means, don't you?"

He looked at her. "No, what does that mean?"

"It means no more walking, Mr. Kavenagh. If my father were here, he would say no walking for at least another week, maybe two."

"Two weeks! A week is even out of the question. Impossible. I can't lay here for that long."

"Brogan," she began patiently, "that's the way it has to be. You have to remember all the blood you've lost. I've seen men ignore my father's orders and pay the price."

"Such as...."

"Well, Timothy Patterson almost lost his leg. How's that for a *such as*. Stop being so hard to get along with. I'm not trying to win an argument here. I'm trying to help you."

Brogan puffed out a long sigh, turning his face toward the small window, disheartened. It was a few moments before he glanced back in her direction. "I'm sorry. I'll do as you say, but you have to make a promise to me too."

She looked at him, perplexed. "What is that?"

"My horse has to be tended twice a day. I put down a lot of extra hay so there's no need to go up to the mow and start forking any down. And just carry small amounts of water at a time, no heavy lifting. And don't, under any circumstances, try to shovel that manure. I don't like leaving it under him any more than you do, but that's the way it has to be for a while. Agreed?"

Now it was her turn to give in, which she did moments later. "Agreed."

"And no snow shoveling. Look," he said when it seemed she was about to object, "you're probably going to be all right. But things can go wrong in pregnancy. You must have seen that when you worked with your father. So why take the chance? We're miles from civilization with no doctor around to help ... or midwife. I want you to be careful. I'll be careful, *you* be careful. I've already got my fingers crossed that nothing goes wrong when I'm helping you birth that baby, I don't need you complicating matters."

Her eyes lit up. "You mean you're going to stay and help me have my baby?"

He gaped at her in surprise. "Well, I'm not going to leave you way out here by yourself. Of course, I'm going to stay with you."

* * *

Maggie woke with a headache pulling at her temples, the house cold because she'd slept so soundly. She'd fallen into that deep sleep from sheer exhaustion, having managed only three or four hours a night for the past week. She'd worked to keep her mood upbeat, mostly for the sake of her son. True to his promise he had returned to school. However, she routinely questioned herself about forcing him to go there every day, because that's what it amounted to. It would be hard for an adult to bear that kind of daily scrutiny, but her prayer was that Luke could continue to rise above it. It would be that mental toughness that would help to build his strength of character. She and Brogan believed that, but she reminded herself that he was an eight-year-old child. However, if she gave in, when Brogan came home, and this would one day be just a horrible memory, he would wonder why Luke had missed school simply because the other children had picked on him.

It was beginning to come light, and she heard something in the kitchen, so she pulled on her heavy robe, sliding her feet into fur-lined slippers. Brogan had given her the slippers two Christmases ago because she routinely complained about cold feet. She looked at them. He'd had them handmade for her and she felt tears spring to her eyes. But she blinked them away. She would confine her tears to the nighttime hours when Luke could not witness them.

Quickly making her way to the main room, she saw Luke piling wood into the hearth, positioning the birch bark as he'd seen his parents do.

"I'll light that," she said hurrying into the room because he was standing a little too close to the fire. A flare-up could easily catch his clothing.

He reluctantly passed her the matches.

"You laid a very good fire, Luke," she told him. "Your pa would be very proud of you."

"That's how he does it," he explained. "I watched him."

"And you learned well, son, but maybe let me fire it up, all right? You made my job so much easier this morning by laying the wood and bark in perfectly, and I thank you."

He glowed with pride, and she promised herself she'd not let the fire get down so far from now on. It was *her* job to keep the house warm. She would never forgive herself if her child had gotten burned.

"What would you like to have for breakfast?" she asked him. "I still have some eggs, and there's bacon in the pantry. Or I could make some buckwheat pancakes. I think you deserve a special breakfast for being such a good boy."

He beamed, but she could still see the sadness in his eyes. "Pa always eats buckwheat pancakes, so that's what I'll have."

Her headache had begun to subside after they'd eaten breakfast and Luke had left for the schoolhouse. Her heart was still heavy, though, as she went about her morning work. At times the worry was almost too much to bear.

Next, she tackled the outside chores because keeping busy did help to pass the time. It would have been wonderful to have her mother to talk to, but she'd passed on to glory last winter. They'd been estranged for some time anyway because both of her parents had forbidden her to *get mixed up with one of those Kavenaghs.* That was how they'd put it. Brogan was a bad boy for sure, but she'd fallen deeply in love with him before she realized he would need some taming if he was going to make a good husband. That taming had taken her longer than she'd ever imagined, but he'd eventually settled down. She couldn't ask for a finer mate. He'd had a hard life growing up, tormented relentlessly at school and again, she felt an ache in the pit of her stomach that they were putting their son through the very same thing.

It was early afternoon when she heard a buggy pull into the yard. She wondered immediately who was there but hadn't bothered to get up from her mending to check. Whoever it was would come to the door and then she would know.

Sure enough, a knock sounded at the door moments later, and she set aside her work to answer it.

She didn't recognize the tall thin man standing there, but she didn't like the look of him. He wasn't dressed especially fine despite the fact he'd arrived in a horse-drawn carriage instead of a wagon like most of the folks hereabouts. He wore a smug expression and appeared much too self-assured for her liking.

"May I come in please, Ma'am?" he asked, "or do I have to stand on the doorstep?"

An even deeper dislike of him surged through her. "Where you are is fine. Please state your business."

His eyes narrowed. "I am Sheriff John Vailor, and my business, as you put it, concerns your husband, Mrs. Kavenagh. He is within days of being captured, and the conversation you and I have here today will have a direct bearing on whether or not he is convicted. You look to be an intelligent woman, so I likely don't have to explain to you that a favourable conversation would bode well for him. If you have your husband's best interests at heart you will cooperate with the law."

Lightning shot through her. They were about to capture Brogan!

She stepped back, pulling the door wide so he could enter, but she would not welcome him. Nevertheless, as he'd just pointed out, she did not want to get in the way of a beneficial outcome for Brogan by being difficult. This sheriff was a vast improvement over that mad dog Percival Ratchford, but there was something about the man she instinctively distrusted. Everyone had liked the man who'd held the job prior to Ratchford. Alden Pomeroy had been a fair man who didn't impose himself beyond his power or influence. Unfortunately, he'd only been sheriff for a short time before political favouritism saw a change of guard.

He stepped into the room, barely glancing around.

"Have a seat, please. I'm sorry I have nothing to offer you," she lied, not wanting him to overstay his welcome. "But I do want to hear what you have to tell me about Brogan. You say he's close to being brought in?"

The sheriff remained standing. "Very close. We know exactly where he is, and it's just a matter of organizing a party to go in and apprehend him."

"But I would have thought this snowfall would be an impediment to the search."

"The law does not stop because of a little snow," he said, dismissing her concern.

She watched him warily, digesting what he'd just told her. Something didn't feel right.

"I can see it in those beautiful eyes of yours that you doubt me, Mrs. Kavenagh."

She was taken aback. "I do doubt that it will be that easily done."

"That's not something you have to worry about, now, is it? What should concern you more are the charges facing your husband."

Maggie put a hand on the back of a nearby chair to steady herself. "I assume he will be charged with the death of Latham Storey."

"That is correct. The brutal slaying of an innocent man."

"He didn't do it."

"Oh? Blind faith in the man you love?"

"Of course, but he told me he didn't do it, and I believe him."

His eyes sharpened, positively gleaming now. "You've been speaking to him?"

"The last time I spoke to him was the day he left. I haven't seen him since."

"Hmmmm. So, you say."

"My husband did not do murder, Sheriff!"

The sly smile was back. "When your husband is brought to justice, Mrs. Kavenagh, he will be charged with three murders – and the assault of a witness. While you believe he might escape the noose for one murder, he will not escape it for three. He took the lives of two deputies who were killed by him in a shootout."

Maggie felt bile rise in her throat. Of course, they would blame Brogan for that. Everything that happened in the county now would be his fault. Her headache began to drum unmercifully in her temples.

"I believe you would do just about anything to save your husband, wouldn't you?"

She nodded. "If given the chance, I believe we can prove his innocence."

"That isn't what I had in mind," he said reaching for her arm, his fingers encircling her wrist in an iron-like grip. "You do as I tell you and there won't be any need to prove your husband's innocence."

Chapter 9

Maggie recoiled as though she'd been bitten by a venomous snake, snatching her wrist away from him.

"I already know my husband is innocent. We just need a chance to prove it."

He smiled and even that made her skin crawl. "What you think you know is of very little importance to me," he told her. "We have two eyewitnesses prepared to swear in court they saw him shoot Latham Storey. And let's not forget he killed those deputies during his escape from a camp where he'd holed up for the night. Now if you were a smart woman, you would see the evidence against your husband is overwhelming. One witness might have gotten it wrong, but not two. I would think you'd want to do whatever you could to save his hide."

Maggie was trembling from head to toe. If Brogan were here right now, there very well *could* be a legitimate charge of murder ... of the sheriff. He would be tempted to break this man in two for even putting his hands on his wife, not to mention the filthy insinuations.

"When my husband is found, we will be hiring a lawyer to represent him at his trial, and I tell you he will be exonerated."

She knew she was talking well beyond what she believed to be possible, but she flung it at him anyway. The chances of Brogan getting a fair trial with the mounting evidence against him were terrible at best. If she faced the reality of their situation head-on it would be almost too much to bear.

And then Vailor struck again, grabbing both her wrists this time. "Don't be a fool. I am offering to speak on behalf of his character, at least give him a fighting chance. If you love him so much, why are you not willing to do whatever it takes to help him? You are a married woman, it's not like I would be stealing the virtue of a maiden. I'm sure you are well accustomed to the duties of a wife."

She spat on him, her liquid missile catching him on one cheek. "You're despicable!"

"And you're stupid," he said releasing one wrist in order to wipe his face with a handkerchief. "What difference does an hour with me make if I promise to set your beloved husband free? Do you really find the cost so high, or are you just trying to drive up the price?"

"Get out of here!" she screamed, wrenching her other wrist free. "I have a gun, and I'm not afraid to use it."

He sneered, knowing he still maintained the upper hand. "I don't see any gun in your hand, Missy."

"It's close by," she said, knowing she would never make it to where the rifle was leaned up against the wall. But she would try.

He caught the dart of her eyes, and with a move as fast as quicksilver, he grabbed hold of her again. "You know what I want, Mrs. Kavenagh. There's no need to shoot anyone."

"I'll claw your eyes out if you touch me!"

He smiled that slow, awful smile again, his eyes unreadable. "It looks like I'm already touching you."

She was breathing heavily as she struggled against his grip, to no avail. "You know very well what I mean."

"Ahh, that means we're thinking the same thing. Smart woman."

"Too smart for you," she said, bringing one knee up with as much force as she could muster and connecting with his groin

Vailor fell to his knees with a howl of pain. This time she did make it to the gun and had it cocked and aimed when he finally found it within himself to get to his feet.

His eyes were black and bottomless. She didn't believe she'd ever seen anything like it before ... in a human.

"Very well, you've bested me," he said clutching his chest, which surprised her. She would have thought he would be clutching something else. "I'm in terrible pain as you can see. You have injured me. Please, help me. I have a very weak heart if the truth be known. It's not something I speak of, but I beg of you to help me with a drink of cool water."

Maggie wavered.

"Please...."

Reluctantly she set down the rifle and started for a clean cup to fetch him a drink of water from the bucket. The last thing she needed was to have him drop dead on her kitchen floor. Filling a cup, she passed it to him.

She never saw the backhander coming, and it knocked her sideways onto the floor. She saw stars and the room spun as she fought to regain her senses. She'd fallen for his trick. There was nothing wrong with him at all, well at least not with his heart. She doubted he even had one.

He dragged her to her feet, his face still pinched with pain, evidently from her kick judging by the way he moved. He pushed her with force back against the wall, his fingers biting into her shoulders.

"You've made a very dangerous enemy, Mrs. Kavenagh. I gave you a chance to save your husband here today but your callous behavior tells me you do not care for him as much as you proclaim to. But it was for naught in any event. I only sought you for my own pleasure because that would be all a Kavenagh woman would be fit for."

Still trembling badly she tore at his arms, seeking release, but he had her well and truly pinned.

"You're vile!"

"Yes? You spit on me again, and you'll find out what I'll do about it this time. I promise you won't like it."

His face still contorted in pain, he reminded her of a wounded bear. But while there was still breath in her, she would fight him.

Her breath came in gulps. "When my husband finds out what you've done to me here today...."

"Your husband be damned!" he bellowed, striking renewed fear in her.

"My husband is an innocent man!" she yelled back, matching his volume. "He's a good man, not that you would be equipped to recognize such a thing if you saw it. He's ten times the man you'll ever be. He has not done one thing wrong. He is the victim of lies!"

"A victim of lies! He's no good is what he is. Make no mistake about it, you'll never see him again."

He had just addressed her worst fear, the possibility that Brogan was lost to her. It was what she wouldn't allow herself to think during those long nights when her tears fell like rain. But no matter how hopeless it might seem she refused to give up!

"I will see my husband again!" she threw back at him recklessly. "He will be found, and we will get legal counsel to help us. If we have to fight every last one of you, we will. I already have a plan in place for when he comes back to his family. We will not allow you to treat him unfairly."

His face curled into the semblance of a smile, but none-the-less reptilian. "What a brave warrior you are, too bad it's all for nothing. You see we are not even looking for your husband anymore, Mrs. Kavenagh. And it's not because of the snow. It's because he's already dead. He was shot during that raid on the camp where he'd found shelter nearly three weeks ago. The bullet came from Sheriff Ratchford's own gun. He saw him fall. He told us all about it before he died. So, we're in no real hurry now, we will simply collect his body when the snow recedes. You've been a widow for weeks and didn't even know it. It's time you were with a real man. You've been wallowing with a pig for so long you don't know the difference anymore."

She felt her body go numb. "You're despicable and a black liar! I don't believe a word that comes out of your mouth."

"Brogan Kavenagh is dead all right, and to the devil with his soul. Percival Ratchford saw him go down with his own eyes. As I've already told you, he fired the bullet that laid him low. It was the one proud accomplishment he took to his grave."

He released her and she sagged to the floor. "I'll see myself out," he told her, grimacing and still not able to stand in a fully upright position, "but I'll be back. You and I have unfinished business. You may have gotten your way this time around, but I can assure you the tables will turn in my favour. Next time, I'll get what I came for, and that's a promise or you'll suffer the consequences. Your husband may be dead, but I'm sure you care what happens to your son."

Getting shakily to her feet, Maggie followed him on unsteady legs at a safe distance as he made his way to the door, and once he was outside, she slammed it shut and dropped the heavy latch into place. When she heard the carriage turn in the yard, she watched from the window until it had clattered to the road and made a right-hand turn to return to the shiretown. Then she headed for the bedroom, collapsing on the bed in tears. Brogan had been shot? He was thought to be dead? She kept her stomach down with an effort. That detestable man was a bald-faced liar. First, he'd told her he'd help set Brogan free. When he couldn't get his way, he'd told her they already knew he was dead and would look for his body in the spring. Which was the truth? And now a new terror seized her, her son. The sheriff's veiled threat was every mother's worst fear.

She had thought Ratchford to be a rogue, but she doubted he could have outdistanced this man. She curled into the fetal position, nausea still washing over her, her headache crashing out of control.

"Brogan," she sobbed, repeating his name over and over.

She wasn't aware she'd drifted off until she was awakened by pounding on the door. "Dear Lord, what now?" she appealed out loud.

The racket at the door started up again, so straightening herself quickly, she hurried to the kitchen, grabbed the Henry rifle, and crossed the room quietly to the door.

"Who's there, please?" she asked in a voice that sounded surprisingly calm.

"It's Luke, Mamma," came her son's voice from the other side. "I can't get in."

Quickly dispensing with the rifle, she threw up the latch and Luke marched into the room. "Why was the door locked?" he asked, setting down his slate on the kitchen table. "I knocked and knocked, but you didn't hear me so I started pounding."

"I'm sorry, sweetheart. I guess I didn't realize the time. Your mamma's not feeling the best today. I didn't sleep very well last night."

He looked at her more closely. "What's wrong, Mamma? You've got blood on your face. Did someone hurt you?" he asked, his eyes becoming fearful.

"Blood?" she asked, pushing a reluctant smile to her lips. "It can't be blood."

He stepped nearer for a closer inspection. "That's what it looks like," he said dabbing the corner of her mouth with his forefinger.

"I was working with beets," she lied, "so that's what you see. It's only a bit of beet juice that must have been on my hand when I touched my face and it made a stain."

She would say anything to spare her son the truth. He was already dealing with enough.

"Why don't you go change into your home clothes, Luke, and I'll get some cookies and milk ready. Are you hungry?"

"Yes!" he answered jubilantly before dashing off to his room to get out of his school clothes.

As soon as he was gone, she hurried to where the small looking glass stood by the washbasin and studied her reflection. Oh no! Not much wonder she'd frightened him. There was indeed blood at the corner of her mouth from where Vailor had struck her, along with a bruise. Her hair was terribly disheveled. She didn't need to look to know her wrists were bruised.

Dampening a washcloth, she quickly ran it over her face and then pulling down her hair, carefully wound it back into place. She was just slipping the last of the pins in place when Luke reappeared in the kitchen.

"All right, a nice glass of milk from our friend Daisy in the barn and some lovely molasses cookies," she said as she poured the milk and set out two cookies on a plate.

"There you are, sir," she said, finishing with a smile. "Enjoy yourself."

Care of her world was forgotten for the moment as Luke made quick work of his snack. When he finished he pushed the plate slowly to where she sat on the other side of the table, in a shameless appeal for more.

She shook her head, working to maintain a lightness she didn't feel. "No, two is plenty for now, young man. You have supper in an hour or two and I don't want to spoil your appetite. You can have another cookie for dessert."

He shrugged with a grin, pulling the plate away. He seemed preoccupied, but she would wait until he was ready to speak about it. Luke was like his father. When he had something he wanted to say, he was not to be rushed. If he was pressed, he might well shut down and wait for another time, or not bother to take her into his confidence at all.

He seemed to have forgotten all about the cookies. "Ma, I heard something at school today about Pa."

Oh no! Surely it wasn't something as terrible as what Vailor had told her, the liar.

She waited, unaware she was holding her breath until he spoke. "They said my pa was shot. Is that true?"

She tried to pass it off as inconsequential. "Luke, you know what people are like. They gossip. We've heard a lot of silly falsehoods already about all of this, so you shouldn't pay it any attention," she explained, realizing she needed to take her own advice. "Every day there seems to be a different story. Even if he was shot, I'm sure he found someone to help him mend."

She grimaced in her mind at the absurdity of the statement. Where on earth would Brogan ever find that kind of help in his present circumstances?

Maggie was grateful when the long day finally came to a close, and after tucking Luke in, she climbed into her own bed and pulled the covers over her head. She thought of the lovely warm beds she and her son had waiting for them at the end of the day. What warm bed would Brogan have out in the middle of those woods? Just yesterday she'd stood in the yard and looked to the hills that stretched for miles beyond their homestead, snowy as far as the eye could see. She'd thought about her husband, out there somewhere ... alone.

* * *

Brogan lay on the bed, his thigh burning hot again. All he'd accomplished was to lose precious recovery time by insisting on doing outside chores. He swallowed a surge of angry frustration. At least he'd managed to set Tilda straight about the horse and any other heavy work that needed doing every day. She seemed like the type of person who believed she could move mountains by herself. It was that indomitable pioneer spirit that kept her thriving out here in the wilderness when most women might fail.

She was even more chipper this afternoon. It was no secret her mood had picked up after he'd told her he would not abandon her. Well, at least until the child was born, and of course, get it through its first delicate weeks and Tilda too. As if he'd walk away and leave a pregnant woman alone away out here, or at all. He just couldn't believe her husband had done that. Something must have befallen the young man, but that was a matter for another day. He wouldn't borrow trouble. There was enough of it around already without looking for more.

Tilda brought the midday meal to him, pleased he was taking her advice and keeping close to the bed. She set the tray on his lap, then returned to the kitchen to get her own.

"So, Tilda," he said after swallowing a mouthful, "how much longer do you think you have before the baby comes? You must be getting signs. You would know how to read them after working with your father."

She chewed thoughtfully. "I would say anytime now."

His next forkful of food halted in midair. He hadn't expected her to say that! "I thought you told me it would be weeks."

"That's right. You've been here more than two weeks, so maybe another week or two."

He was no more thrilled now at the prospect of having to deliver a baby, than he was when he'd first learned he would likely be the one to take on the task. What if something went wrong?

He thought as he chewed his food, waiting to get it sorted out in his mind before he spoke. "Do you have things ready for after you bear the child? What about a cradle ... diapers...."

"All ready and waiting." She smiled.

"And, of course, you'll feed the baby yourself."

"Of course," she agreed, dipping her head, her face crimson.

"What's wrong?"

"I'm thinking about you helping me birth my baby. It will be embarrassing."

Brogan understood. "You can't think of it like that, Tilda. I certainly won't. Believe me, I'll be concentrating on delivering that little one safe and sound. Everything else is just nature. So, try to think about it that way, and certainly don't worry about it. Our main goal is to get that baby born and keep you healthy too. We'll get through it together."

"I've been thinking," she said after a few moments had passed. "If it's a boy, I'd like to name him after you."

Brogan almost choked on a mouthful of biscuit, coughing to clear his throat. "After me! Oh no, name him after your husband. He's the baby's father. I'm not."

"After him leaving me the way he did, I don't think I will. Well, maybe his middle name. I think Brogan Jedediah Loughty would be a very nice name."

"Jedediah Loughty Junior is better," Brogan countered. "It would be only right that he should carry his father's name."

She looked at him, her jaw set. "I like the name Brogan and just so you know, that's what I intend to have him christened as when the time comes. Brogan Jedediah."

"Tilda, come on. I'm flattered, really, but that's a silly idea."

"But I like your name."

"Thank you, but it wouldn't be appropriate under the circumstances to name your child after another man. Besides, it might be a girl. Any names picked out for a female child?"

The way her brow furrowed she clearly didn't expect the child to be a girl.

"I've always thought Fern was a lovely name. My grandmother was called Fern."

"What would you choose for a middle name?"

"Violet."

He laughed despite himself. "Isn't that a little too ... floral?"

"What's your middle name?"

"Nothing you'd want to saddle a girl child with. It's Roderick. But just forget about my names, all right? My own child carries my name, Luke Brogan."

A wave of homesickness swept over him at the thought of his son.

"What's your wife's name?"

"Maggie."

"Tell me about her. You said she was pretty."

He allowed himself a moment to visualize the woman he loved, enjoying the exercise. "She has waist-length auburn hair and green eyes, and she's tall. I like that."

Tilda was quiet as she listened, and her next question surprised him. "Do you think I'm pretty, Brogan?"

He shrugged. "Of course. I'd say your husband is a lucky man to have you for his wife."

His answer seemed to please her. "I'm glad you think I'm pretty to look at. I think that's important."

Brogan's brow furrowed. "Why is that?"

"Because I think you're very handsome. Your eyes are really unusual, light blue with gray mixed in, like some kind of precious stone. And they're always sort of half-closed. Dreamy eyes are what we girls always called such a look. Your hair is as black as a raven's wing, but maybe I shouldn't be saying these things to you."

"I would say not. Save your compliments for your husband."

"You're kind of like my husband now. I mean we're living here together."

My lord, she was young if she had such foolish notions as these. "We're nothing like husband and wife, Tilda, and that's the last I'll listen to any talk like that. It's not proper."

Her cheeks were pink again. "Oh, I was just saying...."

"I can hear what you were saying, and you'll say it no more."

"I'm sorry," she said as her face clouded over.

Now he'd gone and hurt her feelings again. He was glad Maggie wasn't as sensitive as that. They could speak their mind to one another, and she wouldn't run off sniveling. Tilda had a lot of growing up to do. He would quash the notion right off the spur that there was anything between them other than two people helping each other survive. That was all. He belonged to Maggie, lock, stock, and barrel, and he was not interested in making any changes in that regard. She was his wife, and he was as grateful today for that fact as he'd been the day he married her.

He thought of her again and longed with everything in him to be able to hold her. And since they never got close to one another without the flames of desire being fanned, they would be making love. Even at this distance, his body responded to thoughts of Maggie, so he immediately thought about something else. If Tilda were ever to pick up on such a thing, and she was just smart enough to, she might believe his reaction was to her and not his wife. No, never.

"Tilda, come on now. Don't go and get all teary-eyed on me. I'm just making myself clear is all. Don't take such offence when someone is speaking their truth. It's nothing against you. You're a fine-looking woman with a husband, who I have no doubt loves you very much."

"Where is he then?"

He laid his head back wearily. "Good question. Now, I thank you for the great meal but my leg is giving me hell. I don't suppose you have any of that whiskey left."

She shook her head. "Not enough to do you any good. There's less than half a bottle."

His pain had returned with a vengeance. "I need it now, Tilda. Can you get it for me?"

"Are you sure? I think...."

"Tilda, please. Just get the bottle. I've got to have something to take the edge off this."

"Maybe I should look at your leg to see if we need to apply another poultice."

He puffed a short sigh of impatience. "You can do that, just get me that bottle first. Please."

A minute later, he had it in his hands and downed half of the amber liquid in one long drink. He finished the rest seconds later. "Now that should help."

She took the empty bottle away and left him to its painkilling properties. Since they'd finished eating, she dispensed with the dirty crockery and cleaned the cooking utensils.

When she finished tidying up, she returned to the bedroom.

"I'm going to have to take your pants off again, Brogan. You know, to get to your leg. I want to make sure it's still clean."

The liquor had taken effect, and for some unearthly reason, he found that funny. "You want to take my pants off?"

"Brogan! I'm making the suggestion purely on a medical basis. I...."

He chuckled. "I'll take them off for you," he said, undoing the buckle clumsily.

He lowered his trousers halfway, and Tilda took care of the rest, making sure the quilt was in place to keep him decent.

"Everything looks good, Brogan."

"Well, thank you," he replied. "How does the wound look?"

"Very funny. If alcohol affects you that much, you must not drink a lot."

"That's right, it's been a while. Is it bleeding?"

"Yes, I'm afraid it is. Just wait and I'll be back with more bandages."

* * *

When she returned after tearing fresh bandages, Brogan had fallen asleep, snoring lightly. She gently rebandaged his leg and pulled the quilt fully into place, then stood watching him. He was the most handsome man she'd ever seen. Jedediah had his good points, but nothing that would stir a woman's heart like Brogan Kavenagh. She'd also seen him without his shirt on and remembered how good he looked, his chest muscled, hair-roughened and sun-browned. His eyes were his best feature, though, and when he turned them on her, she felt giddy inside. His teeth were white and even, and his lips, she now decided were very kissable. She studied his mouth. Yes, very kissable indeed.

It was then that she realized with horror the snoring had stopped, and he was watching her, his eyes mere slits.

"Tilda," he said gently, "don't. There's nothing between you and I, and there never will be. We're married, both of us, but to other people."

"I'm so sorry," she stammered, mortified and suddenly in a hurry to leave the room. Turning she caught her toe on the leg of the chest of drawers and went down heavily.

Brogan wrenched to a sitting position, swinging his bad leg over the side of the bed, but Tilda was already getting up. Using the bed for leverage, she pulled herself to a standing position.

"Put your leg back up on the bed, Brogan," she said, "or it'll never stop hurting. I'm fine. There is nothing amiss."

* * *

180

Brogan fell back to sleep minutes later, and it was late afternoon when he resurfaced, his head muzzy from the whiskey, his leg still throbbing. The house was quiet. He listened intently for any sound. She had promised she wouldn't go to the barn anymore except to carry small quantities of water to the horse. Put some hay in the manger. That chore should take her no more than ten or fifteen minutes, and so he lay back and waited.

A half hour went by and still nothing was stirring in the cabin. She should have returned by now. Had she fallen again? The path to the barn was slippery. He'd found that out this morning.

"Tilda!" he called out to her. "Where are you?"

There was no answer.

Chapter 10

"Tilda!" he called again more loudly.

He was relieved to hear a stirring in the other room. "What is it, Brogan? Do you need something?" she asked, hurrying into the bedroom.

His relief was palpable. "I don't need anything. It's just that I didn't hear you moving about, so I thought maybe something was wrong. You took a hard fall, earlier. Are you sure everything is all right?"

She looked tired. "I'm fine, no need to worry. I was just resting, is all, but I think it's time I walk out and see to your horse. Luckily, the spring house is on the way to the barn, so I'll carry only a quarter of a bucket at a time. That's what you asked me to do, isn't it?"

"As long as a quarter bucket is not too heavy for you."

She chuckled. "You worry too much, Brogan. Now, I'll only be a few minutes and then I'll come back and start our evening meal."

He heard her go out, and thankfully she was back within the prescribed time.

"Dutch says hello," she smiled as she stuck her head in the room. "He seemed restless. I'm thinking he'd love to get out of that barn and kick up his heels a little."

"There's no doubt he would, but unfortunately the barn's where he'll be staying for the next while. When my leg starts to come around, I'll take him out of there and let him get some exercise."

"I wouldn't mind taking him out. I could walk him around."

Brogan shook his head. "No, bad idea, but thank you for offering."

"I used to have my own horse, you know. Her name was Buttons. She was a nice little mare, very quiet. My father picked her out for me and I rode her everywhere. He even brought a new saddle with him when he went to Boston one time. I loved that horse and I thought my heart would break in two when she got colic and died. Anyway, I'm a very good rider. After I have the baby, and enough time passes, maybe you would let me ride your horse."

"We'll see. Dutch is a very strong horse, very high-spirited."

"I could handle him with no problem."

"I said we'll see, and ... we will see."

"All right. I might be able to show you a trick or two while I'm at it. I used to do a lot of tricks with Buttons, so I'm used to horses."

"I'm guessing Dutch is a little more horse than Buttons was. He's big and strong and he likes to go wide open sometimes. He's not much for jumping around and doing tricks. I think you'd get on his bad side if you tried to do that with him."

She grinned playfully. "I think he would be all right, but I guess I'll have to prove it to you when the time comes. And really, Brogan, I'm experienced enough that I could actually ride him now with no problem, but I'll wait like you asked me to."

"That's a good idea because if I think you're going anywhere near that horse other than to tend him, I won't be very happy. And by the way, I'm not asking you to stay off my horse. I'm telling you."

"A lot of women do ride when they're pregnant. Especially if they know horses like I do. I don't mean to go tearing off on a cross-country race. I'm talking about an easy ride. If I could, it would give him some much-needed exercise. What I'm saying is you don't have to be concerned about me when I'm around your horse. I can handle whatever he throws at me."

His voice was deceptively soft. "Don't do it, Tilda."

She ignored his warning with a dismissive hand gesture. "Don't worry, I have no plans to disobey your orders. I won't try to ride your horse. I give you my word, all right?"

"Good!"

"There's probably too much snow right now anyway. I was hoping it would go down some after that first storm since it came so early, but no. We ended up getting more. I'd like to think it will turn mild one of these days and most of it'll go away."

He thought about the drastic turn in the weather. As much of a nuisance as it was, he reminded himself it was likely keeping the search party out of the woods, or at least slowing them down. He tried not to think about those who were hunting him while he lay here disabled. Ratchford would have seen that he'd hit him with that shot, and he was sure it pleased him to no end. For all he knew, the man was just hours away, bulldozing through the snow. When Percival Ratchford set his mind to something, nothing or no one bothered to get in his way. He realized Tilda was speaking to him.

"I think the snow will stay because it's so cold out. It's going to make for a very long, hard winter if we're snowed in by the middle of October. I'm so glad we have extra firewood stocked up. We're going to need it."

She left him to his thoughts as she went to prepare the evening meal and later was unexpectedly quiet while they were eating. He guessed she was a young woman of many moods, but there was no reason for her to pull in like this. Could she be in pain? Surely, she would tell him if she felt her time drawing near.

"Tilda," he said, "why are you so quiet all of a sudden? Is there something wrong?"

She coloured. "Everything's fine."

He watched her face. She was shy about discussing aspects of her pregnancy with him, the birthing itself. That was to be expected, but he had to know what was going on.

"Everything's not fine, is it? I'm guessing all is not well after that hard fall you took. Have you started to bleed or something? Talk to me."

She nodded, tears springing to her eyes. "I am bleeding a little. Oh, Brogan, I'm afraid."

* * *

Josephine Burk had supper waiting on the table when Amby came in to partake of the evening meal. He had insisted on the children being fed first and then be off with themselves to some other part of the house before he came home. He showed them absolutely no affection. She guessed that's the way he'd been raised. She couldn't remember one single time when they'd all sat down to a meal together.

That meant, in effect, she had to cook two meals. By the time Amby set foot in the house, the vegetables were all but dried up in the pot, and it was hard to keep the meat fresh and juicy. But Amby ruled the roost, and so she did as she was told.

"The new sheriff was here today," she informed him once he was settled into his place at the table.

Amby had been helping himself to boiled potatoes and his hand stopped. Frozen in place.

"What did he want?"

Amby had flown into a blind rage when he'd heard that Ratchford had given up the chase after being injured, and beyond infuriated when he learned of his death. He and Ratchford shared a mutual hatred of everything *Kavenagh*, and Amby knew he'd had a strong ally in him. The two deputies being killed were in his favour, something more to blame Brogan for. He made sure word was spread far and wide that Brogan Kavenagh was a killer who must be stopped.

"He wanted us to know they are calling off the search."

Amby set the earthenware bowl down so hard Josephine was afraid he'd cracked it. He looked at her, his eyes bright with outrage. "They are what!"

"They are calling off the search."

"I heard you. I want to know why!"

Josephine began to tremble, a condition she suffered from whenever her husband raised his voice to its present level. She was sure he could be heard a half mile away.

"Sheriff Vailor explained he doesn't feel it's necessary now because they believe Brogan Kavenagh to be dead."

"And what fool arrived at that conclusion may I ask?"

"I don't know much about such things, but wouldn't he have to discuss it with the magistrate?"

Amby shook his head on an impatient burst of air. "No! Not to bring in a fugitive. They're scared is what they are. Scared of Brogan."

"I would imagine that might be true seeing as how they say he killed those two men."

"Then why stop looking? Surely, it's not because they are worried about a little snow! Everything doesn't stop because it's winter. That's what Kavenagh is hoping they'll do. They're playing right into his hands and too stupid to see it."

"You knew Brogan Kavenagh had been shot, Amby."

"I heard that, but so what? It was only his leg. I hope it went good and deep and hurt like hell, but it wouldn't kill him."

"The sheriff says it likely would if he couldn't get help and then the weather turned bad so quickly. Anyway, that's what they're surmising. That he couldn't survive, and maybe they're right. He would need a doctor and where could he get one of those in the middle of the woods?"

Amby wasn't listening, seeming lost in thought. "I'll go and look for him myself, and I won't let a little bit of snow stop me."

* * *

"You're bleeding? When did that start?"

She didn't raise her eyes. "A little while ago."

"Why didn't you tell me, Tilda? You've got to tell me these things. Are you having any pain at all?"

"A little. It's like monthly cramps. Like that."

"How bad are the cramps?"

"They're bothering me is all I can say."

He remembered when Maggie had fallen off a horse while she was pregnant with Luke. She was a good horsewoman, but in his opinion, she'd been too far along to ride a horse and he'd been furious with her. And she'd started to bleed too, but he'd gotten the doctor straight away who'd put her on complete bed rest. The cramping and spotting had eventually stopped, thank God, and Luke was born fine, healthy, and right on time.

"That's it, Tilda, you have to have bed rest. I'm sure none of this is new to you. Your father would have treated women in a similar condition."

She nodded. "That's right but you know how people think, including me. Bad stuff always happens to someone else, not ourselves. I'm a very strong woman, and I have had absolutely no problems. I slipped and fell a few weeks ago and nothing happened."

"You're further along now, so after we finish eating you have to lie down. In the bed."

"Brogan, there's only one bed."

"I know that."

"And you're in it. How is that going to work?"

He ran his hand over his face. He needed his rest too, if he was going to recover from his injury. He also understood he wasn't able to lie on the floor for reasons previously explored. Every time he considered it, he arrived at the same conclusion. His leg couldn't take it. Same thing with sitting in a chair all night hoping to get the rest he needed. It just wasn't going to happen.

"We'll make it work. We're not a couple of teenagers," although she was closer to it than he was, having barely left those years behind.

"It's not a very wide bed I'm afraid," she said. "I asked Jedediah to build a bigger one, but he said he liked us being so close. It's true too that I would have had to make a bigger mattress, so the bed stayed the size it was."

There was no denying it would be a tight fit, but it was the only solution. He just hoped he didn't make a mistake in his sleep. He'd slept next to the same woman for fifteen years, so it was only natural that it could happen. No, it was not an ideal situation. It would be an arrangement of necessity, although if the time ever came to explain all of this to Maggie, he hoped she would understand. He was not only living with another woman, they would be sharing the same bed.

* * *

Josephine lay awake well into the night thinking about the Brogan Kavenagh case. If Brogan was, in fact, deceased it would solve a multitude of problems. As it stood now, she had to get on the stand at his murder trial and lie. Say the Kavenagh man had shot down Amby's uncle. The more disturbing fact was that she shared a bed with the true murderer.

She thought back to her life at home. She'd earned high praise in Sunday school for her knowledge about the good word. And now, here she was about to commit perjury. Actually, she'd already done it when she'd sworn in front of Sheriff Ratchford that her statement was true when, in fact, it was a product of pure invention. She was accusing an innocent man of murder, and he would hang because of it. But what about the two dead deputies? Was there a chance Brogan had shot them? It was certainly a possibility, but it did little at the moment to ease her conscience.

Was she not raising her own children to be God-fearing? The truth of it was *she* had the most to fear from God because of what she was involved in. And since Sheriff Vailor had been here with the news about Brogan likely having already succumbed to his gunshot wound, hadn't she hoped that Brogan Kavenagh *was* dead? That in itself was shamefully un-Christian. And if she was to be denied on that score and Brogan was found and brought to trial, was she not prepared to lay her hand on the Holy word of God and swear she'd seen him kill another man? When she dared to think about carrying through with such a thing, it washed over her in a sickening wave of guilt. What she was doing was truly wicked.

But, she reminded herself yet again, she had to honour the man she'd married. She'd taken those vows before God as well. Amby was her husband, for better or worse, and this most certainly was the worst part. And again, her more practical side warned her to tread lightly. If she left Amby, she would have to raise six children on her own. How could she possibly care for them, feed them, and clothe them?

She was careful not to toss and turn because it infuriated Amby. His wrath had not even begun to cool after the news brought by Sheriff Vailor. Amby was not to be fooled with. She'd seen him raise the gun and aim it at his uncle but had held onto hope, even in those few seconds, that he would deviate from his original plan. But, of course, Amby had indeed fired that fatal shot. She had not been able to see him in the same light since that awful afternoon. No, whatever Amby told her to do, she must do, and may the good Lord forgive her.

* * *

It was a chilly day, nearing the end of October when Maggie heard a carriage in the front yard. It was time for Luke to be home from school and someone must have given him a drive. They did have some wonderful neighbours, while others were not so wonderful. The Wetheringtons had come by once or twice to see how she and Luke were doing on their own, and the Ralstons down the road a few miles had been kind as well. She would not think about the others.

One took kindness where one could find it, she surmised. Pulling her heavy wool shawl from the hook by the door she went out to thank whomever had driven her son home. She was not prepared for the scene that awaited her.

It was the schoolmaster himself who had brought Luke home, and the young man was clearly very angry. Luke was quietly sobbing as he climbed down out of the carriage.

"What is the problem, Mr. Prescott?" she asked, trying to keep the edge out of her voice.

"What is the problem you ask? The problem is that I can no longer tolerate your son in my schoolhouse. I have discussed the matter with the superintendent, and he agrees the boy should be expelled immediately. He is a troublemaker and a nuisance to the other children. He is not to show his face at school again."

She looked at him dumbfounded. "Luke? Why, he's the one who is the victim, constantly picked on by the other children. It was me who convinced him to return, to try to overlook some of the terrible things being said to him."

The schoolmaster was a tiny, fragile looking man with limp blue eyes that stared out from behind wireless spectacles. Wisps of dishwater blonde hair escaped the confines of a bedraggled-looking winter cap. His nose was bright red in salute to the frigid day.

"He has it the wrong way 'round," the man protested, his thin lips tightly drawn. "I am delighted to be rid of him."

Luke had come to stand by her side, his eyes swollen and red.

"Go in the house, sweetheart. There are a few things I would like to say to Mr. Prescott here. Run on along now," she told him when he hung back.

Luke looked miserably at the schoolmaster, then at his mother, pulling off his mittens to hold up bruised hands for her to see.

She began to take deep breaths to control her rising temper. "Luke, please go into the house and close the door. I will be right along."

Luke did as he was told, and she waited until the door was closed securely behind him before she rounded on the schoolmaster.

"Did you lay the strap to my son?"

"I most certainly did, and I consider it a favour to the lad. Someone has to teach him right from wrong. He is a Kavenagh, so he certainly won't be learning anything of any value here, except for immoral ways. That much we've all seen for ourselves ... his father a murderer and a fugitive from the law. Your son isn't fit to associate with other children. He is a bad example to them. I would suggest it's the way he's been drug up at home."

Maggie felt as though she was about to fly to pieces. "You're a big brave man, aren't you, Mr. Prescott, swinging a strap. Striking a young boy."

"I stand by my actions. It is my right to mete out discipline where I feel it is needed. He deserved what he got."

"He is an eight-year-old child! Why don't you pick on someone your own age for a change instead of beating up children? You are a disgrace to the teaching profession. How they ever came to hire you I have no idea. You are nothing but a vicious bully."

"And you are a loud-mouthed, course, sharp-tongued woman who is not fit to have a child of her own. You are vulgar."

"Call me names if you wish. I would expect no less from the likes of you, but I'm telling you this. Don't you ever strike my child again! He is the victim in all of this, and if you had any sense at all, you would see that and not pile it on against him."

He stuck his nose in the air. "On that, Madam, we can agree. Any child born into the Kavenagh clan would indeed be a victim of happenstance."

"And don't you ever show yourself in this yard again, if you know what's good for you. When our current troubles are resolved, my husband will be having a word with you. Oh, and just so that you know, he's a lot bigger than Luke and can defend himself."

"You are forgetting your place if you think you can threaten me. Perhaps I should have a word with Sheriff Vailor and see what he has to say about all of this."

She jumped out of the way as he clucked to the horse to start forward. Executing a semi-circle, he slapped the horse's rump with the reins to be away as quickly as possible.

Well, good riddance! She took a few minutes to calm herself before she returned to the house, but she was still wound up tighter than a top when she went inside. Luke had gone to his room. And to think she had talked him into going back to school. He had the better sense to want to stay away after his last trouble. She had naively thought matters had resolved themselves when all the while he'd been keeping most of it from her. She felt like the worst mother alive at that moment. She had sent her little boy to a place to be beaten. It was one thing if he'd misbehaved and deserved a whack or two on the hands, but not this.

She found him in his room, face down on the bed and she sat down beside him.

"Luke, I'm so sorry for all the trouble you've had at that school. Your pa and I had wanted so badly for you to get a proper education."

He turned to face her. "I'm sorry too, Mamma. I tried to get along. I did, but the master was the worst one. I'm glad he said I can't go back, but I'm sorry I won't be learning new stuff like you and Pa wanted me to."

"None of this is your fault, Luke. And I agree, until your pa comes home and can sort out a few things, I'm happy you will be staying at home with me. But you're wrong about one thing."

He looked at her warily. "What?"

"You're wrong about not learning new things. It's very important to learn. Don't you wonder what makes a bird fly? How butterflies come into the world? Why there are clouds in the sky?"

"Yeah, I guess but how am I going to do that if I'm not allowed to go to school?"

She smiled. "You know, son, I always wanted to be a teacher. I would have gone on to do that, but I decided to marry your father instead and raise a family. But now I'm going to be *your* teacher. You know all those books I showed you one time that I have packed away?"

She had his attention. "I remember."

"Well, as your teacher, I will use those books to help you learn. Would you like that?"

He shrugged, tears forgotten for the moment. "It'd be fun, but would I still get a recess? Would I still have time to play or do I have to learn all day long?"

"It would be like regular school in a lot of ways, and you'll still have to do your lessons. There won't be any change that way, but I can assure you, you'll be a lot happier here. All of this is for the time being of course, at least for the rest of this school year."

* * *

Long after Luke had gone to sleep that night she thought about the new arrangement. She had already pulled out the box of books and thumbed lovingly through each one. There were books on literature, arithmetic, science, and history and all were geared for young students. She'd been so sure she would go on to the new provincial teacher training college. Then she'd met Brogan and everything else paled in comparison. The truth of the matter was she'd thought she was pregnant while she and Brogan were going together, and that had changed everything. It would have been scandalous to admit that, so to protect her reputation they had married quickly. It had proved to be a false alarm but by then she was kept busy enough as a housewife. She never complained though, only too happy to look after the man she loved.

But there were second thoughts. Brogan's wild ways during the first few years of their marriage worried her that he regretted having taken a wife at such a young age. But he'd eventually got everything out of his system and life had gotten better. After so many childless years, Luke was a welcome blessing.

She picked up the book on spelling. She was sure what she was going to teach him would be far and away more advanced than the lessons taught in the local school. She wouldn't expect more of the lad than he was capable of understanding, but she would show him the world. He would indeed understand that birds used their tails to steer in flight and that their wings acted as both a wing and propeller. He would learn how butterflies are created and the purpose of clouds. She was becoming more excited by the moment. Best of all she would have him here during this time of trial in their lives, so she could better protect him.

She went to bed with a lighter heart than she'd had in weeks.

* * *

Brogan was falling off to sleep when he became aware of Tilda's restlessness.

"What's wrong?" he asked her. "Are you still having pain?"

He felt the movement of her nodding. "The cramping seems to be getting worse."

"Did you check the bleeding before you came to bed? Has it stopped?"

"Yes, I think so. There wasn't much, but the pains seem to be worse since I laid down."

Oh lord, he hoped she wasn't going into early labour. Unless she had guessed her weeks wrong, it was much too soon. This was not good at all.

"You've been through this before with your wife," she said. "Having a baby I mean. This is my first time."

"When Maggie fell, she had quite bad cramps for a day or so. However, they eventually went away, and she lasted until her proper time. Yours could pass too. If you've stopped bleeding, I would say that's a

200

good sign. Your father must have delivered lots of babies, didn't he run into this problem before?"

"I'm sure he did, but I wasn't in his office with him all the time, just a few months before Jedediah and I got married."

"And he didn't think to explain a few things to you before you traipsed off into the wilderness?"

"We talked, yes, but he didn't discuss pregnancy with me."

Brogan shook his head. "I would think that'd be the first thing he'd talk to you about, but it's none of my business."

She moaned again. "Oh, there was another one."

He didn't like the sound of it at all. If this didn't let up it could mean she was indeed going into early labour. And all because she tripped on the leg of the bed waiting on him.

"I'm so scared," she whimpered. "Please, Brogan, hold me. I'm lonely, and I have no one else to turn to. I know it's much too early. I don't want to lose my baby."

He needed to keep her calm, so slipping his arms around her, he tried to do just that. Snuggling closer, she laid her head on his chest.

Chapter 11

Maggie was amazed at the difference in her child after just a few days. She knew he missed his father desperately, as was to be expected, but he was cheerful and smiling for the first time since their terrible ordeal had begun. Preparing lessons for her son also helped take *her* mind off missing Brogan. She was delighted too that she was going to be a teacher at last. Even as late as a week ago, she had no idea her natural teaching skills were going to be put to such good use.

She'd made her first lesson a simple one, to test the water so to speak. Once class got underway on the kitchen table, she was surprised at how well Luke did with it. He would have absolutely no problem keeping up with the slightly more advanced material she had decided to teach him, if he was ready. He applied himself without much persuasion, listening carefully to what his mother was explaining. She had known he was a bright child, but watching him absorb her study materials was truly a gratifying experience.

How pleased Brogan would be when she told him about their new arrangement. It was well into November now and her husband had been gone for many several weeks. But instead of concentrating on what might have become of him, she preferred to believe he had indeed found someplace to stay for the winter and was safe and warm. She knew in her heart he was missing his family as much as she and Luke missed him. What a lot they would have to talk about when they were finally reunited sometime in the future. She refused to entertain any thoughts about just when that future would be, or how such a thing would be accomplished. She simply had faith it would happen. The only way she could deal with any of this was one day at a time, and that's what she steeled herself to do.

As promised, she scheduled the morning break for ten-fifteen, and Luke bounded from the table with a *whoopee* at her announcement that recess was at hand.

"I'm going to eat my apple outside, Ma," he told her as he quickly pulled on his winter clothes and hurried out into the yard.

"Enjoy your time," she called after him before the door closed. "You have fifteen minutes to yourself."

She glanced out the window to see how he would react to his first recess at his new home school. She laughed out loud when she saw him, arms extended, twirling around in reckless abandon, his face to the sun. A typical happy child. But as ideal as this situation appeared to be, she worried it wouldn't be good for him in the long run to not spend time with other children his own age. There were valuable life lessons to be learned there too. But then again, how many valuable lessons had he learned from the meanness of his fellow students at school? He had learned the pain of having his father's character blackened by those who did not know him. He had learned the belittling experience of being picked on, taunted and laughed at. Of being reprimanded and beaten by his teacher when he'd tried to stand up for himself. No, her son needed time to heal and that was what she, his only parent at the moment, would provide for him.

By the end of the week, she was even more encouraged given his progress. He'd reminded her he was supposed to learn about birds, so she understood he would keep her on her toes preparing lessons for him.

It was bright and sunny when he went for his recess break on Friday, tearing from the house with his usual gusto, apple in hand. He'd tried the first two days to beg more time from her for his morning break, but she knew the importance of keeping him to a schedule. To teach him the value of time and how to manage it.

There was no bell to ring, but when she went to call him, he came running, all excited.

"Ma, I saw a bird!" he exclaimed, his cheeks red from the cold air. "There was a whole bunch of them over by the barn, so I watched them."

She was puzzled. "You've seen birds before, sweetheart. These ones would be chickadees, I suspect. Did they have black heads?"

He nodded, eyes still wide. "I saw them before, but when I watched them take off, I was thinking about how they could fly. How their wings worked. I know about that now."

She closed her eyes to hide her rush of emotion. How wonderful was that! He was learning. Remembering his lessons — a most welcome success during a time of great distress. She breathed a silent prayer of gratitude.

"They are called 'black-capped chickadees', and you'll be seeing a lot of them during the winter when they travel in small flocks. Do you know how they got their names?"

He shook his head, watching his mother closely. "No, how?"

"The next time you see them, listen carefully, and they will tell you what their name is. The name of the bird is often in its call. Like chick-a-dee-dee-dee. We call them chickadees for short."

When the afternoon class was finished, Luke cleaned his slate and waited for his cookies and milk.

"I want to talk to you for a moment, Luke," she said sitting down opposite him. "Do you know your birthday is tomorrow?"

He thought for a moment. "I'm going to be nine, aren't I."

"That's right, and to help you celebrate the big day I'm going to bake you a cake. Any special kind you'd like?"

Maggie knew what his response would be before she even asked, and of course, he shouted, "Lally cake!"

Keeping molasses in this house with Luke around was no easy feat.

In addition to his birthday cake, she'd knit him a new pair of mittens. He would be glad to get them because he'd pointed out a hole in the thumb of one of his old ones. She'd found some nice royal blue yarn the last time she was in Sackville and had to work quickly after he went to bed in order to have them done on time.

"Thanks, Ma!" he told her when he opened his present. "Now my thumb won't be cold anymore."

* * *

It was early afternoon two days later, a bright sunny day, although cold, a north wind rattling the branches of the old apple tree in the yard. Maggie worked in the barn shoveling manure, her shawl draped over her shoulders. She took small shovelfuls, best to keep on the safe side of things, while Luke did a thorough search for eggs. Naturally, there weren't any to be found at this time of year, but he was determined to look and so she'd indulged him.

Luke usually cleaned the stall, but this morning she'd decided to be the one on the business end of the shovel for a change. She liked good hard work. It kept a body young.

She thought she heard something outside, and Luke ran to investigate, hurrying back to announce the arrival of a visitor.

"Who is it?" she asked him. "Anyone we know?"

"It's a woman," he said, "but I didn't get a look at her face. She's going to the house."

"Run along then and see her in. Take her cloak and tell her I'll be right there. I'm almost finished."

He came racing back minutes later, and his mother met him on her way from the barn. "It's Aunt Julia, Uncle Tabor's wife," he announced.

"Thank you, dear, now you go and play, but don't go any further than the yard. Promise?"

"I promise, Ma. I'm not a little kid anymore though. I should be able to go a little further now."

She smiled. "All right then, a little further than the yard, but no more. I mean it."

"I won't!" he called over his shoulder, already off and running.

"Julia!" she exclaimed when she went into the house and found her sister-in-law sitting by the hearth. "What brings you out on such a nippy day?"

"It's been a while since I was over and I wanted to see how you were making out, whether or not there was anything you and Luke might need. You seem to be doing all right, although I'm sure the days and nights are still very long."

Maggie hung her shawl by the door, cleaned her hands, and started a pot of tea.

Julia indicated a basket covered with an embroidered sugar bag tea towel that she'd set on the table. "I brought you some doughnuts for a treat. That recipe of my mother's is a big one, and I always forget that fact until after I'm started, silly me. I can't eat them all. Maybe we could have some with our tea."

Maggie smiled. "Sounds like a great idea to me. I could smell them as soon as I walked in. Delicious!"

"If I recall correctly, Luke likes doughnuts too."

"Luke likes food, and he's got a sweet tooth the size of all outdoors. He's a growing boy. I can't keep him filled up."

"I swear he's grown half a head since I last saw him, and he's so handsome. He's a dead ringer for Brogan. Oh … I'm sorry…."

Maggie held up her hand. "No need to apologize, Julia. Brogan's name is bound to come up."

"I feel so bad ... I know we all do. If there was just something I could do."

"There's nothing anyone can do, not until he's brought in, and then I will hire a lawyer. And I assume you've heard the latest, I mean about Brogan being dead. I refuse to believe it."

Julia nodded solemnly. "Good! There's no proof that is the case. There are so many stories going around it's ridiculous! Everyone's got their own opinion, and after it's expressed a couple of times, it becomes fact. As soon as someone repeats something, adding a little flair to their own version, it's gospel. I understand that it would be almost impossible to ignore it, and I'm so sorry you have to go through something like this. I'd heard Tabor and Pate say that Brogan could be a handful at times, but he's a good man. I always liked him."

"Thank you, he is a good man."

"Tell me, Maggie, how is Luke doing in school? I heard there was some trouble there. There's always tittle-tattle, but is it true?""

"It's true, unfortunately," and related the incident in the yard with the schoolmaster.

"Poor Luke. He's such a sweet child. I'm glad you stood up to that little weasel, Prescott. He's entirely too full of himself. If I'd been here, I would have given him a piece of my mind too. Backed you up. He's a bully, picking on a child like that. I'm really happy you've decided to teach Luke at home. He'll be much better off and learn a great deal more than he ever would at that schoolhouse. I've heard the trustees aren't happy with Prescott and that his days are numbered, so good riddance."

"Here! Here! I agree. Now, Julia, I have to ask about you. We didn't get to talk about *you* the last time you were here because of everything that's been going on, but how are things with you and Tabor?"

The older woman sighed, suddenly interested in the pattern on her skirt. "I, too, find the days long. I miss my husband."

"You love him, don't you ... despite everything."

"Yes, or I wouldn't have married him. He's handsome, too, like all the Kavenaghs, but at times he was next to impossible to live with. I'm easygoing so I gave him plenty of leeway, but he could be so mean-spirited toward me. I grew tired of being told to *git* every time he was in one of his dark moods. So, as you know, one day I took him up on it and packed my bags and left."

"Would you ever go back?"

She hung her head. "I don't know. I don't think it matters much now anyway, how I feel. You can't be the only one in a marriage who's in love. I know for him it was a marriage of convenience, but for me ... well ... I've always had a soft spot in my heart for

Tabor Kavenagh. So, when he asked me after his mother died if I wanted to marry him, I naturally said yes. In my heart, though, I knew it was because he didn't want to have to cook for himself, and his son. But I thought there was something else there too. Looks like I was wrong."

"I don't think you were wrong. He wasn't rough with you, was he?"

"Oh no, never that. I'd have flattened him with a rolling pin if he'd ever tried. No, it was just that he was so disagreeable sometimes. He would have to change a great deal if I would ever consider going back to live with him, and I doubt that's ever going to happen. He's thirty-six years old now, me forty-three, so like the old saying goes, you can't teach an old dog new tricks.

"It's been almost two months since you left, has he ever come to see you during that time? You've been married to him for more than six years. That should count for something."

"I was just lucky I still had somewhere to go. It was always in the back of our minds, my brother and I, to hold onto the old house, even with Mother and Father gone. I'm glad we did. Artis will never live there again. His home is in New England now, with Bette, although, of course, the property is still in his name. He's left it to me on what to do with it. It isn't much, but it's a roof over my head. And to answer your question, no, Tabor never even came after me to try to talk me into returning to the farm. I guess that says it all, doesn't it?"

"So where do you go from here, Julia? You're a lovely-looking woman. You might meet someone and want to get married again."

Julia's face fell. "Even if I did, which I don't believe I ever will, Tabor told me as I was packing that he would never give me a divorce so not to bother asking."

"Well? Doesn't that mean something?"

"I don't know. That's the problem, I can't say as I understand my husband. Wouldn't you think he'd want a divorce if he wasn't happy? Then he could be completely rid of me. That, to me, would be logical. It's folly to love such a man. Before I would ever darken his door again, I would expect an apology, and honestly, can you ever see Tabor Kavenagh apologizing for anything or to anyone?"

Maggie pulled a sympathetic face. "No, I can't see it, but people surprise us every day."

Julia was quiet for a moment. "I understand he had a difficult life growing up, although he would never discuss it with me. He just alluded to it from time to time."

"They all had a difficult time of it. That's why Leolie brought her children to New Brunswick in the first place, to get away from the trouble the father was in. To escape the people who'd killed him. And from what Brogan has told me, their father was terribly abusive toward his sons, and Garrett. Tabor, being the oldest, had to withstand it the longest, and often the harshest. Bart Kavenagh was a devil of a man."

"And look how that legacy has followed his family, even here. It's so sad."

Maggie nodded thoughtfully. "Indeed, you are right. The sons, and their sons, are still paying for the sins of the father."

"Garrett did well for himself. He and his wife came by to see us a few years ago. He said he was going to own his own carriage shop in a place called Akerley, quite a distance from here. I thought he was such a nice young man, and his wife, Abby, too."

"I'm glad to see Garrett succeed. I haven't heard from him lately, but I do wish him continued good fortune."

"I thought I'd found my happily ever after too," said Julia, standing to go. "As it turns out, that wasn't the case."

Maggie shook her head. "He is a hard man to understand. Maybe someday he'll change his mind. He's bound to get tired of his own cooking at some point."

"How very romantic," said Julia pulling a comical face. "Be still my heart."

Both women laughed as Julia slipped into her cloak and headed for the door.

"Tabor has been good to Luke and I. The next time he's over I'll put in a good word for you. I'll really praise you up and see what he says. You never know, he might just be stuck in his own way. Maybe he wants to apologize but is too stubborn to do so, or unsure how to go about it. Anyway, it won't hurt to test the water. He can be grumpy, but he's a good man at heart."

Julia smiled at her. "Thank you for your kind intentions, but my hopes are not very high. So, we'll see."

Julia looked up at the sky as they stepped out into the yard. "I wouldn't be surprised if we had more snow before the night is out. It's going to be a heavy winter. We often don't have any snow until December, but we had another foot or so last week. I thought it would never stop." A wind gust nearly dislodged Julia's hat. "Ohhh!" she cried, grabbing for it.

"You'd better leave without delay, Julia, or you might run into something on the way home. Thank you so much again for the doughnuts."

The two women hugged. Julia clucked to her old horse, turned the buggy, and was on her way.

Luke came running into the house shortly after Julia left. "I found a hornet nest in the woods."

"In the woods! I thought I asked you to stay around the yard."

"It's just inside the woods. I could see it from the yard."

"Luke, you are telling me a falsehood. You know you're not supposed to go into the forest alone, especially at this time of year. "

She knew the snow was too deep for him to go far. He would have sense enough to follow his tracks back out, but he could still get turned around. She didn't need a lost child on her hands on top of everything else. Luke didn't need the ordeal of being out in the cold all hours, trying to find his way back home in the dark. And if a snowstorm did blow up, it could change things in a hurry.

"I'm sorry," he apologized. "I just went down that path in back of the barn, to where the pond is at. It's all frozen over now, but the nest was on a tree by the shore."

"Luke Kavenagh! If you walked all the way to that pond, you went a goodly distance, and you did so in deliberate disobedience. Never mind the hornet's nest. You may take the pail and go to the barn and milk the cow. Do so at once, please."

"But, Ma!"

"Don't but Ma me. A promise is a promise, Luke, and you broke it by going where I told you not to go. I would have gone with you if you'd come back and asked me to."

"You were visiting with Aunt Julia."

"That does not mean you were then free to disobey me. I'm disappointed."

"I said I was sorry. If Pa was here, he would have gone with me."

That statement struck a nerve, reminding her once again that if Brogan's absence was hard for her to deal with, it would be doubly so for Luke.

She set the potato down that she was beginning to peel. "Come here, Luke, I want to talk to you."

The two went to the table. Maggie pulled out a chair so that the boy would have to sit directly in front of her.

"Luke, it's very important that you do what I tell you. You don't realize it, but you can get lost very easily. I know you and your father used to do things like that together. I know you miss him. But I'm telling you, if you disobey me again, there will be consequences. Do you understand what consequences are?"

He nodded reluctantly. "Yeah, it means what will happen to me if I do what I'm not supposed to do."

"Exactly right, you will be punished. You are getting to be a big boy, and I should be able to trust you. So, I will ask for your word once again. Do not go into those woods alone from now on. When you are older, much older than you are now, it will be a different story but that is a very long way off. I want you to make that promise for me and I want you to mean it."

He sighed. "All right, I promise."

"I mean it, Luke."

"So do I, Ma," he said solemnly.

She got up. "All right, there's still enough daylight left. Let me get dressed properly and you can take me to where you saw the hornet nest."

His face lit up. "All right!"

"And since the hornets have long ago left the nest, you can bring it home with you. And after that, you can take the pail and milk the cow. Bed her down for the night while I make supper."

* * *

Tilda was still sound asleep when Brogan opened his eyes. In fact, she was snuggled down comfortably beside him. Anyone walking into the room would assume the two were sleeping together. Well, they were of course, but it would look like more to the casual observer. He was glad there were no observers around, casual or otherwise. They were in bed together only as a matter of necessity.

The cabin was cold, the fire having gone out hours ago. The pain in his leg was sharp, and it worked on his nerves, but he was learning to live with it. Oh, what he wouldn't give for some laudanum, but that was outside the realm of possibility at the moment. Of more urgent concern was Tilda's wellbeing. He surely hoped the cramping had subsided, but there was no way to be sure until she was awake to tell him so.

He'd slept soundly over the past few hours, but he knew it couldn't be more than one or two o'clock in the morning. He hoped she'd gotten some sleep too. He knew she wouldn't wake him. She would bear the discomfort in her usual stoic manner. Maybe that's why she was sleeping so soundly now. In any event, he had no intention of waking her and possibly setting things in motion again. This was a critical time. If she went into labour too soon, he worried her chances of survival could be diminished, and also that of the child.

He was relieved to see her sleeping comfortably. That was encouraging. He wished the cabin was warmer for her, but he dared not move. Instead, he gently pulled the quilt up over her shoulder and went back to sleep himself.

And then he had the most wonderful dream. Maggie. He kissed her soft cheek then nuzzled her ear as he settled in closer against her.

He woke with a start, realizing it was Tilda's ear he'd been caressing. All right, it was definitely time for him to find somewhere else to sleep. This could not continue, his body betraying him when he wasn't fully awake to stay in control of his senses. He hoped she hadn't noticed. He knew it wouldn't take much to fan those flames. She'd already made that clear, poor thing. She was lonely.

Tilda stirred and adjusted her position, her breath warm against his neck. He waited until she was fully awake and had finished blinking the sleep from her eyes. She looked up at him.

"How are you feeling, Tilda? Do you still have cramping?"

She hesitated before answering. "No, I think it's stopped." She waited a few minutes, likely to confirm the accuracy of the statement. "No, no cramps at all."

"Thank the Almighty for that," he said, breathing an earnest sigh of relief.

She tossed back the quilt and started to throw her leg over the side of the bed.

"Oh, no, you don't," Brogan told her, pulling the quilt back into place. "You are not moving from this bed for a few days. The cramping could start again, and we don't want that."

She started to protest, but he quieted her.

"Tilda, we don't have a doctor or a midwife we can go and fetch. We're on our own out here. You have to do as I say. That was very scary last night. You could have gone into labour. I'm not even sure you're out of the woods yet, so it's complete bed rest for you, young lady."

She giggled. "So, what are we supposed to do? You can't strain your leg, and I can't move because I might go into labour. We're stuck!"

"My leg is feeling much better this morning," he lied. "So, I'm going to get up and make a fire. Get things going around here. I'll use the walking stick." He raised up and looked around the room. "What did you do with my pants?"

"I washed them."

"Washed them! You mean they're wet?"

"Probably. They're heavy so it'd likely take a day or so to dry. And now with the hearth having gone cold, they're likely still wet."

"Great!"

"They had a lot of blood on them."

"That wouldn't have mattered. Now what am I supposed to wear?"

"If you remember correctly, you were supposed to stay in bed because of what happened yesterday when you did the chores. I didn't think you would be needing your pants for a day or so. I'm sorry."

"No, that's fine. I just wish I had my long johns is all. It was much warmer than this the day I left and I didn't have time to pack. Oh well, I'll start a fire and it won't be so bad. It's going to be a little fresh going to the barn though."

She giggled again.

"It's not funny," he told her, but he did see the humour of it and was soon laughing too. He guessed a body might as well laugh as cry. If ever there was a nearly impossible situation, this just might be it.

"You have a nice laugh," she told him. "You should do it more often."

"I'll have to remember that."

"And I like the way you talk, nice and quiet-like. Jedediah tends to shout when he speaks. It hurts my ears sometimes."

Here she was going with the comparisons again. At times it was hard to believe she was twenty-one, but that's what she said she was. She acted more like sixteen or seventeen.

He made no comment about her compliments. The only woman he wanted to impress was back on the homestead. How he wished it was her he was waking up beside.

"All right, let me up. I've got to get the fire going in the hearth and warm this place up."

She gasped. "Oh no! I just got a pain in my belly again. Ohhhh ... Brogan!"

Chapter 12

Amby Burk looked around his kitchen at the men who'd answered the call for volunteers to search for Brogan Kavenagh. All eyes were on Amby and he watched the others just as closely. If only it were possible to infuse them with the same sense of vengeance that still burned so brightly in himself. A rage born of anger and bitter disappointment.

He'd had Brogan Kavenagh in the palm of his hand, making sure he would pay for the death of his brother at long last. But somehow he'd slipped away. Even Sheriff Ratchford had botched the arrest. The woods were as bare as the back of his hand at the time, no snow, yet Kavenagh had evaded capture. Four men chasing one. How could he have possibly gotten away? And when they did find where he'd been holed up for the night, he'd managed to shoot his way out. Ratchford had died from a broken leg, complications from the injury. His death should also have been blamed on Kavenagh.

And now this new sheriff was too scared to go after Brogan. It was obvious. Too much snow in the woods had been his excuse.

Another was that Kavenagh was already shot and probably dead by now. They'd go in and collect the body in the spring. Right. Like there'd be anything left after the scavengers got hold of it. No, Kavenagh was alive all right. He'd found a place to crawl into for the winter. How hard could it be to find him and his horse?

Three of the men in the room were Amby's brothers. Donnie had already proved himself somewhat useful, and then there were Carl and Merlin. All younger than he was, they were good strong men and well able to suffer a little hardship. Regrettably though, they were not as strong-minded about this as was their older brother. Nonetheless there was family honour at stake. Brogan Kavenagh had killed Tuncy, a Burk. For that they would see him hang, no matter how they were able to bring it about.

"All right men," Amby spoke, calling the meeting to order, "we've had a run of bad luck with snow so early in the season, but there's bound to be a shift. I've never known winter to come and stay this early, and it should turn soon. It's only mid-November."

Nelson Hollaran, a middle-aged man who'd been passed over for a job as a constable twice and thus had something to prove, was the first to respond. "I agree with Amby. Once the temperature moderates, you'll see that snow melts down pretty fast. Besides, even if Kavenagh has found somewhere to hide, he's not going to stay in one place. He'll need to move around, and he'll leave tracks. There's bound to be other signs, too. That's where the snow will be our friend. We can use it to our advantage."

Amby nodded vigorously. "Nelson's right. When you stay out of the woods because of a little snow, you're missing the perfect opportunity to read signs. Kavenagh is probably closer than we know. He's clever. He knows those woods like the back of his hand. He's hunted hereabout all his life, but so have we. His survival skills are no better than ours."

Neely Haines raised his hand as though he was still in school. The youngest of the group he was clearly the most nervous. Amby was still undecided as to whether or not he'd get to make the trip.

Amby acknowledged the young man. "Neely, we're not in the classroom. If you have something to say just wait your turn and speak up."

Neely's face coloured. "What if it starts snowing while we're out there?"

Amby studied him. "Then it starts snowing while we're out there." He looked purposefully around the room. "Anybody else have anything stupid to ask?"

Neely's colour deepened. "Horses don't like snow. I know mine doesn't."

There were a few guffaws.

Amby folded his arms. "Neely, why are you here?"

Neely attempted a smile. "To catch an outlaw ... sir."

Perly Mollins spoke up from the back of the room. "You're reading too many dime novels, boy. Outlaws ain't easy to catch. Might have to get a little dirt on you, get messed up a bit."

Neely could have won the moment by taking the joke, but he chose to act affronted and lost the room.

Amby, his hands on his hips, stared at Neely. "Go home, Neely. It's over."

The young man stared at Amby, open-mouthed. "I'm saying I want to go."

Amby shook his head. "I'm saying we don't want you with us. Go home, and take your snow-shy horse with you. Go on, get out of here and stop wasting my time."

Neely looked to be on the verge of tears as he glanced at the others. Dropping his eyes, he headed for the door and slammed it on the way out.

"All right, boys, we ride out first thing in the morning, unless there's anyone else who wants out ... or that we want out of the group."

Silence.

"All right then," Amby continued. "That makes six of us. Everyone meets here at first light tomorrow morning. Bring plenty of hardtack and jerky with you. And put some coffee in your saddlebags, I'll bring the pot. We ain't going to no city, so we've got to be ready for some rough travelling. And, of course, pack plenty of ammunition."

Perly spoke up again. "What's the sheriff think of our little expedition?"

Amby's jaw was working. "Who cares what he thinks. I would imagine he's glad someone's got the guts to go and do his job for him. That way he can stay nice and safe back in the town. I'm guessing he'll not be striking a medal for any of us. He'll probably be ready to step up and take all the glory when we bring Kavenagh back. At the end of the day, though, we'll know the truth of it. We'll have brought in a dangerous criminal. If we leave that Brogan Kavenagh out there, there's no telling who he might kill next. I wouldn't put it past him to ride into town when we're all asleep some night and kill us in our beds. He's just liable to."

Perly crossed his arms across his chest. "Do we shoot on site, or are you still thinking we bring him back alive?"

Amby cleared his throat. "You can't hang a dead man, and I aim to see that killer swing. I won't be done out of him hanging. If you have to bring him down, make it a leg shot. Something that'll stop him. The hand, the arm even, but nothing vital. We bring him in alive, is that understood?"

Carl and Merlin Burk were known to be on the quiet side, but brother Donnie was a chip off the old block. "Don't forget he killed Uncle Latham," he said looking directly at

Carl and Merlin. "That's what he's going to swing for."

Amby's gaze shifted to Donnie. "Of course, and he should have swung for Tuncy. Too bad we can only kill him once."

* * *

Josephine had taken up residence in the corner of the parlour, out of the way of the men in the kitchen, although, she heard every word they said. An innocent man would be hunted to ground for something he had not done. There was a conspiracy afoot, and she realized with stomach-turning clarity that she was part of it. She had no call to look down her nose at them. She was no better herself.

She'd known what was going to take place in that woodlot back in September. Amby had schooled her on what she was to say — what would happen to her if she didn't. Yes, she'd known the murder was coming and it was all she could do to keep her stomach down. She had tried to brace herself for the actual killing. She'd closed her eyes against the gruesome spectacle, but the aftermath was lying there, waiting to be acknowledged. She had to play her part. And she had done so, facing Brogan Kavenagh with that damning falsehood. That would haunt her until the day she died.

227

Trembling, she adjusted the pair of trousers she was mending, the needle missing its mark and jabbing deep into her finger. She stifled a yelp as she stuck the injured finger in her mouth. A simple pinprick was painful, what must that bullet have felt like?

She listened to the men plotting Brogan's capture. If these men were successful, returned him for trial, and inevitably execution, she would have to testify in court. Again, she hoped the search party would find Brogan's remains and this nightmare could finally be over.

* * *

The following morning, Josephine cooked a substantial breakfast for the four Burk brothers and poured coffee for Perly Mollins and Nelson Hollaran when they arrived. There was a general melee of last-minute plans being hatched, and soon the six were off into the overcast November morning.

They rode along the shoulder of the main thoroughfare until they came to the old logging road as planned, then formed into a single file. The going was relatively easy for the first few yards. They were surprised to find the snow, wet and heavy, more than two feet deep when they reached the cover of the forest. Onward, they went at walk speed, heading for the site of the choppin' where the tree cutting had taken place. It wasn't long before Amby, at the head of the group, raised his hand. "We'll rest the horses once we get to that clearing yonder," he announced. "We don't want to wear our mounts out on the first day."

"Or the first hour," Perly added wryly, but Amby let it pass.

Amby was a man who was used to having the last word, a beaten-down Josephine was trained long ago to let him have it. "I hadn't expected it to be quite so slippery underfoot. That's hard on the horses' feet."

There was a general grumble of agreement from the others, although it was still early in terms of a mutiny.

It was a good half hour before they gained the clearing, and the men climbed down off their horses. The temperature, which had been pleasantly mild when they'd gotten underway, had begun to drop off somewhat. But soon Amby had a fire going and the coffee pot on. Within a half hour, the mood had shifted back to a more positive frame of mind.

"All right," Amby told the men, "so the snow is a little deeper than we expected. We've got time on our side. We can take it slow, and that's how we're going to go about this thing. It takes patience to capture an outlaw, especially one as wily as Brogan Kavenagh. Now we're giving the horses a good rest, and we'll try for another couple of miles before we stop for lunch."

Perly drank deeply from his metal cup, the hot coffee sending up a cloud of steam around his bewhiskered face. "Don't see any tracks hereabouts."

Amby regarded Perly impatiently. "Did you think he'd be sitting on the side of the road waiting for us?" he asked the older man. "We don't see any tracks because we haven't found where he's holed up yet."

Perly sighed, glancing up at the sky. "Looks like more snow to me, and I'll bet it's not too far off."

Amby dismissed him with a wave of his hand. "At best, we might have a few flakes. We'll be fine. All right, men," he said raising his voice, "let's mount up again and have at this. We'll head west. The lakes back that way should be frozen and will give us good travelling."

Donnie Burk spoke up. "I know which lakes you're talking about. There's a good many miles between them from where we are now."

Amby never took his eyes off the trail. "That's right, Donnie, so slow and steady as we go."

A half hour later, they came upon moose tracks and again proceeded in single file along the well-travelled game trail. It was easier on the horses with the trail broken for them, although packed and slippery in places. The horses were tired after an hour of heavy going.

They'd covered a fair distance by the time they stopped for another break, the horses slowing their pace and shortening their stride considerably. It was obvious to the men they couldn't push them any further without a rest if they were going to get anything more out of them today.

The men were quiet at lunch and once they'd eaten, each found a comfortable spot to sit back and rest. An hour later, they were on the move again. Amby led the pack, plainly driven by an insatiable need to find Brogan. The others seemed content to plod along behind, the air of camaraderie long gone.

Another game trail brought them to Ezekiel Loughty's camp, where Ratchford and the deputies had come upon Brogan weeks ago. It was now under a deep blanket of snow, but it was apparent from Ratchford's description this was the place where the firefight had taken place. The men were off their horses and inside the camp in a heartbeat. At least they'd have cover for the night and that cheered them.

Soon there was a fire burning in the hearth. They found food in the abandoned larder, cooking a large evening meal for themselves.

Amby couldn't seem to stop smiling. This was proof they were on the right trail. Ratchford and his deputies had gotten no further, but *they* would. If Brogan had indeed been shot, and Ratchford had sworn he'd seen blood fly, then how far could he have travelled in that condition? He had to be nearby! Besides, they'd find Brogan's horse before they found him. Even if Brogan was dead, the horse was likely still alive. There wouldn't be much for the horse to forage on but he would find something to eat. However, if the horse was indeed still around, there should have been tracks and there weren't any.

No matter, after they'd had a good night's sleep and the horses refreshed, they'd go at it again. Things were going much better than he'd anticipated, and much faster. They would have Brogan by tomorrow night if all continued to proceed smoothly. The men bunked down early after imbibing liberally from old Ezekiel's liquor supply, the walls soon rattling from a cacophony of snoring. An early start the next morning might be in doubt, but the good cheer of the group had been restored, at least temporarily.

It worried Amby how quickly the men's moods had deteriorated today. Last night, in the kitchen, he'd had them properly fired up, but after only an hour or two of hard travel, they had quickly lost their zeal. He knew the going could get a lot more difficult than what they'd experienced today. Truth to tell, they likely wouldn't want to leave the warmth of the hearth behind, not to mention the larder with its ample stock of fresh meat. The old man who'd lived here had certainly gotten in plenty of winter supplies.

* * *

When daylight filled the camp the next morning, Amby was the first one to come fully awake. Something wasn't right, he could feel it in his bones. Getting quickly to his feet, he crossed the room to the window and let out a string of curses. It was a world of white outside, snow falling so heavily it wouldn't be long before they would be socked in good and tight with another foot on top of what was already there. If they'd found the going getting tougher on the way in, continuing on after this storm would be completely foolhardy. They could only push their horses so hard. If they gave out on them completely, they'd all be stranded in the teeth of winter.

Perly was the next one to shake out the cobwebs from a hungover brain, awakened by Amby's loud expletives.

"It could end as quickly as it started," the older man suggested, although he didn't sound convinced. "But if this weather keeps up, we should head back home, otherwise we'll be stuck here until spring. It looks like it's going to be one of those winters."

"And Kavenagh will get away."

"Kavenagh has already gotten away, Amby. We could be looking for a ghost. Anyway, this snow might just be a squall and pass in a short while. I'll go out and see how much is already down."

Perly was back a minute or two later, his hair and shoulders coated with large white flakes. "I'd say it's been snowing all night, it's making fast, and there's already seven or eight inches more on the ground. So, we should probably wait it out here instead of getting out in the middle of it. This is poor luck all right. You can't see your hand in front of your face out there. The horses have taken shelter in the trees, and I would imagine they've been able to dig up some dried grass. When it's over, we can decide if we want to keep going or head back. We've got our snowshoes, so we can lead the horses if we have to and break trail, but they should be all right if we take it slow. If it was just a short distance it wouldn't matter, but we're already several miles in. We can't ride them to death."

Amby was not in the mood to be spoken to as he kicked a nearby stool and sent it crashing into the wall. "We'll wait until it stops snowing," he announced. "I don't know about you men, but I'm going on as soon as this lets up. We're close to him. I can feel it. If we tuck our tails and turn back now, we might never get another chance."

Perly shrugged. "Suit yourself, Amby, but I'll tell you one thing. My decision's going to be what's best for me *and* my horse. If I think we can go on, we'll go on. I'm not going to run a good animal into the ground chasing a ghost."

Again, there was a rumble of agreement, all the men awake now. Amby found something else to kick.

* * *

It was still snowing when darkness fell, and the more the snow piled up the worse Amby's mood became. And then came the sound that none of them wanted to hear, the clicking of freezing rain against the camp's one windowpane. That meant there would be a crust on the snow, and if the horses might walk through snow the height of their bellies for thirty or forty minutes at a time, crashing through a layer of ice on top of that snow, it would abrade their legs. Rub them raw considering the distance they needed to cover to even get back. This was quickly going from bad to worse. There was nothing to do but wait it out, only then would they know exactly what they would be facing.

Donnie Burk tried to mollify his brother. "It's not looking good, Amby. The weather turned against us and we'd be asking a lot of the horses."

Amby could barely contain his anger. "They'll harden up. The exercise will be good for them."

Donnie shrugged. "That may be so, but even if we catch up with Kavenagh, how are we supposed to get him back? We'll be doing everything we can to get *ourselves* back. Look, it's only a few months to spring. If we're affected by the weather, so is he. If he's still alive, how far do you think he's going to get in this mess? Come on, Amby. We've got to use reason here."

Amby glared at Donnie. "You were all hepped up in the kitchen, but now that you've got a little bit of weather to get through you're giving up. That's just what Kavenagh wants us to do."

Donnie folded his arms. "I'm just as hepped up as I ever was, you know that. But you think he's sitting in the bushes somewhere watching us? Laughing at us? No. Maybe Vailor was right. Maybe we're just looking for a body anyway, and how are we supposed to find it under all this snow?"

"But we're so close," Amby protested. "I can feel it. He was right here."

Donnie shook his head. "That was weeks ago! He could be sitting up in Moncton for all we know, his feet up and us out here slogging through this. If he's laughing, that's where he's doing it. I want to get him as badly as you do, but I didn't think the going was going to be so hard. None of us did. I talked to the others. They want to turn back. I'm sorry, Amby."

Amby raised his voice as he looked at the other men. "Those horses are going to be fine. You're all worried about yourselves. You're all lily-livered."

Perly watched him through narrowed eyes. "I'd watch my tongue if I were you, Amby. None of us made it snow, but that's what it's doing. This has turned into a fool's errand, or will be if we continue on. We're going back. You can come or you can stay, or go on. It's up to you."

Amby turned on Perly. "I'm leading this search party, not you."

Perly didn't back down. "Then lead it. Do what's best for everyone, not just yourself. We were damned lucky to find this camp. If we hadn't, we'd have been stuck out in that all night," he said gesturing toward the window. "I don't know about you but I'm much more comfortable in here than lying in some lean-to freezing my hind end off. Look, Amby, the weather's not with us. We'll try again."

* * *

The storm had played itself out by morning, but the men had heard trees crashing to the ground all night long, brought down by a heavy layer of snow and ice on their branches. When they emerged from the camp, the clearing was filled with deadfall. What trees had managed to keep standing were weighted to the ground, most bent double. Others were still breaking under the load. Rounding up the horses in the deep ice-covered snow was an exhausting task, accomplished by the men wearing snowshoes. They tore up bed sheets and whatever rags they could find in the camp to wrap the horses legs and feet against the sharp edges of the ice-crusted snow. Walking ahead of their mounts, they broke trail to spare them some of the ordeal.

Both men and animals were tired after only a couple of hours. That included two challenging detours around massive fallen trees that blocked their path and slowed their progress to a crawl. At one point, a large spruce tree fell, its sprawling branches narrowly missing Amby and Nelson Hollaran. Night was gathering steadily around them when they stopped to make camp, erecting a makeshift lean-to. An icy wind added to their misery.

Donnie Burk had brought along a second bottle of rum from the larder, and it helped warm the exhausted men. The horses sought shelter in the woods nearby.

The next day dawned overcast and as impossible as it seemed, it looked as though more precipitation was ready to fall on the already beleaguered countryside. They again attacked the trail, winding their way through the heavy forest. Each step required the men to stomp on the slippery ice-covered snow in order to break through. The horses followed. At times, whole stands of young trees had succumbed to the weight of the ice, forcing the party to backtrack and find an easier route.

And then it began to rain, the temperature having rebounded in the other direction although far from warm. It soaked man and beast alike until each step was a hardship.

Once they'd made camp on the second night the men were so worn out, they ate some hardtack and jerky, washed it down with water and quickly fell asleep.

The third day back was no better, cold and windy, clothes still damp and heavy from the previous day's rain. But at least the coverings on the horses' legs and feet had spared them damage from the punishing icy crust.

The search party finally hobbled into Amby Burk's yard late in the afternoon of the third day, completely dispirited. The failed mission had accomplished something though. To a man, they all vowed to return to the chase in the spring. Brogan Kavenagh had won this round. He would not be so fortunate next time. They would not be denied again.

* * *

Josephine saw the men filing into the yard, and she flew to the stove to get a pot of coffee going. It didn't appear as though they had a prisoner in tow, so they must have had to turn back because of the weather or had simply come up empty-handed. She could only imagine what Amby's state of mind would be like now. He'd been harbouring a hatred of Brogan Kavenagh since his brother Tuncy's death. It was affecting his thinking, and she was becoming increasingly more frightened of him.

* * *

Brogan watched Tilda, as her face contorted in pain.

"You've only just wakened," he said. "Did the pain wake you up?"

She nodded. "I feel pressure, here," she said, laying a hand on her lower abdomen.

"Are you having any pain in your back?"

She shook her head. "A little but not bad."

"All right," he said in an affecting calm voice that he was far from feeling on the inside. He hoped with everything inside him that this was what Maggie had experienced after her fall. It was called false labour, and the discomfort eventually passed. With any good fortune at all, that's what was happening here. "Just try to relax and hopefully it will pass. Don't try to push or anything, and see if the feeling goes away."

Easing himself past Tilda, he carefully extracted himself from the bed. Even the slightest movement caused the pain from the gunshot wound to escalate. However, a glance at the bandage told him it had stopped bleeding, hopefully for good this time.

"I'll build a fire because if that baby does decide it wants to get born, I'm going to have to boil some water. So just try to take it easy. I'll be back in a few minutes to check on you."

The first thing he noticed when he limped to the kitchen with the aid of the walking stick, was that his trousers were dry. Sitting down, he gratefully pulled them into place and was glad of the warmth. There was another cry of pain from the bedroom.

With an effort, he gathered enough wood to start a fire in the hearth and it was soon crackling and snapping merrily. It was a truly welcome sound and the cabin warmed up quickly.

"Brogan!" came Tilda's troubled cry minutes later.

He hurried as fast as he could into the bedroom.

"I'm soaked," she wailed. "I think my waters have broken."

Chapter 13

Brogan's heart sank. Tilda was already in labour. He had to help her through this as best he could, relying almost entirely on his knowledge of animal births. He'd had a mare once that was having trouble foaling and he'd had to step in and come to her aid. She'd finally delivered a fine-looking filly, however he hadn't been able to save the mother from a rupture during the birthing process.

And of course, it could be challenging when heifers had their first calf. Back on the farm they would pen up the bull when heifers were not yet old enough to be bred. The bull however, answering the unrelenting call of nature, sometimes jumped the fence. The result was calves being born to heifers much too young to have them. There had been three or four of them over the years and although there were calving difficulties, they'd managed to help them through it without any loss of life. And now that limited knowledge was to be put to the ultimate test.

He hurried as best he could into the bedroom where a terrified Tilda regarded him with saucer-wide eyes. "I'm going to have the baby, aren't I Brogan?"

He nodded. "I would say so, but it likely won't be for some hours yet. "

She gritted her teeth, holding her belly. "That was another cramp."

"Labour pains, Tilda. It's only been a few minutes since you had the last one, so it's starting to happen all right. I've got a good fire going now. I'll have some water in the pot all set to boil when the time comes. You said you had things ready for the baby, where are they?"

"They're all in that big cupboard across from the hearth. There's a cradle and flats — you know, diapers, and I sewed two nighties for him."

He left to find the baby supplies and returned minutes later as Tilda clenched her teeth on another wave of pain. He sat on the edge of the bed, holding her hand until the contraction subsided.

He knew she would likely object to what he had to tell her next, but it had to be done. He was no more anxious to perform that duty than she would be to allow him.

"Tilda, I'm going to have to check to see how far you're dilated. I know it's embarrassing for you, but it will help me know where we're at with this thing. How far along you are."

She turned her head away, but he guessed, under the present circumstances, she was beyond caring about the details. "Just do it!" she told him. "I know it has to be done."

And so, pulling back the quilt, he gently arranged her clothing so he could determine how close she was to giving birth. Just as he expected, there were still many hours of labour left. Maggie had endured hard labour for almost twenty-four hours. He well remembered the agony of waiting. Believing something had gone terribly wrong, but the midwife had assured him that for a first-time mother, it was not at all unusual.

All through the day, Tilda rode the waves of contractions, her small body wracked with pain. Her progress was slow, and when nighttime approached, she was still far from being close to delivering. He kept the fire stoked, had the water ready, and left her side only to do chores. Other than that, he sat in the chair he'd pulled up next to the bed and patted her face with a cool damp cloth. He didn't know if that was usually done, but she seemed to appreciate it.

It was well after midnight when he checked her again, and she was now close to being fully dilated. She was almost there. This was going to happen soon, within the next hour or so he guessed.

"Tilda, did you help your father during any births?"

She shouted with pain again as another contraction seized her. It was a moment before she could answer. "Not really," she was finally able to tell him, "but he told me how to tie off the cord. The proper way to go about it."

"I have a general idea but I've never seen it done. Tell me how your father explained it to you."

She managed to do so as he held her hand, mopped her forehead, and did everything he could to keep her as comfortable as possible. At times like this, men felt helpless. But he did keep the cabin good and warm.

Another hour passed, and Tilda looked exhausted. Kneeling down, he examined her again and could see the baby's head, he'd heard it called crowning. But Tilda was such a small woman and this baby looked anything but small. That would bode well for its chances once it was born. It was just getting it out that seemed impossible at this point.

"Try to push harder, Tilda. Come on. The head is right there, I can see it. Try to push a little more. Harder! Harder!" he encouraged her when she bore down, shrieking with the effort.

There was movement. He could see more of the head. He'd let her rest for a moment before urging her to bear down again.

"All right, Tilda, push, push, push!" And then the baby's head was out, resting in Brogan's hands and seconds later she was fully ushered into the world.

"All right, honey, you did it. Very good! It's a girl, and she looks strong and healthy.

I would guess she weighs at least seven pounds."

"*We* did it," Tilda sobbed. "You and I."

This was not a premature baby in any sense of the word, so at least they were spared that situation.

When he'd finished with the cord, Brogan wrapped a soft baby blanket around the infant and laid her on Tilda's chest. If ever there was a more beautiful picture, it could only have been when he'd seen his own sweet Maggie holding their son like this for the first time.

The baby, golden fuzz apparent on its tiny head, eventually found a nipple, and within a remarkably short time, she began to suckle.

Brogan saw to the cleaning up and despite the fact that his leg was in no mood to calm down, he felt better than he had in weeks. He had brought a child into the world, a beautiful little baby girl. He left the baby at Tilda's breast for nearly an hour before placing it in the cradle and gently covering it over. The newborn didn't seem to be much of a crier, other than that lusty howl she'd given just after she was born. After he'd cleaned her up, she'd settled down right away.

Now it was time to tend to Tilda, get her back into the warmth of her nightdress, and get some fresh bedding on the bed. Within a half hour, she was resting as comfortably as she could after having gone through labour and childbirth. There'd been some hemorrhaging, but not more than could be expected he supposed. In any event, she looked very tired now, but happy as only a new mother could. They had gotten through this together, and both mother and child had survived. He couldn't have been more thankful.

He would let Tilda sleep after he'd cooked her something to eat. He recalled that Maggie had told him how hungry she'd been after giving birth to Luke. Birthing was hard work, not to mention staying healthy because her body had to feed their son. He remembered that whole time fondly.

Brogan would make up a bed for himself in front of the hearth. He was sure he'd have no trouble sleeping because after seeing to Tilda and the baby, he still had the horse to take care of. Dutch had let him know, too, that he was unhappy with the poor service, pawing the barn floor impatiently. He'd fed and watered him, only able to push the manure aside for the present time. He would do a better job of it tomorrow. And then there'd been water to carry and stocking up on wood for the night. He'd kept a sharp ear for Tilda, and the baby while he worked. He didn't like to leave either of them alone for too long in case they should need him, although Tilda was getting some much-needed sleep. It was soon time for the baby to be fed again anyway, and he was glad all was going well in that regard.

Back in the cabin, he'd just taken off his coat and boots when Tilda called out to him. He made haste to the bedroom.

"I'm here," he told her. "Just taking care of some chores. I've been in the barn so let me wash my hands, and I'll bring the baby to you."

He hurried to do so and within minutes had the baby at her breast again.

There were tears in Tilda's eyes, they shone bright in the weak sunlight. "I am so grateful she is healthy, Brogan. I have you to thank for seeing me through her birthing. I don't know what I would have done if you weren't here."

He smiled, his own eyes bright. "I'm just as thankful as you are," he told her. "I've always heard of the things that can go wrong, as I'm sure you have."

"I am so appreciative of everything you did to help me. If it was a boy, I would have named him Brogan for sure."

He was relieved that was not going to be an issue. He sat on the side of the bed. "So, are you still going to call her Fern?"

Tilda nodded. "Yes, Fern. I'll also use my mother's name. Martha. So, Fern Martha Loughty. I think that's a pretty name, don't you?"

"A very pretty name for a very pretty little girl. And she's feeding real well, too. That's a relief."

"That's one thing I remember my father talking about, women complaining they couldn't get their babies to nurse properly. From what I understand, it can be quite a problem sometimes."

He nodded. "I can see where that *would* be a real problem. Our little boy, Luke, took to it quickly too. You couldn't keep him filled."

He excused himself to get some venison in the fry pan for an early supper. He'd just finished peeling the potatoes and had them in the pot when it was time to take the baby from her.

She felt so tiny and fragile cradled in his strong arms, a wiggling Fern, making low-pitched, contented sounds.

Tilda watched wistfully at him, holding the baby. "I wish you were her father, Brogan."

That took him by surprise. "Now, Tilda, you shouldn't be saying such things. It isn't right. I'm a married man. I already have a wife and a child. This little mite has a father, too."

Tilda looked away, and he could see tears shimmering on her lashes, but she made no further comment.

It felt good holding a little baby again, and he couldn't help but recall the day he'd become a father. There was no feeling in the world quite like it. He also knew neither he nor Tilda would get a lot of sleep tonight, and he'd already been up more than twenty-four hours. Newborns were fed every two to three hours. That much he knew from experience, but as exhausting as it was, a parent would say it was the most beautiful sound in the world. And as Maggie had often teased him, more often than not, he'd slept right through the baby crying.

Tilda ate every scrap of her supper, and that pleased him. Soon, it was time to bring Fern back to her mother for her evening meal, and the baby was eager for nourishment.

He set about washing up from supper and after finishing, took the baby back to her cradle.

He sat down on the edge of the bed, the clock in the kitchen chiming out seven bells.

"I think you should come to bed early, Brogan," she told him. "I'm sure I'm not the only one who's tired."

"I have a bed made out in front of the hearth."

"No!" she objected. "You said it hurt your leg to get up off the floor. How is the wound by the way?"

"Don't worry about my leg. It's fine."

"I don't believe you. Let me look at it."

"Tilda, my leg is all right. There's still pain, and there likely will be for quite some time. It hasn't started to bleed again, so I would say it's on the mend. I changed the bandage myself earlier. All is well."

"But you'll make it worse trying to get up from the floor."

"I've solved that problem too," he told her. "I've placed a chair beside me, so I'll use that to pull myself up. It doesn't hurt my leg at all. I've already tried it. So, you see, there's nothing whatsoever to concern yourself about. Now, you just worry about getting your own strength back."

There were tears in her eyes. "But I want you to be in bed with me, Brogan. I feel safe with you next to me."

No, turning to her in his sleep, nuzzling her ear while he dreamt about Maggie had been enough. It would not be repeated.

"Tilda, we were together because we both needed a bed and this was the only one. You could hardly sleep on the floor in your condition, and my leg needed that extra day's rest. Now you must have the bed because you've just had a baby and besides," he grinned, "it's your bed. My leg is healing nicely, so there's no more reason for us to do that. It won't be happening again."

She was into a full cry now. "Brogan, please. I want you with me."

"Tilda," he said quietly. "Calm yourself and try to keep your voice down. Let the baby sleep."

She was not to be comforted. "I'm lonely," she wailed. "Is it so much to ask for someone to hold me?"

She reached for his hand, and he held hers for a moment, then gently pulled away. "Tilda, listen to me. It's not too much to ask someone to hold you, but it is too much to ask that of someone else's husband. I'm married to Maggie, and I love her very much.

I'm not about to sleep with another woman just because my wife and I are not together at the moment, any more than it would be proper for her to sleep with another man under those circumstances. And you have a husband, Tilda."

The thought of Maggie ever doing such a thing was like a knife straight through the heart. Lord, he missed her! If she were the woman in this bed, there would be no need to beg. He would never want to leave it.

Tilda cried softly. "I know you're right, Brogan, and I'm sorry. You must think I'm a terrible person to be so bold."

He took hold of her hand again. That was the least he could do to comfort the young woman. "On the contrary, Tilda. You're a very brave, smart woman to stay out here on your own like you do. I can't think of any other woman who would have the fortitude to do such a thing, and you expecting a baby. I can understand you're lonely. I'm lonely too ... for my wife. It's a natural thing for people to get lonely, but there are certain lines that shouldn't be crossed. It wouldn't be right."

She looked at him. "Your wife is a very fortunate woman to have you for a husband, and that you love her so much. I can't say the same about my husband, but then you never know."

"No, sadly you don't, but look, nothing says we can't be friends. I'm here now, and I'll look after you and your baby as best I can.

Now dry those tears and think about the sweet new babe you have lying in her cradle just a few feet away. This time last night you were not yet a mother. That's quite a remarkable thing that happened in the last few hours, wouldn't you say?"

She was smiling now. "I'm a mother. I have a child. Last night, I was so scared to go through childbirth. Now it's over and my baby and I are fine."

"That's right. Now we should try to get some sleep. I know a certain little girl who will want to be fed in another two or three hours. You'll have to get your rest while you can."

* * *

He had just laid down for the night when Fern's wailing woke him, but how could anyone be annoyed with a newborn? He was still filled with the wonderment of bringing a child into the world, without mishap. The edge hadn't even begun to wear off that.

His leg ached with a steady throb because he'd put it through more than enough punishment today. At least, there had been no more bleeding. He still checked his pant leg to make sure the wound hadn't been torn open again.

It was close to the end of November now he thought as he waited to take the baby back

253

to its cradle. There'd been plenty of weather in both October and November so far, snow, freezing rain, rain.

He was deeply grateful he'd had such good shelter during all of that, both he and Dutch. If he had been forced to deal with the elements, he reminded himself yet again, it would be a much different story. It wouldn't make much sense to strike out while they were in the throes of one of the worst winters in recent memory. He could never hope to duplicate what he had here, either for himself or his horse. Dutch couldn't be expected to navigate this kind of snow for any length of time. He was shod, so therefore snow would ball up in around the shoe and eventually make walking both arduous and painful. No, they would wait it out.

However, when he did go in the spring, if he hadn't been captured before then, how could he leave a young mother and baby alone way out here? And he couldn't take them with him. It would be ludicrous to think he could. And in which direction would he go this time? It had only been a couple of months since he'd left so quickly that September afternoon, but it felt more like years. He hated to think about what lay ahead. No matter how he examined it, his predicament still seemed truly hopeless.

* * *

254

The ice storm had brought a big old fir tree down onto the barn. Fortunately, thought Maggie, it hadn't done any more damage than breaking a small hole in the roof. That meant wet hay in one corner, considering it rained all the following day. She and Luke had forked what hay was there, away from the opening. They hadn't lost much. With only the milk cow to feed now, there was an abundance of hay in store.

She thought about Dutch and how Brogan was managing to keep the horse fed while hiding in the woods. All of this heavy weather was like salt in an open wound. It would be hard enough for him to survive in the wilderness during the winter, especially since he hadn't any time to prepare. Why did it have to be so terrible?

Tabor and Pate had come by when the weather cleared to see if she'd suffered any damage on the homestead, and they had the roof patched in no time.

"I was talking to Julia the other day," she told Tabor when they were alone. "She came by to see if we needed anything. She misses you, Tabor."

He bristled, she could see it in his face. "The house is there. She can come back if she has a mind to. I'm not going to stop her."

Her heart skipped a beat. Maybe there was a chance for them after all.

"Should I mention that to her the next time I see her?" she asked him carefully.

"You can decide that for yourself," was his reply before he strode off to help Pate.

Yes, Tabor was a hard man. All of the Kavenagh boys had suffered. Julia was probably right. Perhaps Tabor had suffered the most.

* * *

It was early the following afternoon when Peterson Gault pulled into Maggie's yard in his farm wagon. The kindly old neighbour with his penchant for gossip was simply making his rounds, but Maggie was not fooled. He had information for her, and she steeled herself that it might not be good. It was the only way she could make it through these weeks. She feared if she let down her guard, the pain of receiving bad news would hurt much worse. If she prepared herself, there might not be as far to fall.

Answering his light rap on the solid oak door, Maggie welcomed him inside to sit by the warmth of the fire. "It's nice to see you, Mr. Gault. I just happen to have a fresh batch of Cornish pasties made. I could offer you a plate and a cup of coffee if you had a mind to stay for a few minutes."

His eyes lit up, but it was apparent he had news he wished to deliver before he accepted the hospitality of a warm meal.

"Where's your boy, Mrs. Kavenagh?"

"Luke? He's out in the barn, why?"

"Wouldn't want to say this in front of him is all. I heard them talking up at the sawmill about Amby Burk going after Brogan. Do you want me to tell you what I heard?"

Her stomach instantly soured. "Of course."

"Well, Amby and three of his brothers and a couple of other men went into where Sheriff Ratchford reported that Brogan had been shot."

Her voice felt as though it was coming from a far distance. "Was there any sign of Brogan?"

"No sign, but then there was lots of snow on the ground. That's as far as they got when the storm moved in. It was very bad slogging, especially for the horses. Perly Mollins got pneumonia out of it, but they say he'll live."

Maggie realized she had been holding her breath, waiting for him to tell her they'd found Brogan's horse. That would likely mean her husband was also dead.

"I'm sorry for Perly Mollins' sickness, but I can't feel any pity for the men who are chasing my husband like a pack of bloodhounds," she stated, her hands in a white-knuckled grip on the back of a nearby chair. "Brogan is an innocent man. It's a constant nightmare to think he's out there somewhere, suffering through this terrible weather."

Peterson Gault studied the floor. "And maybe his suffering is over, Mrs. Kavenagh. I just don't see how he can have survived these past two months with the winter we're having. Not from what those men said. It's bad going out there where they think he is."

She felt tears spring to her eyes but willed them to remain unshed. "Brogan is a survivor, Mr. Gault. I have to believe he'll get through this and come back to us."

He looked at her sadly. "I so dearly hope you're right. Brogan is a tough man and if anybody could make it through something like this, he could. I'm not meaning to upset you. I thought you'd want to hear what the latest talk is. That's two search parties that went out there, and they still don't have him. I'm thinking with him shot and all you might want to be preparing yourself. On the other hand, I have to admire the faith you have that he'll come back alive and well. Sometimes the good Lord works in ways that are mighty hard to understand, like when the sickness took my family. But I do believe one thing, if it's not Brogan's time to go, he'll be spared. Let's hope it's not his time to go."

* * *

The first week of December was ushered in by spring-like temperatures that gave the hope for a respite, but the weather turned mean again a few days later. There had been no more precipitation save for the odd light dusting of snow, but biting cold with a north wind bent on punishment. Maggie was glad Luke didn't have to go out in bad weather anymore to get to the schoolhouse, a two-and-a-half-mile walk. No, her son was here with her in a nice warm house, with plenty to eat. At least she was able to keep one of the precious people in her life, safe.

Luke was doing well in his studies and, with the resilience of a child, seemed to be adjusting fairly well to life without his father. It had become obvious he preferred not to talk about Brogan. That told her he was hurting much more than he let on.

She was glad when Julia dropped by one fine afternoon. The sun shone brightly and there wasn't a cloud in the sky, the snow sparkling as white as frosted porcelain.

"Come in by the fire," Maggie welcomed her friend. "It's a bitter day to be out in a buggy."

"I have a robe for my feet," Julia told her pleasantly. "I made bread and guess I forget I'm only baking for myself, so I made too much. You wouldn't help me out by taking a couple of loaves, would you?"

Maggie smiled. Julia lived to help others, and she appreciated her creative way of sharing without making people feel beholden.

"Thank you, Julia. That will really come in handy. How did you weather that awful ice storm we had?" she asked as the two women took a seat at the table, waiting for the tea to steep.

"A few limbs off trees, nothing more than that. I heard some people had considerable damage. How were things around here?"

Maggie told her about the barn, and that Tabor and Pate had come to take care of the repairs. She saw interest flare in the other woman's eyes at the mention of Tabor's name. And that flare blossomed into undisguised hope when she told Julia about the brief conversation that she'd had with him.

"Did he really say that?" she asked Maggie, her face alight.

"That very thing," Maggie assured her. "You know Tabor, he's a man of few words. He gets right to the point, and I believe he did."

Julia tried to suppress a smile, without success. "Hmmm.... I'll just have to think about that. I guess his pride won't let him come to me."

"I believe you're right. I think he's let himself get closer to you than he has any other woman since his wife died, but he's way too proud for his own good."

Julia nodded knowingly. "Now tell me, how are *you* faring, Maggie? I've heard about how well Luke is doing with his studies, and how the barn got repaired. I'm wondering about you. How are you holding up during this terribly trying time?”

Maggie was silent for too long, and she could see concern on Julia’s expressive face.

“What is it, Maggie? What’s happened?”

Maggie fought back tears. “I’m pregnant, Julia, a little more than three months along. How can I bring a child into the world at a time like this?

Chapter 14

Early May, 1877

Baby Fern was a happy healthy baby, her eyes as blue as the sky and her hair pale blonde like her mother's. She was now nearly five months old and sleeping through the night. Brogan remembered very well that cold November night when she was born. How worried he'd been because he'd never delivered a child before. But all had thankfully gone well, the proof of that sleeping peacefully in her cradle.

He thought of Maggie often, of Luke, and wondered how they'd made it through the winter. Had the barn held up in that dreadful ice storm in November, or the one that coated the countryside with ice again in March? Was the cow still milking? How was Luke making out in school? Maggie would hold everything together as she was so capable of doing, but it would not be easy being both mother and father, not to mention worrying about *him*. At times, he felt like a caged animal, especially with the weather improving. He longed to see his wife and child, even if it meant stealing home to surprise them. But he just as quickly discarded the idea. They would get him for sure. Ratchford would be watching the homestead with that very thing in mind. So he would spare Maggie and Luke the nightmare of watching him being arrested, or worse.

He'd given a lot of thought to returning, maybe get up as far as Moncton and find a lawyer who would defend him against the charge of murder. He would turn himself in if he thought he would get a fair chance to plead his case, but he was not optimistic about that. Ratchford was anything but fair. He knew he didn't stand much of a chance as his mind continued to go in circles on the matter, and always arriving at the same dismal conclusion.

And how could he just walk away from Tilda and Fern? They depended on him. He felt honour bound to protect them, seeing as how Tilda had given him shelter and care when he needed it. It would be fundamentally wrong to abandon her, but still, his life was on the line.

Brogan knew it was not a good idea to bond with the child, but it was impossible not to spend time with her. He couldn't very well ignore her, and Tilda was eager for him to be part of her life. He knew it would be hard on both him *and* the baby when the time came to go and they would not see each other again.

Tilda and Fern had been his family for the past seven months and it was difficult not to form an attachment, but the time was coming for him to move on. There would no doubt be another search party underway soon. Ratchford would be on his heels before he knew it. He wouldn't be surprised if they had tried again during the winter. With the terrible weather they'd had this past season they likely hadn't gotten very far. He knew his respite from the law would soon be over now that spring had arrived.

"You seem very deep in thought, Brogan," Tilda said, looking up at him from the washboard. "I guess I don't have to ask you what you're thinking about. You're going to leave us, aren't you?"

He glanced over at the baby, and then back at her. "I have to go, Tilda, and soon. If the sheriff and his men come here it could be bad for you both ... dangerous if they actually found me here. You could face the law too, for harbouring a fugitive. I have to leave."

She looked away quickly and Brogan knew it wasn't what she wanted to hear. They'd had this conversation before, and his leaving wouldn't get any easier no matter how much time went by.

"Tilda," he said gently. "You know this is the way it has to be."

She sniffed. "I know," she said, pulling her hands from the water and drying them on her apron. "Do you have any idea when you'll be going?"

"Probably in another week or so. I'll let it warm up a bit more, and then I'll have to be on my way."

"But where will you go, what will you do?"

He shrugged, not any happier to be announcing his departure than she was to hear about it. What man would want to leave a safe harbor when he knew the law was after him? Men who would capture him and take him back to hang. That was if he even made it back to hang. It would likely be easier to give them cause to shoot him, although he still felt the pain of the bullet he'd taken back in September. He'd wish for a fatal shot rather than endure the agony of the hangman's noose. He couldn't bring himself to think about that all the way through.

"I suppose the answer to that is to stay one step ahead of the law for as long as I can."

"That's a terrible way to have to live, Brogan. I can hardly bear to think of that kind of fate for you."

"I'm not too happy about it myself," he said, trying to inject lightness into the conversation, but it was proving to be impossible. "I have no other choice. They're after me, Tilda, and they'll find this place. I'd say with the ground drying up as quickly as it is, they'll be along soon. Time is running out, and the best way I can protect you and Fern is to get as far away from here as I can. That Sheriff Ratchford is ruthless. I can't take the chance he would involve you in this. He would do it all right and not lose a moment's sleep over it. Now that I think about it, I should probably leave tomorrow or the next day."

"No! Not that soon!" She began to cry.

Laying down the gun he'd been cleaning, he went to her and put his arm around her shoulders. "I know it's hard, Tilda. I appreciate everything you've done for me, but we both knew this was how it was going to end."

She turned quickly, laying her head against his chest, crying softly, and he comforted her.

Suddenly the door to the cabin was thrust open. A man of medium height stepped boldly inside, pointing a rifle squarely at both he and Tilda. Brogan's eyes shot to his own gun, but it was too far away to get to quickly, and it wasn't loaded. He didn't move a muscle, keeping his eyes on the man.

Tilda had turned to stone, her back to the door and the stranger who had thrust himself so aggressively inside. Brogan knew his time would be up soon, but he just didn't think it would be this morning.

"I caught you, didn't I!" the young man shouted.

At the sound of the voice, Tilda wheeled around, shocked. "Jedediah! What are you doing? Put that gun down!"

The young man turned blazing eyes on her. "You ask what I'm doing? Like I had no right to walk into my own home? And when I do I find my wife in the arms of another man."

Brogan held up his hands. "Now wait a minute. There's nothing going on here. I needed shelter and your wife gave it to me. She saved my life and that's all there is to it."

Jedediah did not lower the gun. "Is that a fact! You look all right to me, certainly healthy enough to put your hands on my wife."

Brogan was relieved the husband hadn't walked in on him and Tilda sleeping in the same bed. Now that would have been completely damning.

Jedediah stared at Brogan. "How long you been staying here?"

Brogan kept his hands where they were. "A few months I guess."

Just then Fern let out a wail.

The man's eyes widened as he sought to grasp the situation. "A few months! So that baby is yours! I'm going to kill you where you stand for what you did."

Tilda was beside herself. "Jedediah! Stop this! Brogan isn't...."

"It's Brogan, is it? Well, Brogan, you've been lying with my wife, haven't you? Gave her a baby."

Brogan started to lower his hands, and Jedediah raised the rifle another inch for a perfect head shot.

Brogan tried again. "Listen to me, you fool. I am not the father of that baby. You are!"

Fire was also flying from Tilda's eyes. "How dare you accuse me of such a thing, or this fine man standing here! That is your daughter, Jedediah. Now put that gun down before you hurt someone or I'll take the frying pan to you. I swear I will!"

Jedediah didn't look convinced. "I've been gone almost long enough for such a thing to happen."

Brogan rolled his eyes. "Not quite, but your wife says she was with child when you left. Now put the damned gun down!"

Jedediah did not appear convinced but slowly lowered the weapon anyway and set it against the wall.

In a heartbeat Brogan was on him, grabbing the front of his shirt in a painful twist. "You and I are going to have a conversation, sonny boy," he told Jedediah as he propelled him through the open door and out into the yard.

Tilda hurried after them and Brogan turned on her. "Go back inside, Tilda, and shut the door. Jedediah and I are going to have a little talk. Go on now, go back in the house."

Tilda reluctantly did as she was told, and once the door was closed, Brogan turned Jedediah around and marched him all the way over to the back of the barn. Dutch, tethered nearby, lifted his head, watching from where he was munching on dried grass.

"What kind of a man walks out on his wife and leaves her all alone way out here for almost a year?" Brogan demanded, his hand gripping the front of Jedediah's shirt again.

The young man looked genuinely afraid, accurately reading the fury in Brogan's eyes. "We had a fight."

"You had a fight! Every married couple has fights. You go somewhere and cool off. You don't abandon your wife."

"She told me to go. She said she never wanted to see me again."

"We all say things we don't mean when we've got up a head of steam. But to leave her way out here alone ... and pregnant."

"Pregnant! Tilda was not pregnant when I left."

Brogan shook his head, his grip tightening. "Of course she was pregnant. How else did she get that way? I've only been here since October and I helped her deliver the baby in November."

Jedediah sneered. "I'll just bet you enjoyed that."

Brogan's eyes burned into his. "You dirty little whelp. Your wife would probably have died if I hadn't come along to help her. She couldn't have birthed that baby all by herself."

"My mother did."

"And that would be you, would it?"

"No, my sister, Lulu."

"Women shouldn't be left to do it alone because a lot can go wrong. You have a duty to see to your wife. To help her through such things, or find someone who can. Women can die in childbirth. So can babies."

Brogan was relieved to see that Jedediah had gone pale. Maybe he'd gotten through to him after all.

"Tilda could have died?"

"Certainly, she could have. Any number of things could have gone awry. She could have bled to death for one thing. Even if everything went well, your wife would have needed you to help her with the baby. Help her get something to eat. Clean up after the birthing. She couldn't have done all of that on her own. You are one stupid little bastard!"

"I am not stupid."

Brogan was still seething. "Well, selfish then and I can't abide either. It makes me sick to look at you." He could well understand Tilda's attraction to another man if this was what she had to live with. "I'm thinking you were doing something you shouldn't have been doing all those months away. Admit it. You were with another woman, weren't you, although I can't imagine who would have you."

Jedediah's face coloured guiltily. "What if I was, that's none of your business."

"I'm making it my business for the sake of that young woman in there who believes she loves you. And you have a child now. You have a responsibility to take care of them both."

"You heard her, she threatened to hit me with a frying pan."

Brogan's anger hadn't even begun to cool. "I should take you in and let her get on with it. It's what you deserve. You were with someone else, weren't you? While your wife was out here in the woods, alone all this time and pregnant. Leaving her to birth the baby on her own. Where's this other woman now?"

"I said it's none of your business!"

Brogan tightened his grip until Jedediah was wincing in pain.

"I did spend the winter with someone I used to know," he said. "I was getting ready to head back a few times and then the weather would turn bad again. I came back as soon as I could in the spring. That should count for something. I lost, Caesar, my best dog. He sickened and died over the winter and I couldn't very well leave him alone."

Brogan let go of Jedediah's shirt and gave him a shove, the young man fetching up against the barn with a jolt. "You'd leave your wife to fend for herself but you stayed with your dog!"

"What was I supposed to do?" he whined.

"What you're supposed to do is take care of your wife. That's what a real man would do, and that's what you're going to do from now on. If you don't, I'm going to come back for you."

"I'll shoot you dead if you do."

"Then you better make that shot count because if I get past it...."

"I'm sorry, all right!" Jedediah yelled. "Leave me alone."

"That's not a problem," Brogan agreed stepping back. "I'll leave you alone as soon as you start doing the right thing."

"And what's that?" he asked, overly concerned with straightening the front of his shirt.

Brogan glared at him. "All right. Seeing as how you're not smart enough to know the answer to that, and you can't be trusted, I'd say move your family back to civilization. That way Tilda will have someone to turn to if you decide to take to your heels again when you two have another fight. And I don't want to hear of you ever laying a hand on her ... ever ... or that baby."

Jedediah was now more contrite. "I would never hurt Tilda, or the baby. You have my word on that."

"You've got a lot of growing up to do, boy. How old are you?"

"I'm twenty next month."

"You're going to have to get over that. You have a wife and now a child. You sure you're going to do the right thing by them? I want your word as the man you might become someday if you try hard enough."

Jedediah kept his head down. "I'm going to do the right thing by them, all right? I promise."

"Good, then you get on in there and start doing it. And if you ever stick a gun in my face again, you'll get more than a dressing down. Understood?"

Jedediah nodded, still defiant. "You're the one the law is looking for, aren't you?"

Brogan took a step closer. "That's right, I am."

Jedediah's false courage evaporated, likely imagining Brogan to be the desperate killer described by the law. Looking even more frightened, he agreed to treat his wife with the utmost respect and be a loving father. Good, let him be scared into doing what he should have been doing all along.

Jedediah Loughty was the type of person most people took an instant dislike to. Brogan knew when the search party came looking for him, the kid would be only too happy to set them on his tail. He would do it in a heartbeat instead of being grateful for what he'd done for his wife and child. That meant there was no time to be lost. He had to leave the cabin at once.

* * *

Brogan said his goodbyes that night, slept in his usual spot in front of the hearth and was gone by daybreak. It had been hardest to leave the baby. Jedediah had sulked when Fern had acted strange with him, holding her arms out for Brogan instead. Maybe any man would, but the child would get used to her father after a while. He doubted he'd ever see Tilda or the baby again. He hoped the young couple would work out their differences.

There was no mistaking the look of love in Tilda's eyes when she gazed at her husband. The air had begun to clear when she finally calmed down and Jedediah apologized for his long absence. For what he had mistakenly assumed was going on between her and Brogan. He'd left them alone to do that, but he could hear from outside the house that proper amends were being made. Good. He didn't feel so bad now to leave Tilda and the baby behind if the family unit had been restored. Now he had to worry about himself.

Tilda had packed him a good lunch of biscuits and jerky and he would have to make it last as long as he could. So far, he'd been very fortunate in his flight from the law, but the chances of coming across another cabin in the wilderness was remote. Especially one as well equipped as the Loughty place was. She had saved his life, but he liked to think he'd pulled his share of the load as well.

He found a deer trail not far from the cabin and followed it for a mile or more. The ground was soft for the most part, still snow-covered in places. He hoped to hide the horse's tracks in the leaf litter. Other than that, he was leaving a trail a blind man could follow. Further along, he came upon a stream and walked that for as long as he could before the footing became too treacherous. The water would still be frigid at this time of year and he had no wish to end up in it. He would have to be careful about a fire. He would only use his gun to shoot game should the opportunity arise. He couldn't do anything to draw attention to himself.

The first night he bedded down in a thicket, using boughs for a bed and spent a reasonably comfortable night were it not for the steady thrum in his leg. He was using those muscles again, riding, and they protested in full revolt. It was a pain he would have to bear though. There were no doctors around to prescribe laudanum. He would just have to grit his teeth and get through it.

As he lay there waiting for sleep, he solidified his plans to start heading toward Moncton, skirting Memramcook. Perhaps there he would blend in with that more populated area. He had no real money with him. He might be able to get a job in order to keep himself until he could afford to hire a lawyer. That was his only chance now. Even that was slim at best. Back home, there would be a pack of bloodthirsty hounds waiting for him, led by none other than

Sheriff Ratchford. He wasn't naïve enough to think they only would be looking for him there, but they might not think he would make it all the way to Moncton or somewhere in the other end of Westmorland County.

On his way early the next morning, he found another brook and walked that, although the stones were larger and could be hard on the horse's feet. When it began to deepen, he climbed the low bank and set off through the forest again. He thought of Maggie as he spied a beautiful patch of yellow trout lilies. He'd also seen plenty of purple violets and trilliums. How she loved wildflowers. There was always a vase of something or other in season on the middle of the table. Even in the fall, she would bring in coloured leaves, and during winter it was a sprig of spruce or fir and pine when she could find it.

He thought about Maggie and Luke alone at Christmas. His wife would make the most of it for the boy. It would have been a lonely time for them, just as it was for him despite having Tilda and baby Fern to keep him company.

Onward Brogan and Dutch travelled until he felt he'd pushed his horse far enough for one day. A sharp wind had come up and the air felt like rain, so he would seek shelter. It was much easier to stay dry than to get dry. To do so would mean having to light a fire, and that would be a dead giveaway to anyone pursuing him. He knew the searchers would come upon Tilda and Jedediah's cabin any day now. He thought again how the young man would delight in turning the tables.

"How about it, boy?" he asked his horse, leaning ahead in the saddle to pat his neck. "You ready to call it a day? I would say that fallen tree over there would make for good shelter."

The horse tossed its head and Brogan smiled. Dutch could communicate with him just as though he was speaking. He was probably the smartest horse he'd ever owned.

When he got to the site, he was pleased to see there were actually two large partially fallen spruce trees together, with enough space under the canopy for both he and his horse. Tonight's shelter was likely compliments of last winter's ice storms. He'd already come across a lot of deadfall. These two would serve them well tonight, so he slid off the horse, uncinched the saddle, pulled it off with the blanket, and made camp for the night.

* * *

Maggie was miserable. It had been a very difficult pregnancy with morning sickness lasting the whole nine months. Well almost, seeing as how she had not given birth yet.

She'd had a relatively easy time carrying Luke, but it was an entirely different experience this time around. By her calculation, she was already two weeks past due. She was nervous about what might lie ahead.

There was a new doctor in Sackville, and Julia had gone for him a few days ago. Doctor Mains had examined her, listened to the fetal heartbeat, and declared both her and the baby healthy. He had left her with instructions to fetch him when her labour started. It couldn't start quickly enough to suit her. She was huge, much bigger than she'd been for Luke, and he'd been a large baby. That, too, had been a difficult birth, so she wondered how on earth she was ever going to safely bear what she had inside of her now.

Luke was a tremendous help, taking care of all the barn chores, fetching wood and water, and helping his mother with meals. She had continued with her teaching as well as she could. Normally school would be out in another month and a half anyway, so she wasn't too concerned about the slow pace she was keeping in the classroom.

"I've got the crockery all laid out, Ma," Luke told her. "And I think the potatoes are almost ready."

"That's wonderful, son. I'll be right there to dip everything up," she told him with a tired smile. If her back hurt any worse she would cry, she was sure of it. "Just maybe get some of that cornbread out and put it on a plate."

Luke was unusually quiet during the meal, and she could tell he was thinking about something. He would chew on it a while longer before he felt ready to share what was bothering him.

"Are you going to die, Ma?" he asked her unexpectedly.

"Die! Why wherever did you get such a notion as that?"

"Pensy Roberts' ma died bearing her."

She reached across and laid her hand on her son's arm. "I don't want you to worry about this. I didn't die having you, did I? Women have babies every day. Now, I wanted to speak to you about something," she said, changing the subject. "When I go into labour, that's what it's called when the baby decides it's time to be born, I have made arrangements for you to go and stay with Uncle Tabor and your cousin Pate for as long as it takes. All right? Once I've had the baby, I'll need you back here to do the barn work."

He nodded solemnly.

"You've been such a big help to me, Luke. I don't know how I would have managed without you. And just think, when you come back home, you will have either a new brother or a sister. Isn't that exciting?"

"Will I have to feed the baby too?"

She smiled. "No, I'll take care of that, and Aunt Julia is going to stay for a while to see to my needs and look after the barn. That means she'll also take care of getting the meals and such while she's here. Having a new baby is a very happy time."

"What will I do now?"

She looked at him, perplexed. "About what?"

"I won't be your little boy anymore. You'll have a new little boy or girl."

She chuckled, taking his hand in hers. "Luke, my son, no matter how old you get, you will always be my little boy and don't you forget it."

He smiled at his mother. "What will Pa say when he comes home and finds another baby here?"

She chuckled despite her discomfort. Luke had a way with words.

"He'll be very surprised, but he'll be pleased. I can promise you that. Now Aunt Julia is coming tomorrow to stay. She'll be here until the baby is born and then stay here afterward like I said."

* * *

Two days later Maggie went into labour. Mild contractions started after the evening meal and lasted through the night into the early morning. As planned, Julia drove Luke down the road to Tabor's farm, then went for the doctor in Sackville. Doctor Mains was an efficient young man, a well-read scholar who enjoyed helping his patients. From a wealthy family and the son of a medical doctor, he had actually attended medical school in Boston and later apprenticed with his father. When Julia got there, however, the doctor was away from his office delivering another baby. By the time he'd finished and arrived at the Kavenagh homestead, Maggie had been in hard labour for more than twelve hours. And then everything stalled. By midday the next day she still had not given birth.

Chapter 15

It was Dutch's whinnying that roused him from a deep sleep, the cold metal against his ear that brought him fully alert. The chase was over. It had just come daylight, and as his eyes fully focused, he was aware of men milling around. Many men.

The gun was still shoved hard against him. "Don't you move a muscle, Kavenagh," came a voice he didn't recognize. "We're going to put irons on you, and if you fight us, I'll shoot. We can take you back dead as well as alive. It's all the same to us. Matter of fact, it'd be much easier with you slung over the saddle, so you choose which it's going to be ... hard or easy."

It would have been a waste of time to fight with this many men, so he decided it would be the easy way as he reluctantly put his hands behind his back. The cold steel was locked in place, biting painfully into his wrists. That accomplished he was hauled unceremoniously to his feet, his leg throbbing, and shoved toward his horse. Someone had already saddled Dutch.

He could see no sign of Sheriff Ratchford. He had to be somewhere about, though, and although he had no wish to make conversation he did wonder what had become of the man.

"You're looking mighty well fed," a tall thin man who seemed to be in charge told him. "Where have you been holed up all winter?"

Brogan looked away. They might be arresting him, but all he had to do was cooperate, he didn't have to make friends with them.

The tall man struck him sharply on the side of the face. "I asked you a question, Kavenagh. If you're wise, you'll answer it. We want to know who's been keeping you."

"Nobody's been keeping me," he lied to protect the Loughtys. "I found a deserted cabin with some food still in the larder."

"That where you dug out the bullet from your leg? Sewed up the hole in your pants?"

Brogan didn't miss a beat. The Loughty's safety depended on it. "That's right. Found all the doins' I needed there and got through the winter. Where's Ratchford?"

The tall man said, "Sheriff Ratchford is in his grave. I am his successor, Sheriff John Vailor."

Deceased! Now that was a revelation! "How did he die?"

Vailor was in his face. "I ask the questions around here, not you."

"Well, Sheriff Vailor" said Brogan, "you're arresting an innocent man. Amby Burk knows who shot Latham Storey, and it wasn't me. His wife knows, too, because she was there and saw the whole thing."

Vailor smiled like a Cheshire cat. "And speaking of wives, Mr. Kavenagh, I must say yours is very beautiful. But not very friendly, at first. I found my way around that."

Brogan's blood ran cold. "You're a dirty liar! So, help me, if you've hurt her...."

Vailor took a step closer. "It will do you no good to threaten me. You are being charged with three murders. We're here to see you don't commit a fourth."

Brogan was breathing heavily, nausea rifling through him. "Three!"

Vailor watched him, clearly enjoying himself. "Have you forgotten so soon? Latham Storey, and the two deputies you left dying in the woods. It's a pity we can only hang you once." He turned to the men standing around. "Someone, get him up on his horse. I want to start back right away."

The ride back was torturous. When they rode into the shiretown, a crowd quickly gathered to watch the outlaw being brought to jail. Brogan refused to hang his head as the people jeered at him and he tried to block out their ugly words. No one appeared to be interested that the accused is presumed to be innocent until proven guilty in a court of law.

A light spring rain began to fall as he was pulled roughly off his horse and marched into the jailhouse. The heavy iron door screeched loudly on its hinges as it was pulled open, the irons removed. He was shoved inside, the cell door clanging shut behind him. He stumbled, falling hard against the wooden bench meant to serve as a bed. The key was turned noisily in the lock before the jailer ambled away.

Never in his life had he felt more dispirited. He feared now for Maggie's life and wondered if he would ever see his beautiful wife again, or Luke. A farce of a trial would be next, and then it would be the gallows for him. He sat down heavily on the rough wooden bench.

* * *

Maggie knew she was in trouble. Something was wrong. She felt the heavy pressure of the baby inside her, but it did not seem to want to be born. She had every confidence in the doctor, though, as he carefully examined her.

"I can see the problem, Mrs. Kavenagh," he said. "I'm afraid this is going to be a breech birth."

Breech birth. She knew the dangers that went with such a delivery. In many instances, the child did not survive. Its lower anatomy couldn't prepare the way for the much larger head which sometimes became wedged in the birth canal, fetched up on the mother's pelvic bone. She'd read about that very thing.

"Does that mean I'm going to lose the baby, doctor?" she asked worriedly.

"It means it might not be easy to get that child born," he said. "From my examination, I can see it's going to be what we call a footling breech birth. That means the baby is coming out feet first, not buttocks first. We have to catch the feet and hopefully guide him out as best we can, hope the cord doesn't get compressed while that's happening. But it can be done. This isn't the first breech birth I've attended. Now you rest for a few minutes. You've been at this for many hours and I don't want you to exhaust yourself."

Ten minutes later, the entire process began again and when she didn't think she could push anymore, the doctor declared: "All right, I have the feet in my hands. It's coming. Keep pushing! More! More!"

And she did just that, suffering through some of the worst pain she had ever felt in her life. She felt as though she was going to shatter into pieces if she bore down any harder. Julia held her hand through the entire ordeal, mopping her brow, and encouraging her.

Moaning loudly and almost completely spent, she finally felt the baby slide from her body. It had been born without complications and she sobbed with relief.

"You have a lovely new son, Mrs. Kavenagh. He appears none the worse for wear having been born feet first. I think he's going to be just fine."

And then the most beautiful sound in the world, the baby's wail, lusty and loud.

It was a few minutes before the birthing process finished and the doctor got the bleeding stopped. He attended to the umbilical cord before the infant was wrapped and placed in her arms.

What are you going to call this son of yours?" the doctor asked cheerfully.

"Jake," answered Maggie through tears. "Jake Roderick after his father. Roderick is my husband's middle name."

* * *

Amby Burk strode into his house wearing a satisfied smile. "As you can see, we got him," he announced to his wife who was boiling water to make a pot of coffee. "Take that sour look off your face, Brogan Kavenagh had it coming for what he did. Besides, it's just a Kavenagh. It's not like they're worth anything. People around here will be happy there's one less of them to worry about, and that Brogan is the worst of the bunch."

Josephine was shaking like a leaf. "And I imagine there'll still be a trial."

He looked at her as though she'd lost her senses. "Why wouldn't there be? That would have happened months ago if he hadn't run off like he did. And now they're charging him with three murders, so he'll swing for sure. I won't lose any sleep over that."

She sat down, her legs unsteady. "What I mean is we may not have to testify now. I don't see why we should have to anyway."

"What is in your head, you fool woman? What makes you think we won't have to give our testimony in court? Nothing has changed. They got him, and now we do what we have to do to sew things up. I've waited a long time for this."

Josephine was on the verge of tears. "What I mean to say, Amby, is if they try him for the murder of say one of the deputies, they don't have to try him for anything else. They can only execute a man once. So, if they convict him on one charge of murder, why bother with the others?"

"Uncle Latham was the first, so that's the one they'll go with. The trial will be for *his* death." He looked at the steam flying out of the kettle atop the cast iron stove. "The water's boiling. Get up and make the coffee and stop bothering me with questions. I swear! You get more addle-brained every day."

In minutes, the coffee was made, and she set out the cups, sugar, and cream, just the way Amby liked it. Truth be told, though, she didn't care anymore whether that was the way he liked it or not. The most important thing was to not have to listen to the hullaballoo he would make if it wasn't.

"And how about some of that cornbread? I'll take a piece or two of that with a little butter. It was a long ride back and I'm hungry, but that should hold me until suppertime."

Josephine stared at him nervously, almost wringing her hands.

"What's wrong with you? Go get the cornbread."

"I'm afraid there isn't any cornbread left, Amby. The children finished the last of it with their noontime meal."

He rolled his eyes impatiently. "What else do we have?"

"I made some nice fresh biscuits this morning. How about some of them with butter and strawberry preserves?"

He considered her suggestion for a moment before nodding his approval. "All right, bring those. Then I'd like you to get busy making another pan of cornbread for supper. Go on," he declared when she hesitated, "and stop standing around looking terrified. I'm not going to bite you."

"I have something to tell you."

He threw up his hands with a sigh. "And what might that be?"

Her hands shook. "I've been doing a lot of thinking over the past few weeks, and I don't think I can testi...."

He moved so quickly that she shrieked in alarm. "If you're going to say what I think you're going to say, don't bother," he said, his face inches from hers. "You better remember what I warned you would happen. Just settle yourself down for once and stop flitting around like a moth scared to death of the light. And keep your mouth shut, very tight. Do you understand me? If you don't, I can explain it to you in another way."

She tried to back up but he caught hold of her.

"Do you understand me, Josephine?"

"Yes, I understand," she answered him, scared nearly senseless by the look in her husband's eyes. He released her and she stepped away.

She thought again about when she'd first met Ambrose Burk. He was so good looking and she liked the way he took charge of situations ... people. Before long, she realized he'd taken charge of her, and the blush had gradually faded from the rose. He didn't ask her to marry him, rather, he'd said she *should* marry him, and she didn't feel strong enough to refuse. 'Everything will be different once we're married and I can show him what a good wife I am,' she'd foolishly told herself. However, nothing changed at all and Amby was now in control of her life from one end of it to the other. As the children kept coming, she knew she was tied to this man for the rest of her life.

She hurried into the pantry to start the cornbread.

* * *

Word soon reached the outlying rural communities that Brogan had been captured. Tabor brought the unsettling news to Maggie at the homestead. Julia met him in the kitchen.

"Tabor," she said, suddenly ill at ease. "Is everything all right? I feel you have something troubling to tell us."

If he looked happy to see her, he hid it well. "I have news for Maggie," he said. "Is the boy around?"

"Luke's out in the barn milking the cow and collecting eggs."

"Good. I've come to tell you they've captured Brogan. They've got him in jail up at the shiretown."

Julia's hand flew to her mouth. "We had so feared he was dead."

"Well, he's not dead. He's very much alive but I don't hold out much hope for his life," he said, providing her with whatever details he'd been given. "You can tell Maggie the news," he finished before turning on his heel to leave.

"Tabor," Julia said reaching to take hold of his arm. "Have you not got a moment to spare? I want to talk to you. I miss you."

He faced her again, his jaw set. "Then you shouldn't have left. Women who run once will run again. Good day."

"Tabor...."

"That's all I have to say."

Anger flared to life inside her. "You listen to me, Tabor Kavenagh! It was you who drove me away."

His eyes were flat. "Then stay away if I'm such a villain. I can't think of anything else to tell you. I say again, good day," and with that, he left.

She was good and angry now, following him out into the yard. "Tabor Kavenagh, stop behaving like a child. I love you, and I'm asking you here and now if you love me. I think we can resolve our differences, but you have to meet me halfway."

He stopped, his back to his estranged wife. "I would say this is about half way to where you live now, give or take a few yards. If you want to come the rest of the way back to the farm, then do so. Suit yourself, but if you do, don't you ever go running off again."

She moved to step in front of him, then leaned in to kiss him. It was like kissing cool granite. Then miracles of all miracles, he put his arms around her and kissed her properly right there in the yard. "Come back, Julia," he told her moments later, still holding her. "I will try harder. I'm sorry."

"And so am I, Tabor. I'm here with Maggie during her lying in, and then I'll do that. Return to the farm I mean. Now I must get back inside," she said, kissing him quickly again. "I have to tell her about Brogan."

Her step was lighter as she hurried back into the house, but went heavy again as she reached the bedroom. The newborn was asleep in his cradle in the corner of the room. Maggie was sound asleep. Dare she wake her? She finally decided she must do so. If it were her man she would want to be told immediately.

She shook Maggie's shoulder gently, and when the younger woman's eyes fluttered open, she sat down on the edge of the bed.

"Maggie," she said smoothing the hair back from her sister-in-law's brow, "they've arrested Brogan. He's in jail up at the shiretown. I know you feared he was dead but he is very much alive and as well as can be expected under the circumstances. Tabor was here with the news just minutes ago. I understand he was brought in yesterday afternoon."

Maggie began to weep, great gulping sobs. "Brogan is alive," she kept repeating aloud as though trying to convince herself it was indeed true.

Julia stroked Maggie's hair to soothe her. "Try to stay calm, dear. You've just been through the ordeal of childbirth. You must not strain yourself. I will tell you that Luke does not know. I came directly to you with the news. I assume you want to keep it from the child until matters can be sorted out."

Maggie nodded as she threw back the covers. "That's right. I don't think it would be wise to tell him just yet. Now, I must go to Brogan at once. Help me up, please."

"Maggie! You can't travel anywhere. You'll bleed to death. You hemorrhaged after the birth, and the doctor had a difficult time getting it under control. You must stay in bed."

Maggie swung her legs onto the floor. "I'm going to him, Julia. It may be the last time I ever see my husband again if the law has its way. I also need to find a lawyer."

"Maggie, be rational, please. You can't travel by wagon all the way to the shiretown. It's many miles and the roads are in their usual terrible condition. You would not survive it. I beg of you to lie back down. What use will it be to kill yourself getting there? I know you love Brogan and are desperate to see him, but you have two children to care for now. You can't rob them of both father and mother. That's what you have to think about, dear. I'm so sorry, but I cannot allow you to do this. You wouldn't get a mile before you started hemorrhaging again."

"I'm tired is all, and the bleeding has stopped."

"For the moment! The doctor himself said you were to lie quiet. Women who've just had babies have to do their proper lying in to allow their body to heal. And you had a particularly strenuous delivery. It is only by divine dispensation that you and the baby survived. And even foregoing all of that, you're nursing Jake. I will go to the shiretown and take your message, and find a lawyer for Brogan. Please. Maggie, listen to me. To try to do this would be utter suicide. I know how much you love him, but like any mother, you love your children more. You have to do what's right for them."

Maggie sagged back against the pillow, as pale as a ghost. "I want to see him so badly. I'm not thinking clearly. I have missed him unbearably these past months. I hardly dared believe he'd survived and to be told he's still alive and that I can't go to him is almost unendurable. The suffering I just went through to bring our darling Jake into the world is nothing compared to how badly my heart is hurting now."

"And I have no doubt he has a sore heart as well for you, and his son. Now I will get the materials for you to write a letter, and I will take it to him."

After careful consideration, Maggie still thought it was best not to tell Luke that his father had been taken prisoner. Naturally, he would want to see him. Maggie did not want her son's last image of his father to be him languishing in a jail cell. She had no idea what he would look like after living in the wild for months. Withstanding a harsh winter. Somehow surviving a gunshot wound. His appearance might frighten the young boy and leave him with a terrible memory.

* * *

It was arranged that Tabor would travel with Julia to the shiretown to visit with Brogan. Adelia Powell, a neighbour girl, would come and stay with Maggie and the children while Julia was away.

It was a pleasant day as they set off in Julia's buggy. The main road was now completely dried up from the deep muddy ruts of early spring, but still unfit for smooth travelling. Not surprisingly, it was a quiet ride, both Tabor and Julia deep in thought about what lay ahead for Brogan.

When they finally arrived, jarred to the bone and dusty, Tabor went in to see his brother. He agreed with Julia that it would be better if she explained about Maggie and the baby.

When Tabor came back to the buggy an hour later, he looked drawn and sat quietly while Julia took her turn.

She felt a pall settle over her as she was taken to the cell where Brogan was being held prisoner. What a dreadful place. It was half-decently kept, as much as a place such as this could be she imagined, but it reeked of bad times and desperation. She thought he might be thin, being on the run these past months, but he looked remarkably fit in that regard. His hair was longer and somewhat bedraggled though and he had a full beard, now unkempt. A trickle of blood had dried from a cut on his cheek. She had to admit he did look fearsome. His eyes were those of a hunted man. It had been a wise decision to spare Luke the trauma of seeing his father like this.

"Did Maggie not want to come?" he asked, disappointed as he looked past her through the bars. "I asked Tabor about her, but he said you would talk to me about it. What has happened to her? That new sheriff, Vailor, said some things about her...."

"The new sheriff is as bad as the old sheriff, only in a different way. He did pay your wife a visit and let's just say Maggie handled herself well. He didn't hurt her, not like you might think, but she hurt him and he left on the limp. That's when he told her you were presumed dead. That almost took the ground out from under her, but you know Maggie. She stiffened her spine and carried on."

"So, is she all right? I mean other than the run-in with the sheriff? Why didn't she come?"

"Maggie wanted to be here, but it was not possible for her to make the trip," Julia explained quietly. "You see, Brogan, Maggie was with child when you left. She wasn't sure enough to tell you yet, but it turned out she was. She had the baby only two days ago. It was a very physically demanding birth, but both she and the child survived. You now have another son, a fine strong lad, whom she named Jake Roderick."

Tears sprang to his eyes. "I have another son?"

Julia smiled through tears. "Yes, a son, and he's dark-haired, too, like Luke. It will take Maggie some time to get back her strength as well as the blood she lost. The doctor says she'll make a full recovery."

Brogan ran a hand wearily over his face. "I can't hardly take it all in. And what of Luke? Is he well?"

"Luke is growing like a weed and has been such a help to his mother since you've been away. You would be so proud of him."

"I kept thinking the whole time how hard the other children would be on him at school, with everything that's taken place."

Julia held his gaze. "I will not lie to you, Brogan. Luke has had a very hard time at school. Maggie teaches him at home now, so your son is safe with her and no longer the victim of bullies."

"Maggie has kept everything together this whole time. Did she have a message for me by any chance?"

Julia smiled. "Better than that." She pulled the letter from her reticule. "She wrote you this," she said passing it to him. "She wanted to come so badly, fought to do so in fact, but she would never have survived the trip after having just given birth. I have no doubt if I hadn't tried to physically restrain her and spoke some common sense to her, she would have been in the wagon trying to get here. That woman loves you desperately, has been through hell with the wanting of you."

Brogan sighed, swiping at his eyes with the back of his hand. "And I love that woman more than I love my own life."

"I suppose they wasted no time ordering you to stand trial."

"That's right. They'll go through the motions of a trial, but they already have their minds made up. Amby Burk and that lying wife of his will say they saw me shoot Latham Storey. And now I've had charges laid against me for those two deputies. I never shot them, Julia. I haven't shot anyone."

"Have they set the date for the trial?"

"Two weeks from tomorrow. I have a lawyer, Lemuel Hildebrand, from here in Dorchester. He's agreed to represent me but has already said the Crown has an airtight case in those two eyewitnesses for the Storey murder. It's what they call an open-and-shut case, and will be very easily decided. But even if I did manage to beat that one, there are still the other two."

"But surely, you'll have an opportunity to speak in court. You express yourself well, Brogan. It should convince the jury of your innocence on all three charges."

He swung away from the bars, agitated as he paced back and forth in the confined space. "Where do you think they'll find twelve impartial jurors? Twelve people who don't look down on the Kavenaghs? Twelve people who don't already believe I'm guilty before they ever parade me into that courtroom. Even the food they're feeding me isn't fit for a dog. You're looking at a dead man."

"I'm going to speak to your lawyer, today, Brogan. I will tell him I'll be a character witness for you and so will Tabor and Pate. I'll find more people. Peterson Gault for one. We will tell that jury what a hardworking man you are — a good father and husband. We will all be there for you."

"Julia, I'm not optimistic about the lawyer. I just don't see him being all that effective, but he's the only one who would take my case. So, I'm going to tell you the same thing I told Tabor. Go home and start forgetting about me."

"Oh, Brogan! No!"

He continued as though she hadn't spoken. "And take this message to Maggie. Tell her I couldn't love her more, but she is not to come here ... especially with her still recovering from childbirth. Those rough roads would be too much for her." He turned away, and it took a moment or two before he continued, "and hug Luke, and tell him it's from me. And that I love him too, and to be brave and strong, and to always be there for his mother. And when Jake is old enough, tell him about me. I never got to meet him, but make sure he knows he was always in my heart. Now go, Julia. Thank you for coming, but I want to be alone."

"Brogan, please...."

"Go, Julia, and don't look back."

Julia and Tabor found the office of Lemuel J. Hildebrand, barrister and solicitor, and fortunately he was available to speak with them. They made their intentions known, but left disheartened after the brief meeting. If Brogan's life was in his hands of this inexperienced young man, both agreed he was doomed. Still, they would be present in court and ready to do their best.

Julia had never felt more forlorn in her life as she and Tabor slowly made their way to the buggy for the sad trip back to the homestead.

Chapter 16

Josephine had been under such strain these past months, it was little wonder she fell ill. She felt worn out and would actually welcome death rather than go through with getting up on that stand and committing perjury. She was simply too weak at the moment anyway. She just couldn't do it. But she was wise enough not to bring the matter up to Amby again. She knew he would make good on his threats. Besides, he was well aware she also held his own fate in her hands. And speaking of hands, she thought deliriously, she would not have Brogan Kavenagh's blood on hers if she was unable to testify. They might not be able to convict him. She now realized that coming down with a fever was nothing short of divine intervention. She had been spared from condemning an innocent man to death. Still, there was that damning statement....

Doctor Seeby diagnosed her with pneumonia and by that afternoon her fever had risen dramatically. Nellie, her eldest daughter, looked after her mother while Amby fretted about her being well enough in two days to attend court. It certainly didn't seem likely with her being so sick. He roundly cursed her in any creative way that came to mind.

* * *

Court day arrived and would proceed as scheduled. Both sides agreed that because Mrs. Burk was seriously ill her written statement, taken under oath, would be deemed sufficient in her absence.

And so with all and sundry in their places, scrubbed and neatly folded, the trial began. Brogan was paraded into the courtroom to the prisoner's bench in shackles. He was still unshaven and now unclean, having been left to fend for himself in the dingy jail cell. The spectators, every available seat filled, gawked at him from the public gallery.

The lawyer for the Crown put on a fine show in his starched winged collar and tabs, black gown, and overlong sideburns. His first witness was, of course, Amby Burk, and the court indulged his long-winded spiel about the vicious, cold-blooded murder perpetrated upon his dear unsuspecting uncle.

"I've had trouble sleeping ever since," he told the court, his voice shaking with emotion.

'If he had trouble sleeping,' thought Brogan, 'it should be because he'd placed his hand on the Holy Bible and told a downright lie.'

Amby's performance finally came to an end, the jurors appearing to hang on every word.

Brogan was pleasantly surprised at the change in his own lawyer and realized he may have misjudged the young man. Lemuel Hildebrand appeared very self-assured when he cross-examined Amby. However, Burk, like any practiced liar, had told the story so often that he now believed it himself. Hildebrand was not able to shake him.

Mrs. Burk's eyewitness account was then read aloud, and you could hear a pin drop in the courtroom. The defense lawyer might have been able to successfully challenge her account of that afternoon if she'd been present. Brogan was not pleased that opportunity had been allowed to slip away. Hildebrand should never have agreed to rely solely on her sworn statement, although legally it carried the same weight. He still didn't like it though.

When the prosecution moved on to the shooting of the two deputies, counsel for the prosecution produced notes made by the late Sheriff Ratchford. The late sheriff's accounts indicated that Brogan had gunned down his men while they were carrying out their lawful duties.

It was all Brogan could do to sit there quietly and listen to what was being said, none of it true.

Then it came time for the defense to present its case. The suitably robed Hildebrand called Doctor Seeby to the stand and first had him qualified as an expert witness. Doctor Seeby subsequently confirmed he had not only performed autopsies on the two deputies, but also on Ezekiel Loughty, the owner of the camp where Brogan had spent the night.

"In my expert opinion it was not Brogan Kavenagh who killed the two deputies," said Doctor Seeby in his low-pitched, calm voice. "I say that because both men were killed with a shotgun. I saw the pellets in the bodies. I understand Brogan Kavenagh was carrying a pistol. That was not the weapon used to shoot those two men. There were no pistol bullets in either of them. The likely shooter was the owner of the camp, Ezekiel Loughty. He himself died during that gunfight and was found with a shotgun in his hands. Sheriff Ratchford told me so himself, and also verified that he himself had killed the old man in self-defense."

The Crown objected, citing first speculation and secondly, hearsay, but the Magistrate overruled him.

Doctor Seeby's testimony was held up under cross-examination.

And then it was Brogan's turn, and Hildebrand walked him through that fateful

September day in great detail. On the stand for nearly two hours, which included a rough cross-examination, he felt he'd comported himself quite well. At least, he'd had an opportunity to tell his side of the story.

As the day wore on Hildebrand called one character witness after another to the stand on Brogan's behalf. However, when Brogan dared to glance in the direction of the jury again, he was met with scowls. Their hostility toward him was glaringly apparent. He was glad he had spared Maggie this demoralizing spectacle.

In his summation, the Crown painted Brogan as a vicious killer, one who must be punished for his crimes against society. Lemuel Hildebrand, far and away, outdid the prosecutor with an impassioned plea for his client's acquittal. He accurately called Amby's account absolute nonsense and questioned whether Mrs. Burk's statement had been given under duress. He reminded the jurors there was still reasonable doubt as to Brogan's guilt, and therefore they could not convict him. When both lawyers had finished speaking, the magistrate provided the appropriate instructions to the jury to help them reach a verdict.

And then it was over. The jurors filed from the courtroom to begin deliberation, and Brogan was returned to the jailhouse.

The wait for the verdicts seemed interminable when, in fact, it was less than an hour before he was walked back down the narrow corridor from his cell and over to the courthouse. The jury foreman passed the envelope containing their decisions to the magistrate. After reading them himself first, he addressed the court.

Brogan was relieved to be found innocent of the deaths of Deputy Edward Cassidy and Deputy Homer Whitlong, but guilty as charged for the death of Latham Storey as well as the assault of Ambrose Burk.

The magistrate told the prisoner to rise while he imposed sentence, and he did so.

"Brogan Kavenagh, in addition to the charge of assault against Ambrose Burk, you have also been found guilty of the murder of Latham Storey. The sentence of this court is that on the morning of May twenty-seventh you will be taken to the place of execution and there hanged by the neck until you are dead. May God have mercy on your soul."

Brogan felt ice-cold, but none of this was a surprise. He kept his face expressionless as he, now a condemned murderer, was led from the courtroom. He refused to make eye contact with anyone, not even his family. He left with his head held high and walked with purpose back to his cell. He would not shuffle in despair or give any other outward sign that would suggest they had broken him. And it would be the same when they put that dreaded rope around his neck. He would stand tall and proud. They might kill him, but they would not defeat him.

Once it was made known there were no further funds available through the family to seek an appeal in the newly minted New Brunswick Court of Appeal, work got underway on the gallows. Construction began a few hours after the trial had finished. He could hear a bird singing outside the window of his cell, not put off, it seemed, by the constant ringing of the hammers. The magistrate had said May twenty-seventh, and today was the twenty-fifth. That meant he had less than two days left to walk this earth. More to the point, he would sit in this stinking cell and wait for his time to run out.

He would have thought there would be a permanent gallows for those who were sentenced to hang. It would certainly be more practical. But maybe that was all part of the punishment. A man having to endure the agony of hearing the gallows being built, a constant reminder of what was to follow.

He had known this would be his fate since that awful September afternoon. Had known this moment would come eventually. Running for his life had only delayed the inevitable. So here he sat, his final hours dwindling away. He reached into his pocket and pulled out Maggie's letter. He had saved it, knowing when he would need her comfort the most. It wouldn't be the same as the sound of her voice, but it would be the next best thing.

He willed the tremble from his hand as he unfolded that one precious page and recognized her neat cursive scroll. There were only a few lines, but there didn't need to be more. Maggie was a woman of few words. She had always shown him the depth of her love.

"Kavenagh, you've got a visitor," the jailer, a surly man well-chosen for the job, called out to him.

He refolded the letter and slid it back into his shirt pocket as he went to the front of the cell and waited.

"Hello, Uncle Brogan. They got you locked up good and tight haven't they," said Pate, scowling at the jailer who glared back at him before leaving them alone.

"Yeah, they sure have," he told his nephew. "They got me good this time."

Pate looked around him, up and down, as though inspecting the strength of the jail. Made solidly of brick and stone with an iron-box like holding area, it was well designed for its purpose.

"I think I could get you out of here," he told Brogan in undertones. "It wouldn't be easy but I could do it."

Brogan shook his head. "No, Pate. It's not going to happen. That jailer out there would just love to hear you say something like that, then you'd be in here, too. No, our family has suffered enough. There's no way around this that I can see. I've got two people lying against me and a whole bunch of other people who believe them."

Pate was near tears. "They're going to hang you, Uncle Brogan! We've got to do something to save you. We can't let them do it!"

"It's already been done," Brogan explained. "There's nothing we can do about it. I didn't have any witnesses to help me in September. Besides, with the way most people feel about the Kavenaghs, they were only too happy to jump on the bandwagon and convict me. One less Kavenagh will be no hardship for them."

"But how can they hang an innocent man?"

"They do it all the time, Pate. It's just a bunch of men saying something is so, and then other more important men taking it for gospel truth because it was sworn to with hand upon the Good Book. And all these nice iron bars you see around me, are here to protect those same good people of the town from me, a killer. It's what they believe. It doesn't take much for people to become hysterical. It just takes one crazy man to get things started and then it picks up speed from there."

Pate looked ready for a fight. "It's that Amby Burk who done all this! I should go and have a word with him. Find out where he's hiding, which hole, and dig him out."

Brogan shook his head again. "It doesn't work like that. See, you and I know he's a worm, but he's got everyone convinced he's the injured party. He shot his own uncle in the back. What man does that!"

Pate folded his arms. "Yeah, he does that and you're the one in jail. I hate the people who done this to you. I hate every one of them."

"You know, Pate. You can't let that hate build up inside you. If you do, you'll be no better than they are."

"Looking back, Garrett was the smart one to get out of here. As long as we live around here there's always going to be someone after us. You know that as well as I do. We should have fought back more."

"You think we didn't fight everything they were doing to us? Everything they said about us? It all started in the schoolyard, and it just kept on from there. Those children who said things that weren't true about us are all grown up now, and still singing the same old tune. Maybe it makes them feel better about themselves, I don't know."

"None of it is fair."

"No, it isn't. Maybe it will die out someday, who knows?"

"It just might, but not in time to save you, Uncle Brogan. So, they hang you, and then what? Come after the next one? And when we fight back, they'll hang us too. It makes me hopping mad."

"I can see that, but I'm telling you it's not going to do any good. Remember, we've also got friends in these parts. Not everyone is against us.”

Pate threw up his hands in frustration. “Other than your character witnesses today, it doesn’t seem much like it.”

“No, it doesn’t.”

Brogan sighed. This conversation could go on all night. As good as it was to have his nephew with him, he knew he had to get him out of there. The boy was getting up a head of steam. He would get himself in trouble if he wasn’t careful. That Sheriff Vailor would love to get his hands on another Kavenagh. Clean up the county as he put it. He couldn’t let Pate play into his hands.

“Pate, I thank you for coming to see me, but I want you to go back home. *Now*, before you get yourself in trouble. I know you’re mad about all of this. Lord knows there’s plenty to be mad about, but it’s not going to help any to have them arrest you for getting into something trying to save me. You can’t. It’s too late for that. So, if you want to make me feel better, start on the road toward home. If you get yourself locked up, it’s going to make me feel worse, not better.”

Pate was not easy to convince, well-armed with a good helping of Kavenagh temper. He finally raised his eyes to meet his uncle’s. “All right,” he said at length. “I’ll leave. But that means this’ll be the last time I ever see you.” Tears filled his eyes. “Where are they going to bury you?”

"Someone will likely have to come and get my body." He didn't bother to tell him murderers were not permitted to be buried in consecrated ground. "You'll find somewhere to bury me. Now go. Look after those horses of yours. You're well on your way to raising some of the best in these parts."

Pate sniffed noisily. "I've got a mare getting ready to foal. I want you to name the baby."

Brogan thought for a moment. "Call it Freedom."

"Freedom?"

"That's right. It's the best, most precious word I can think of."

Pate reached through the bars and grasped Brogan's hands. The strength with which he squeezed them showed how much he loved the man. And then he was gone.

The light of late afternoon had faded sufficiently to prevent letter reading, and so Brogan contented himself by simply holding it.

Sleep was out of the question as he either paced the small cell or lay on the hard bench. A prisoner having to sleep on that makeshift bed was punishment enough. It wasn't deemed necessary, apparently, to show any form of human kindness.

It rained hard all the next day, which meant the workers got wet finishing the job. Too bad. By nightfall, he was relieved that another torturous day was at an end.

The sun made a brief appearance the next morning before being swallowed up by mauve grey clouds lying in wait just above the horizon. So, the day he died was to be overcast, and well, maybe that was fitting. Sunny days were usually good days, so he didn't want to waste a sunny day on an execution. His execution. No matter how many times he told himself his life would end in mere hours, his brain refused to accept it. What would it feel like when they placed the rope around his neck? Released the trap door? And would the Almighty be waiting for him on the other side? That thought soothed him somewhat, because *He* would know he had not done the terrible deed he'd been accused of. That thought was followed by what Amby Burk could expect when *his* time came. He smiled. He didn't figure his enemy would fare too well for what he'd manifested in this life.

There was no hammering now. He assumed all was in readiness. Minutes later his breakfast arrived, but he turned it away. The truth was it made his stomach lurch just to look at it, let alone eat it. Besides, who could possibly be hungry at a time like this?

He'd decided to save Maggie's letter for the day of his execution, to find at least some measure of peace in what she'd written. There wasn't much light in the tiny cell, even during daylight hours, so he stood with it held up to the window.

"My Dearest Brogan: I knew we were meant to be together the first time I laid eyes on you, and I have never stopped loving you since then. And I never will. My heart is breaking as I write this to you, but I know you will be strong. As much as it hurts me to say this, I fear you will not come out of this alive. But I know you will go to your death a brave man, just as I must be brave to carry on without you. Know that I will take good care of your sons. I will keep your memory alive. Remember this, my beloved Brogan, we will be together again someday. Until then, you will always be in my heart. Your loving, devoted wife, Maggie."

The tears did come then, dripping onto the cold stone floor.

He heard the footsteps growing closer, a solemn pace. Folding the letter, he put it in his shirt pocket. Maggie would be with him to the end.

The jailer opened the door, the sheriff quickly fastening Brogan's hands behind his back. The clergyman, eyes downcast, quietly invited the prisoner's confession. Brogan ignored him as the party began the long walk to the gallows. He purposely looked at those who had gathered on this cloudy day to witness the hanging. He had never understood the mindset of someone who would, of their own free will, attend such a thing. Watch a man lose his life. What type of person would find such a gruesome act entertaining, and yet they were here in numbers.

He looked into their eyes as they walked him from the jailhouse. Many looked away, others stared back, defying him. Their expression clearly said a deadly killer was receiving the punishment he deserved. Some were even laughing, smiling, enjoying the suffering of another. Even if he were to be spared this very moment, how could he not lose faith in mankind. And then he searched his own soul as he imagined others did in similar circumstances. Had he always been the best kind of man? The answer slapped him in the face. No, he hadn't, but he had never purposely harmed another. His conscience was clear.

One thing he understood as he held the gaze of those who at least had the backbone to look back. He saw no pity. He had been convicted by popular opinion back in September. This was simply bringing the matter to a close. But something else occurred to him. He had seen something akin to compassion in the eyes of the magistrate during the trial. A man couldn't mistake that, but the jury had spoken.

And now they were at the bottom of the steps and he shook off the clergyman's hand to guide him up the thirteen steps to the platform. What was the worst thing that could happen to him? Stumble and scrape a knee? Sprain an ankle? They were going to kill him. What else mattered?

A crow was cawing loudly in a nearby tree, a child giggled, and a man coughed. All these sounds burned into his mind, every sound sharp and clear in a brain catapulting through space trying to make sense of his own mortality.

* * *

Josephine's fever broke in the night, and although she was weak, she knew she would pull through. She'd listened to the building of the gallows, who could avoid it? Each blow of the hammers penetrated deep into her soul. She could see the look of disbelief on Brogan Kavenagh's face that day in the woodlot. It haunted her. He'd been as shocked as she was at the killing of Latham Storey. That same incredulity was also there when she'd told a lie that would bring them to this point in their lives. The look in her husband's eyes had been much worse, maniacal.

She crept out of bed, pulling on her dressing gown and slipping her feet into the slippers Nellie had so lovingly placed by her bedside. Her children adored her, and she loved them back just as passionately. Yet, she thought, just to keep food on the table, she was letting them be brought up by a man such as Amby. A cold distant man who struck out at them for the slightest infraction. She

317

was weak-willed, she knew that about herself and perhaps would never change, but that's what she was teaching her children. Her daughters *and* her sons. They might also be afraid to stand up for themselves thanks to her pitiful example as a mother.

Once she was on her feet, she felt stronger than expected and made her way to the window. "Oh, dear God!" she exclaimed aloud.

Brogan Kavenagh was standing on the platform, and Amby was out there somewhere in the crowd. He'd bragged that he planned to be good and close to watch. This was a moment he'd been waiting for, and he would not be denied his prize.

Was it too late to save Brogan? She knew in that moment she had to try or face eternal damnation. She would be no better than a murderer herself. There was no time to get dressed, so descending the stairs as quickly as her weakened condition allowed, she grabbed her woolen cloak from the hook beside the door, stepped out of her slippers into shoes and opened the door. The magistrate's office was closer than the gallows, but would she make it in time?

* * *

Brogan stood tall and straight just as he'd planned. He saw the black hood in the hands of the executioner, himself similarly attired. The hemp rope was rough against his throat and fitted into place under his beard. The hood was pulled over his head. Everything went black. An appropriate colour so that his tired brain mocked him. It reeked of sweat and fear. Death. The macabre garment was evidently not worthy of being laundered.

* * *

The magistrate looked up in surprise when Josephine burst into his office nearly in hysterics.

"They're hanging an innocent man," she cried out breathlessly, all but collapsing into the tufted leather chair in front of his desk. "It was my husband who shot and killed his uncle. He blamed it on Brogan Kavenagh because he had a grudge against him. It was all a set up to frame Mr. Kavenagh. He threatened me that if I didn't lie and say I had seen Brogan do it, he would harm me ... or the children. Please, you've got to stop the hanging. Hurry before it's too late. It's Ambrose Burk who is guilty of slaying Latham Storey, *not* Brogan Kavenagh. And he only hit Amby to save himself."

* * *

And then Brogan was being asked if there was anything he had to say. He did, but

319

why play around and continue the torment? "Get on with it."

"Very well then."

"Stop!" shouted the magistrate, a portly man not given to mad dashes, but that's what this situation demanded. Josephine trailed along unsteadily behind him. "Take the rope from around that man's neck this instant! Remove that hood!"

The rope was removed and then the hood, everyone gaping at the magistrate as though he'd lost his mind.

The magistrate struggled to catch his breath. "New evidence has just come forth that...."

Amby suddenly burst from the crowd, heading straight for Josephine. "You stupid cow! We had him!"

Josephine was also working to catch her breath, clutching her shawl tightly. She faced her husband. She was trembling from head to toe, but her voice could be heard clear as a bell amid the shocked silence of the crowd. "You shot your uncle, Amby, and you know you did. Not Mr. Kavenagh. I was there. I saw you do it. You shot him in the back and then you had me lie so they'd arrest Brogan. So that this," she said pointing to the gallows, "would happen. You had a plan all along to frame him for the murder that you committed."

Amby could barely contain his rage. "My brother died because of him. He deserved ... *this*," he shouted, gesturing wildly at the gallows. "We had him," he shouted at her again, his face a menacing shade of scarlet, "and you ruined everything! Yes, I killed my uncle, and I ought to kill you too, with my bare hands. A bullet in the back would be too good for you."

The magistrate turned to the sheriff, Vailor oddly silent in the face of this stunning turn of events. "Unbind Mr. Kavenagh's hands," he told him, and then to Brogan: "Mr. Kavenagh, you are free to go."

Now it was Brogan's turn to gape. He stood transfixed, watching as Amby Burk was still trying to get past the magistrate to seize his wife.

"Sheriff!" shouted the magistrate, "arrest Mr. Burk here for the murder of his uncle, Latham Storey, and jail him immediately!"

Amby was apoplectic, struggling with the sheriff all the way to the jailhouse, the jailer stepping in to help subdue him.

"Josephine! You betrayed me!" he screamed. "I'll kill you too!"

The magistrate helped Josephine to her door, her energy now spent.

"Mrs. Burk, you know you broke the law by giving a false statement under oath and there will be consequences."

She nodded slowly. "I realize that, but I will face it. I'm not afraid anymore."

"The court will take into consideration the extenuating circumstances. Your husband will stand trial, and it will be your testimony that will convict him. You also realize that. Are you prepared to do so?"

"I am," she said, her voice barely a whisper.

"Go in and rest, Mrs. Burk," he told her. "You have a difficult time ahead."

She thanked him as she let herself into the kitchen. She was badly shaken but felt as though the weight of an ox had been lifted from her shoulders.

* * *

It was a long ride home, but Dutch was full of spit and vinegar and Brogan let him have his head until the big horse slowed to a more reasonable pace. It seemed the gelding was in as much of a hurry to get to the homestead as he was. The events of the day were still reverberating through Brogan's brain at top speed. Not more than two hours ago he'd been seconds away from a gruesome death, and then suddenly he was free. Gloriously free.

He drank in lungfuls of sweet fresh air. The trees were now in full leaf and the sun had managed to break through as if in salute to this most remarkable turn of events. If anyone ever asked him what the meaning of utopia was, he'd say it was this: the wind in his hair, the sun on his face, and the sound of Dutch's hooves pounding their way back home.

It was mid-afternoon when he and Dutch walked into the yard. He tied the horse at the rail by the old apple tree and ran for the house.

Julia screamed when she saw him walk in. She looked as though she was seeing a ghost. Maybe she believed that's what he was, but she recovered quickly. "Oh, my lord, Brogan. I'm not even going to ask how, just go to Maggie. She's in the bedroom. She thinks you were hanged. We all did."

Maggie was weeping quietly, a soggy handkerchief pressed to her face when Brogan walked in and sat down on the edge of the bed.

She looked up, thinking it was Julia. She'd heard the scream but assumed it was the same spider that had frightened her sister-in-law yesterday.

"It's me, sweetheart," he said, his tears matching hers as he cupped her face gently.

She shrieked and flew into his arms.

"It's all over and I have been declared innocent," he whispered against her ear. "I'll tell you all about it later. I am a free man and now I promise you, with all my heart, that we will never be apart again."

Epilogue

Brogan and Maggie Kavenagh eventually recovered from their ordeal and settled back into a contented way of life on the homestead. Maggie continued to home-school her children.

Tabor and Julia Kavenagh were happily reunited.

Pate continued to do well raising horses. The mare who'd been about to foal delivered a handsome black colt with a perfect white star on his forehead. He called him Freedom.

Ambrose (Amby) Burk was sentenced to death for the killing of his uncle, Latham Storey, and was hung on the gallows constructed for his sworn enemy, Brogan Kavenagh.

Josephine Burk was found guilty of giving a false statement to the sheriff, with extenuating circumstances. She was shown mercy with a greatly reduced prison sentence. Ten year-old Nellie Burk kept house for her brothers and sisters during their mother's brief incarceration.

Tilda and Jedediah Loughty eventually left their home in the wilderness with their eight children and moved back to the shiretown.

The End

Eden Monroe loves giving voice to the endless parade of interesting characters who introduce themselves in her imagination. She writes about real life, real issues and struggles, and triumphs against all odds. A proud east coast Canadian, she enjoys a variety of outdoor activities and a good book.